DARK SHADOWS OVER CORONATION CLOSE

LIZZIE LANE

First published in Great Britain in 2023 by Boldwood Books Ltd.

Cover Design by Colin Thomas

Cover Photography: Colin Thomas

A CIP catalogue record for this book is available from the British Library.

Paperback ISBN 978-1-80483-415-2

Large Print ISBN 978-1-80483-414-5

Hardback ISBN 978-1-80483-416-9

Ebook ISBN 978-1-80483-413-8

Kindle ISBN 978-1-80483-412-1

Audio CD ISBN 978-1-80483-421-3

MP3 CD ISBN 978-1-80483-420-6

Digital audio download ISBN 978-1-80483-418-3

Boldwood Books Ltd
23 Bowerdean Street
London SW6 3TN
www.boldwoodbooks.com

1

APRIL 1938

Her daughters having gone to bed, Jenny Crawford drew the curtains against the night and prepared to sit down and do some mending whilst listening to the wireless but swiftly changed her mind.

'This is the twenty-eighth of April 1938 and this is the third news of the day. The time is 9 p.m. Neville Chamberlain stated that he was hopeful that they could agree on a mutual strategy regarding the Sudeten region in Czechoslovakia and that rumours of the likelihood of war were greatly exaggerated by those who—'

'I don't want to know!' Jenny Crawford snapped.

She turned it off with as much fervour as someone might wring a chicken's neck.

War. The word of the moment. She heard it from neighbours and even from women waiting to be served in the greengrocer's. The sooner it went away, the better, but all she could do for now was not listen to the news.

Broadcasts on the BBC began at 10.15 in the morning with the morning service. The first news of the day wasn't broadcast until 6 p.m. After that it became crammed in every evening. She used to listen a lot more before all this talk of war. Bram Martin and his orchestra was pleasing. A play or half-hour of comedy was uplifting. Listening to the wireless on an evening had always constituted her own private hour or so after her daughters, Tilly and Gloria, had gone to bed. Nowadays, she was careful what time she tuned in.

It wasn't that long since the Great War, when millions from all over the world had died – and not just those in uniform. Zeppelins had flown over London and the Home Counties dropping bombs that had done notable damage and killed a thousand people. The very thought of it happening again – perhaps to a greater extent thanks to the proliferation of more modern weapons, more ways of killing, of destroying cities and lives – was terrifying.

Some people were suggesting that those who prophesied war were exaggerating, and that this man Hitler, who sought a purist German state, could be appeased. Having heard of some of the horrors, she didn't think so. Like many others, she was worried about her children being killed in their home and the young men likely to be called up to fight for king and country – just like before. Did men never learn?

It seemed not. At least those at the top didn't seem inclined to learn. And as for everyone else, small people could do nothing but hope and pray.

Without the wireless, the only sound was the ticking of the clock on the mantelpiece. As it ticked away the seconds and minutes, Jenny felt the distance between her and the wireless announcement widen. It was behind her. She could forget it.

A good night's sleep should set me right, she thought.

At first, she tossed and turned. Nothing seemed to settle her until she turned her mind to planning the following day. The garden beckoned. On sensing yet another day of spring sunshine, the plants had rushed into the exuberant bloom one would expect in summer. So had the privet hedges which surrounded every house on the estate, small cascades of white flowers with a strong smell. They needed trimming.

* * *

A bright day came with the dawn. Once the girls had left for school and the laundry was hanging on the line, Jenny prepared everything she needed. Her old gardening boots had seen better days, but they were waterproof and comfortable – mainly because they were two sizes too big.

After collecting a pair of shears, she headed out front. She had every intention of attacking the hedge with a vengeance. Her hope was that a combination of physical effort and enjoying the fresh air would blot out the rest of the world and its troubles. Her world would narrow down to the everyday things, the insignificant things that she had some control over – such as the privet hedge.

Privet leaves and bits of twig flew up her arms and around her face and she began to relax and then to hum to herself and dance tunes that she'd heard on the wireless. It seemed that the shears snipped in time to the music. The world suddenly seemed a better place.

Mondays remained laundry days to the sticklers for convention, though what difference the day made Jenny found amusing. As far as she was concerned, as the long as the weather was dry and a stiff breeze blowing, it didn't much matter what day the laundry was hung out. Today looked just perfect for hanging out a line. She'd pegged hers out early before the girls were up.

At ten fifteen, she went back inside and made herself a cup of tea and took the last two biscuits from the biscuit barrel. Peace had returned to her own personal space.

The short break was much enjoyed. Now back to the garden.

Coronation Close was quiet at this time of the day. The

milkman had been and gone and the vegetable man, fresh fruit and veg piled on the back of his horse-drawn cart, wouldn't be around until midday.

Jenny set to with the shears, lopping off the longer pieces that dared escape the nice level hedge she required. Once satisfied that the top of the hedge was neat and flat, she wiped at her forehead.

She would have dipped straight back down and trimmed the lower hedge until she saw movement, then a figure standing straight and still, outside number one Coronation Close.

She paused wondering what he wanted. She didn't recognise him. He wasn't a neighbour. So who was he?

The Close formed a horseshoe shape so the numbers ran consecutively all around the circle of green grass from one to twelve. Although standing outside number one, the stranger seemed transfixed by number twelve.

It occurred to her that he might be selling something, though she hadn't seen any sign of a case. Most of the tally men who came banging on doors carried their goods in suitcases unless they were calling to collect the money due. They sold everything from household goods to books. Few of her neighbours could afford to buy books. It was household goods they favoured – new bedding, towels, crockery or children's clothes.

'Well, I'm not buying, so he needn't think that,' she murmured.

Laying aside her shears, her attention turned to picking the last of this year's daffodils. She began humming again as she cut a few choice blooms and smiled when she thought of the cobalt glass vase Robin Hubert had given her. The glass had been left as a pledge at his second-hand furniture and pawn shop at Filwood Broadway and never reclaimed. Either they'd moved away or decided they didn't need it anyway. The money given in exchange for the pledge had been more useful. It was like that for a lot of people. Valuable objects couldn't buy food or pay the rent. That's the way it was.

It was a lovely vase. Robin had remarked on it being Bristol glass.

'Bristol glass was mostly blue. Dark blue.'

He'd looked deeply into her eyes as he'd said that. She'd found herself blushing – just as she did now at the memory.

Robin had refused to accept payment and the thought of what he'd said broadened her smile.

'Call it a bonus,' he'd said. 'Or a late Christmas present.'

She'd pointed out that it was getting towards the end of April.

Unperturbed, he'd responded, 'Easter then.'

'That's been and gone too.'

'Imagine it's your twenty-first birthday. Sorry I missed it.'

She'd laughed then and smiled now. Robin always had an answer. They shared the same sense of humour, had been childhood friends but had grown apart and married other people. Fate had since intervened. Her husband, Roy, had become a career soldier, informing her that he much preferred brothers in arms to a day job and living a domestic existence with her and the children. He'd assured her that he still loved the children, but that his heart was elsewhere.

They'd grappled with poverty and unemployment during their marriage. Those things alone drained whatever affection they might once have had, which in turn had led to violence and love turning to fear and even hate. It had taken several years before the parting of ways and had been a relief for Jenny. Roy's temper and frequent bouts of violence had been a marriage made in anywhere but heaven. She couldn't blame him entirely for how he was. He'd come back from the Great War in 1918 fully expecting the promises made by those in power to come to fruition. Why shouldn't a man be given some kind of reward for having served his country?

His hope had been short-lived. Not only could he not find a decent job but finding somewhere to live had been difficult. From one series of cramped rooms in a shared house to another – until their last room in Blue Bowl Alley in a crumbling slum close coupled with other ageing slums in the medieval heart of the old city. By hook – or even crook, in the guise of a council official who also happened to have been one of Oswald Mosley's Blackshirts – they were offered a council house.

It had meant a new start though at the time Jenny hadn't known just how new. Shortly after coming to Coronation Close, the truth came out and Roy had declared proudly, excitement shining in his eyes that he'd joined the army. That was what he wanted. Jenny had simply wanted a decent house in which to bring up her daughters.

While Jenny's life had been governed by Roy, Robin's had been governed by Doreen. Their marriage had been based on a lie but Robin had believed Doreen when she'd told him that she was pregnant and that he was the father. His parents had still been alive and had insisted he married the girl. That's how it was. Young men were expected to 'do the right thing'. Young women were expected not to get into trouble in the first place.

It had been a case of marry in haste, repent at leisure. Eighteen months after their wedding day, Doreen's declaration of being in the family way at last proved true when she gave birth to their daughter, and a son had followed.

'Longest pregnancy in history,' Robin's mother had grumbled.

Happy ever after had not happened. Doreen became bored not only with domestic life but with marriage in general and Robin in particular. There were rumours of her having 'fancy men'.

Robin was mortified but had put up with her for the sake of the children. No amount of arguing or threats had any effect – not that Robin was the type to ever raise his hand to a woman. And Doreen knew it.

Her behaviour never improved. She started quarrels just so that she could stomp out of the door and disappear for a time – sometimes for a few days.

'I've been with friends,' she would tell him when she bothered to return. 'Can't stick yur in this bloody 'ouse all day waiting for you to come home.'

It became a waste of time to accuse her of starting the quarrels deliberately. Over time, it got that he couldn't care less. Not that it seemed to bother her. She preferred her companions at the Black Horse, the George and the Bunch of Grapes to him. She came back displaying the attitude that she was doing him a favour, keeping him dangling on a string. 'Like a bloody puppet,' he often stated. And he had been that, accepting her back from whatever company she'd been with, for the sake of the children.

Jenny fully accepted that she and Robin had made regrettable mistakes. Both were now separated from their spouses and fate had thrown them back together again but only as friends. Good friends.

She now worked part-time for him at his second-hand furniture and pawn shop, which gave her independence plus a little money. Doreen who, even though living elsewhere, still demanded maintenance from him, thus Jenny was only paid a few pounds.

If he dared complain, Doreen's riposte would be, 'Wouldn't want the kids to do without would you?'

It was sheer blackmail.

Being of a kindly nature, Robin did his duty by his wife and his generosity wasn't only confined to his family. Sometimes he gave furniture away to those who needed it. He sold and exchanged furniture at the front of the shop and had a pawn shop at the rear, just as his mother had done down in Stokes Croft – a busy area of shops and bustling traffic close to St James's Church. He was the man someone went to for a bit of furniture or a few shillings to last them until payday.

On his mother's death, Robin had carried on with the business, moving it out of the city centre and to the heart of one of the new council estates to the south of the city. The bevy of shops on either side of the expanse of green at Filwood Broadway, including his, served the post-Great War sprawling red-brick council estate of Knowle West. Business was as brisk here for him as it had been for his mother trading in the heart of the city.

His mother had always said that being in the pawnbroking business was like being on a merry-go-round that never went anywhere and never stopped. Those a bit short of cash at the beginning of one week came in to pawn their valuables, retrieved them on pay day – usually a Friday – and brought them along again on Monday. Those were the ones Robin never made much money on, but at least a regular shilling was better than ten rarely seen.

The business was doing as well as could be expected. His marriage was not.

Robin and Doreen were currently living apart. Robin's wife had insisted on staying in rooms in a tenement owned by a man she termed a friend. Robin learned that indeed he was far more than that. Robin's young daughter had told him so.

'Ma sleeps with Uncle.'

It shouldn't have come as a massive surprise, but to hear the truth from the mouth of his ten-year-old daughter had knocked him sideways. Yet another man passing through Doreen's life – one of many. He'd finally faced up to the fact that Doreen wasn't suited for marriage and never would be. Unlike most women who persevered for the sake of their children, Doreen chose to go all out for what she really wanted. And she wanted other men. She liked a fun time and a bit of variety.

Many people ostracised those who threw in the towel and became separated or divorced, but Robin had held his head high, bought the shop in Filwood Broadway and threw himself into his business and providing for his children. Because he had to work, the children had remained with their mother. He made sure he saw them frequently, though Doreen couldn't have cared less one way or the other so long as he paid her maintenance.

Marriage, thought Jenny as she snipped the last daffodil, is not necessarily made in heaven. Hers certainly hadn't been and neither had Robin's.

Enough daffodils cut to fill the vase, Jenny straightened and slipped the scissors into her apron pocket. She was about to go back into the house but her attention was taken by the man she'd seen earlier. He was still standing on the pavement outside number one Coronation Close, the house that used to be occupied by Mrs Partridge.

Mrs Partridge had died in coronation year, 1937. Mr Partridge, who had spent years pretending to be her sister, had been imprisoned for deserting from the trenches in which he'd served during the Great War. Explosions, death, blood and destruction had broken his nerve. He'd deserted and with the help of his wife he'd lived as a woman for years – until his wife had died. Then he'd thrown in the towel, given himself up.

He'd been led away on the day of the coronation when King George the Sixth and Queen Elizabeth had been crowned in the glory that was Westminster Abbey. Everyone presumed Mr Partridge was still in prison, but nothing had been heard from him since.

Her former neighbours had been keen gardeners, but things had changed since the rough-and-ready Arkle family had moved in. Gone were the blossoms from the front garden that used to fill the air with perfume and colour. Gone too were the vegetables from the back garden. The Arkle kids had been seen selling bunches of flowers outside the cemetery, the vegetables sold door to door for a few coppers.

Whilst the man's attention was fixed elsewhere, Jenny took further stock of his appearance. He was of average height and average build. In fact, everything about the man leaning against next-door's privet hedge was average including his clothes. He was dressed in a brown gaberdine mac, the collar turned up around his face. His hands were buried deep in his pockets.

It occurred to her that he might be from the council come to read the riot act to Mr or Mrs Arkle. Not that he'd get much joy there. Mr Arkle avoided anyone of authority. If he was home, he'd send out his wife Rosellia. Mrs Arkle would beam and say, in amongst the machine-gun-quick Spanish, 'Me no speak English.' It was a lie. She could certainly speak it when she wanted to.

But while it was the privet hedge of number one he was leaning against, he was staring across the road at number twelve. Yes. There was no doubt in her mind now that his attention was fixed on Thelma Dawson's house. But why would he be watching Thelma's place?

In her mind, Jenny sought for possibilities that might entice a council visit. Precious few queued up to be recognised. Thelma paid her rent on time and besides the fact that she was an honest woman, she had an ongoing relationship with Cuthbert Throgmorton, senior rent collector. If anything was amiss, she would hear it from him first. Nor was she a problem neighbour. She kept her house neat and tidy, had a steady job and was not unduly noisy. On the contrary, she exercised her authority when someone wasn't keeping their pig bin clean or leaving a trail of clinker around the base of their ashbin. Thelma liked things just so.

'What if the King and Queen came visiting,' she was fond of saying. 'Want it all neat and tidy when they turn up, don't we?'

The chances of royalty ever making its way into Coronation Close were slim. But Thelma, a keen collector of coronation memorabilia and fervent royalist, lived in hope.

Thelma had made Jenny more than welcome when she had first moved into Coronation Close. She knew something of Jenny's life before she'd moved into the Close, as it was termed. So Jenny felt she owed her friend a few favours and keeping an eye on Thelma's house when she was at work was one of those she didn't mind doing at all.

But what now? Should she ask the man outright why he was so interested in her house? No, but she had to question him in some way, perhaps say something friendly, that wouldn't betray her suspicion of him.

She took a deep breath. Flowers clutched in her hand, the blooms nestling in the crook of her arm, she trailed along the hedges to the front gate of her own garden.

Across the road at Thelma's house, the buds of a yellow climbing rose only just coming into bud were nodding in a smiley manner above the privet hedge. A few had dared to burst open despite it being too early in the season for roses.

'Beautiful, aren't they?' Well, he was looking in that direction.

He started, turned his head and stared at her.

'The roses across the road at number twelve. They're beautiful. And so are these for that matter.'

He looked surprised to see her there, as though he'd been so engrossed in his mission of watching Thelma's that he hadn't noticed her. His eyes were blue, his face very pale. She got the impression that his hair was reddish though couldn't tell for sure on account of the brim of his trilby.

'The daffodils,' she said and nodded at the flower heads, bright as suns against the dark green of her cardigan. 'I know people say that snowdrops are the first sign of spring, but it's not until the daffodils begin to dance in a March breeze and are still cheering us up in April, that's when I think spring has finally arrived and that summer is on the doorstep.' She patted the daffodil heads affectionately. 'Of course, it's nearly the end of April and a surprise that they're still blooming. The daffodils are late and those rosebuds across the road are early. The weather's been wonderful for the time of year. Really warm.'

It was as if she'd awoken him from a deep sleep. He hunched his shoulders, pulled the brim of his brown trilby hat further down over his face and then was gone.

Like a rabbit, she thought.

Through narrowed eyes, she watched until he turned left at the end of the cul-de-sac and disappeared. There was no doubt in her mind that he'd been surveying Thelma's house and that she'd taken him by surprise.

Creepy, she thought. Why had he been staring so intently? It crossed her mind that he might be contemplating breaking in and taking whatever valuables he could find. Thelma would be heart-broken if anyone stole her royal crockery collection. She'd built it up over several years and guarded her mugs, cups, saucers and plates like the Crown Jewels. Jenny had only ever known one item of that collection being broken. A coronation mug depicting King Edward the Eighth had been her most treasured possession back in 1936. Not because it had been a present from Cuthbert Throg-morton – which it had been – but because Thelma had thought King Edward the handsomest of the royal family. It had been to the amazement of the world, parliament, the lords and the commons that Edward declined to be king, instead declaring his intention to marry an American divorcee. Thelma's anger had boiled over. He'd let the country down, but worse than that he'd let her down. Furious beyond belief, she had smashed the mug to pieces.

Turning thoughtfully back to the house with both the cut flowers and her shears, Jenny tried to convince herself that there must be a perfectly logical reason for the man being there, and for him running off like that.

Back in her living room, she turned the wireless on. Music for now but when the pips sounded for the news, she would turn it off.

It was as she was arranging the flowers in the pretty glass vase that her thoughts turned back to the man she'd failed to recognise and another possibility, which made her pause and go quite cold.

Way back at the beginning of last year, during a severe snowstorm in nineteen thirty-seven, a man had attacked Thelma and left her in the family way. The pregnancy had not come to fruition, but angry that he'd taken advantage of her and fully aware that the police would do nothing, Thelma had found out where he lived. His name was Sam Hudson and, to Thelma's horror, she had discovered that he didn't live that far away.

'I want to face him down,' Thelma had said, yet again stoutly refused to report him to the police. Jenny understood that. She'd heard many a tale of the police not wanting to know. Their belief seemed to be that women were hysterical creatures but also too licentious for their own good. It was always their fault. They led men on. Women only had themselves to blame. That seemed to be the opinion of the police and men in general. 'I'll face him and then I'll announce what he is to all and sundry.'

'Do you think you should?' Jenny had cautioned.

Eyes blazing, Thelma had ground her teeth. 'I have to, love. Otherwise I'll go mad!'

Jenny had heard all about it, how Thelma had stood on the pavement outside staring at that closed front door. Even the rows of stone gnomes in the front garden of his house had failed to make her smile. They were too much like him, grinning faces that mocked rather than welcomed.

Going there on a weekday had been a mistake. He was at work. Of course he was. She had ended up meeting his wife, Beryl, a poor disabled woman, downtrodden, sometimes confined to her bedroom and living a life of hell. Instead of confronting her attacker Thelma had befriended his wife.

Jenny considered now that the stranger could be him. She imagined mentioning the man to Thelma. 'Some bloke weighing you up for a weekly payment for a pair of bath towels,' she would quip and leave Thelma to surmise who it might be. Her comment would be met with a quick-witted response. She could imagine it now, right down to the words Thelma was likely to use and the expression she was likely to pull.

'I don't give a jot as long as he wasn't weighing me up for a coffin!'

It almost made Jenny burst out laughing until she wondered again whether it might have been Sam Hudson. She herself had never seen him so she couldn't know for sure.

She went out into the kitchen to peel vegetables for this evening's meal and make sandwiches for midday when the girls came in from school. Doorstep sandwiches. Cold meat with pickle. Enough to keep them going for the rest of the school day until they came home at four o'clock.

As she scraped potatoes and sliced carrots, she decided that, yes, of course Thelma had to be told, but not until later this evening. Thelma's son George and his wife were coming to dinner that evening. If she mentioned it at all it would be after George and daughter-in-law Maria had gone back to the two rooms they were renting in Montpelier.

And what shall I tell her? He wore a brown hat and coat. I didn't get much of a glimpse at his face but think his hair might have been sandy – or reddish. She wasn't quite sure which.

After putting the potatoes and carrots into the same saucepan, Jenny wiped her hands and went into the living room. Looking out of the front window across the road to the closed front door, she thought of Thelma. She would be blithely looking forward to an evening with her family after a long day at work.

Just leave her to enjoy it, she thought and no doubt Thelma would. She loved all three of her children, but at times it seemed that George was her favourite.

There were some things Thelma wasn't looking forward to. She conveyed these to Jenny in private.

'Maria wants to do the cooking. Something Italian. Do you think I should let her?'

She'd wanted to burst out laughing at this, but stopped when she saw that Thelma was deadly serious.

Instead of laughing, Jenny had done her utmost to reassure her. 'Why not? It'll be nice to let someone else wait on you – besides Mary and Alice, that is.'

Thelma had nodded. 'Yes. They're good girls.'

'And George is a good boy. Give his wife a chance.'

'Yes. I suppose you're right. It'll be good to have the whole family around the table even if we'll be eating something Italian.'

George had returned from the merchant navy with an Italian wife. At first, Thelma had been somewhat disappointed that her son had not married a local girl. To some extent, it was a jealous wish. A Bristol girl was likely to remain in her home city, which meant Thelma would get to see her beloved son on a regular basis, and if grandchildren did come along, she'd get to spoil them rotten before handing them back. It's what grandmothers did.

Thelma's greatest fear had been that Maria would persuade George to live in Italy, where her own relatives would be on the doorstep. Women were nest builders no matter where they came from and girls especially liked to be close to their mothers. Maria's mother was back in Italy. Even though Thelma had never known her own mother, she knew what a draw it could be. Being close to family meant a lot.

So far, Maria had given no sign that she had any intention of returning to her native country, taking George and whatever children they had with her.

'But that doesn't mean it won't happen,' Thelma had declared gloomily.

Jenny had asked if she'd asked George about his plans.

'It all depends on if he decides not to go to sea again. I'm hoping he won't, but he's in two minds. He loves the sea, but he's got himself this temporary job at the tobacco bonds. He wants to see if he can stand being a "landlubber", as he terms it. But that doesn't mean he won't go to sea again or return to Italy.'

'Can Bert help them get a council house? They'd likely stay in this country if they've got their own place. Their rooms in Montpelier are reasonable and the rent's cheap, but a family should have a proper house.'

'I don't know. I haven't asked him. But I will.'

In a few months' time, Maria would give birth to Thelma's first grandchild, an event she was very much looking forward to. Thankfully, there was no way for the foreseeable future that either George or Maria was going anywhere.

The clock on the mantelpiece struck twelve, interrupting Jenny's random thoughts and concerns. The sandwiches were ready and waiting on the table. Now all she had to do was put the kettle on and make herself a cup of tea. She would enjoy midday with her daughters, a happy time when she listened to their chatter about school, friendships and that morning's arithmetic test. She had no doubt that twelve-year-old Tilly had done well. What the fickler and younger Gloria had done was a different matter. She had a devil-may-care attitude to the world. In some ways, it could be her downfall. In others, it might get her far, mused Jenny.

Teapot ready, water boiled, Jenny was just about to spoon two scoops of tea from the caddy into the pot. The simple task was interrupted by the sound of something falling through the letter-box. The second post of the day had arrived.

Once the water had been poured and the tea was brewing, she went to check what had fallen onto the coconut mat immediately inside the front door.

A sudden something – like a whispered warning – caused her to pause. Rarely did she receive second post. People like her didn't get much drop through their letterbox unless it was from the council. Gas and electricity were paid with pennies or shillings into meters in the hallway.

Shaking her head did little to dislodge the premonitions that idled there. Silly really. She told herself she was being daft, but the feeling of an impending problem wouldn't leave her.

The chill of the hallway met her as she opened the door. And there was also the coconut mat with an item of post settled on it. The item that had fallen through her letterbox was not a letter but a postcard.

A weird wobbly feeling cramped her stomach, a sign of premonition, but a premonition of what?

Jenny didn't know anyone likely to send her a postcard. Nobody she knew was on holiday and even if they were, it would probably only constitute a day trip to the seaside and a saucy postcard to tell her how bracing it was.

She was vaguely aware of the picture on the front being a handsome white building surrounded by tropical trees – palm trees, no doubt. A road ran in front of the white building where Chinese men pulled rickshaws. Two men wearing uniforms and turbans on their heads stood either side of the entrance. She presumed them to be Indian.

Even before she saw the familiar handwriting, the sight of which pierced her heart, she knew who was writing to her. She only feared why.

Heart pounding, she turned the postcard over and almost dropped it when she read the words.

Jenny,

A nurse is writing this for me. I've been taken ill. Arrangements have been made for me to come home. I've been discharged. See you soon.

Regards, Roy.

No dear Jenny, dear wife or with love.

Rain began to patter against the window and trickle like tears down the cold glass. The sunshine had gone and, to top it all, her husband was coming home.

2

Thelma turned the corner into Coronation Close full of apprehension about Maria's meal. Tonight, they would usually have cold meat left over from the weekend joint with bubble and squeak made from potatoes and other sundry vegetables from Sunday dinner. The meat would have been served cold with piccalilli and the vegetables, boiled the day before. The whole lot would have been fried in a frying pan with a good dollop of lard. The smell of something being fried in lard would have laid heavy on the air.

So absorbed was she about what might happen in her kitchen she didn't hear Jenny calling across the road the first time but heard her the second.

'I need to talk to you. It's urgent.'

Thelma looked at her, looked at her front door and back again. 'Can it wait until the family are gone? We're eating an Italian meal this evening,' she called back. 'It's something called spaghetti Bolognese. Maria is cooking.'

'I know. I remember you telling me.' Jenny grinned. 'Stop looking so worried about it. She's not going to poison you. I'll see you later.'

Thelma had never eaten foreign food of any description and wasn't sure what to expect as she entered her house.

'I'm home,' she called, shutting the door behind her.

The smell hit her the moment she entered the living room. So did the sound of clattering dishes, excited chatter and Gracie Fields singing full throttle on the wireless.

Mary and Alice were seated around the dining table. George was keeping the girls occupied with a game of snakes and ladders.

The smells were delicious, a significant improvement on what they might normally have had this evening.

George noticed his mother's distraction. 'She's a brilliant cook, Ma. Stop worrying.'

The sound of Maria singing in Italian drifted in from the kitchen.

With a wry smile, George commented that his wife was very fond of singing from morning till night.

'Ain't got a bad voice neither,' he proudly remarked to his mother.

'You're right there,' returned Thelma, though, if asked, she'd have to admit she hadn't a clue. Someone had once suggested she was tone-deaf, but she wasn't quite sure.

The expectancy on the faces of her daughters added to the sense of an impending adventure.

Alice inhaled deeply and licked her lips. 'Maria's cooking smells lovely. Don't you think so, Ma?'

'Wish she'd hurry up,' grumbled Mary.

George directed his mother to her favourite armchair. 'Come on, Ma. Take the weight off yur feet. Maria don't need your help. This is supposed to be a treat. Now, come on. Sit down. I'll pour you a sherry.'

'Just a small one.'

There were occasions nowadays when her children made her

feel as though the times for indulging them were over. The time for indulging her – like an old granny, though she felt far from that – had come.

Maria poked her head around the door. 'Hello, Mama. I have all ready in an hour.'

Tresses of her daughter-in-law's hair were plastered to her forehead. Her cheeks were red and her swelling belly thrust against her pinny. Thelma had been told she was going to be a grandmother at the end of last year. She'd been counting the days ever since. It wouldn't be long now.

Thelma offered her help in the kitchen.

Maria shook her head. 'I do this.' She promptly disappeared.

George tutted at his mother and shook his head. 'Relax, Ma.'

It was easy to say but hard to do. Thelma fidgeted, fingers tapping a beat on the arms of the chair. Not exactly in time with Gracie on the wireless, more in time with the seconds and minutes ticking past before she went to see what Maria was up to.

The kitchen was ostensibly her domain, although since they were quite young, Mary and Alice were in the habit of preparing an evening meal for her on her return from Bertrams Modes – the dress shop where she worked.

However, she knew what to expect from them; dishes she'd taught them to make. She was used to them cooking good old-fashioned West Country feasts like faggots and peas, shepherd's pie, pigs' trotters, mutton stew and boiled ham with cheese and leek sauce.

Although itching to see what was happening out in her kitchen, Thelma asked her daughters what sort of a day they'd had at school.

In the past, they might have chatted thirteen to the dozen, telling her every little thing that had constituted their day at Connaught Road School. Halfway between being children and becoming young women, these days they were less open about their lives. Alice, perhaps because she was younger, was more enthusiastic than Mary, who had become more reticent. Of late, Thelma had found herself nudging them into telling her things, though on this occasion she was only half taking things in. The sounds and smells coming from the kitchen were impossible to ignore.

Finally, when the girls had fallen to silence, their hunger taking precedence over the happenings of the day, they began fiddling with the cutlery.

'It's no good. I must go out there.'

She was up in a flash, edging her way around the large oak dining table that took up most of the space in the living room.

George leapt from his chair and placed himself between her and the door into the kitchen. 'Oh no you ain't. None of you are going in there. Maria wants to cook a traditional Italian dish for you without anybody's help. She can cook,' he added. 'Look at this.' Grinning from ear to ear, he patted his belly lovingly – love for his food as well as his wife.

Thelma pulled a face. She wouldn't say it out loud but had to agree that he'd put on weight since being married to Maria. 'As long as she can cope.'

'Of course she can cope. Italian girls are brought up to be wizards in the kitchen.'

Thelma whispered, 'I'm just a bit worried I might not like what she's cooking. I wouldn't want to offend.'

George shook his head at her. 'Mother, there's no need to worry. She wants to cook you something they cook in Italy most days of the week. Pasta – in this case spaghetti.'

'Pasta?'

'They eat it as regularly as we eat potatoes, but it's made of wheat – I think.'

Trying to look or behave meek and mild – obedient even – had never come easily to Thelma. Pushing forty she was still a force of nature, a whirlwind around the house, a more sedate one when working in Bertrams but quite capable of holding her own with the posh women that came in. She could speak to people on all levels and with great confidence. But this... she was all a-flutter simply because her kitchen had been invaded.

There was one more option open to her.

'I need the bathroom.'

There was no avoiding going through the kitchen to the bathroom. It was downstairs and tucked away.

George threw her a look of outright disapproval and shook his head dolefully.

'Got a bit of a waterworks problem today,' she declared and swept past with a determined and slightly smug look on her face. Her curiosity was almost killing her. What in the world was Maria doing to make all that racket?

'All right,' Thelma said cheerfully and nodded at Maria.

'*Si*. Yes.' Maria took no notice and carried on with what she was doing.

Thelma sauntered on, aware that George was standing in the doorway.

Well, she thought as she shut the bathroom door behind her, it comes to something when a son watches to make sure that his mother goes to the WC.

Her brief intrusion into the kitchen had revealed that a great deal of stirring and clattering was going on. Steam filled the room and gathered in clouds close to the ceiling. The vapour turned to water trickling down the walls and windowpanes. Even though the window was open, it hung there, only slowly dissipating out into the back garden. Whatever was being cooked smelt spicey, appetising and not at all British.

What with the steam and pretending she needed the bathroom she'd not had enough chance to get a good look at everything; she made a fresh attempt as she exited the bathroom.

Few of the ingredients were known to her, except for the grated cheese and a bundle of chopped up parsley. A quick stretching of her neck in the direction of the stove revealed something that looked like tomato soup bubbling in one of her larger saucepans. Something else bubbled away in her biggest saucepan, a heavy cast-iron one that she could barely lift. Maria was pressing dough through a kitchen tool she had never seen before. It had a handle on the side and when Maria turned it, strips came through.

'Are you sure you don't need any help?' Thelma asked. Although it did look as though she had everything under control.

'No, no, no,' returned Maria, shaking her head, her attention firmly fixed on stirring each saucepan in turn. 'I can manage.'

Curiosity unsatisfied, Thelma grimaced. The urge to poke her nose in was overwhelming.

'Ma?' Suspicious of his mother's intentions, George appeared in the doorway between kitchen and living room. He crooked his finger at her. 'Come on. Sit down and stop interfering.'

Meekly, though still itching to be involved, Thelma went back into the living room and sat down obediently when George pulled back her chair and pointed at the seat.

This is my house, she thought to herself. *I've got rights to go where I want.*

Going and doing what she wanted had been her dream back in the orphanage, which had been, and still was, in an outer suburb of the city called Fishponds. It had been surrounded by The Duchess's – a place of green grass and trees, a weir and the ever-flowing water of the river Frome. Back then, Thelma had made a vow that she would always go and do whatever she wanted in life. Years had passed but that vow had stayed with her.

She began to rise from the chair. 'I really think—'

'No you don't.' Placing his hands on her shoulders, George pressed his mother back onto the chair. 'You don't want to be an interfering mother-in-law do you, Ma?'

'Well there's a thing to say! I am no such thing!'

Some of her neighbours had complained of an interfering mother-in-law. She'd even heard of one who had accompanied their son and his bride on honeymoon, treating it as a kind of holiday.

'You sit, whilst I 'elp Maria with the plates.'

She let herself be persuaded, though only because it seemed the food was about to be dished up.

Composing herself with a deep breath and sitting straight at the table, she addressed her daughters, whose eyes were fixed on the kitchen.

'Well, isn't this nice. It smells as though we've got a treat in store,' she declared with great enthusiasm that she hoped would hide her anxiety. The fact was she so wanted to put Maria at her ease and reassure her son that she no longer cared that he hadn't married a local girl. She decided a bit of praise was in order.

She turned to her daughters and repeated what she'd already said. 'I think we're in for a rare treat. What do you think, girls?'

'It smells nice,' said Alice.

The sound of Mary's stomach rumbling was proof enough that she too appreciated the smell and made both girls giggle.

A crescendo of clattering resumed in the kitchen.

I wonder if Italian cooking always makes that much noise, thought Thelma. *Or sends so much steam up in the air and condensation running down the windowpanes.* She looked at the living-room windows. The steam had travelled in from the kitchen and misted them too.

Knives, forks and spoons had already been set out on the table.

A cast-iron trivet had also been placed in the middle of the table, ready to take a saucepan.

'We need another trivet for the sauce,' George shouted.

An outstretched brown arm came through the door and passed him a smaller one, which he placed beside the first one.

'All set,' George shouted to his wife.

Thelma restrained herself from asking what was going on. The only time she put trivets on the table was for a saucepan of stew thick with doughboys. Rarely had she placed two trivets on the table, except perhaps for a hot meat platter at Christmas – one for the chicken and one for the roast potatoes.

Two saucepans. The ones she'd seen on the gas stove. Those were the reasons.

Regardless of her inner turmoil, Thelma kept smiling. She didn't want to appear the disapproving mother-in-law. She wanted to be friends with her son's wife.

'It is ready,' cried Maria. Using both hands, she entered cradling a huge bowl against her belly. Thelma recognised it as the one she normally used for making pastry – certainly not as a serving bowl. It was just too big.

Sensing this was an opportunity for her to help, she rose to her feet. 'Maria you shouldn't be carrying that in your condition.'

'Ma.' Placing his hands on her shoulders, George pressed his mother back down in the chair as he had done before. 'Sit down and stop fussing.'

'Spaghetti! The food of Italy,' trilled Maria with smiling face and flashing eyes. It was as though she hadn't noticed Thelma's offer of help at all. The food seemed to be all that mattered. 'Use fork and spoon.'

Mary and Alice stared round-eyed at the steaming bowl set in the middle of the table, whilst Thelma did her very best to hide what she was feeling. Trepidation for a start, plus the sense that something was missing.

'We need plates, Georgie!'

George followed his wife back out into the kitchen and brought the plates in. Maria came back carrying the smaller of the large saucepans. This she placed on the smaller trivet.

'This is the Bolognese sauce.' She sighed with satisfaction, her eyes holding a yearning for validation. 'Now, help yourselves. There are things to use for serving or we can do it for you.'

'Sit down, darling.' George gently pressed his wife down onto a dining chair in the same way that he had his mother. 'Dig in, everyone. Use the tools provided. You might think it all looks a bit haphazard, but trust me – trust us – they'll all work fine.'

There were indeed some useful implements. To Thelma's surprise, she recognised the tongs she used to lift the laundry from the boiler. The handle of the only ladle she owned stuck out above the smaller bowl. Everyone had been provided with knives, forks and spoons.

She'd never tasted spaghetti and was worried she might not like it. What if it wasn't to her taste? What if she disliked it so much that she spit it out? Maria would be mortified if she did that.

'Right,' Thelma said, determined to tuck in with gusto and hope for the best. 'I think it might be better if you two serve it up. We don't want to drop any do we.'

Exchanging looks of love, husband and wife began to dish up.

'You will like it. I am sure you will,' Maria declared in staccato accented English.

Thelma's heart went out to the girl. She was desperate to impress her English relatives – especially her mother-in-law.

Thelma watched as George deftly handled her laundry tongs, dipping them into the bowl and bringing out long strips of what did look a bit like white worms. Not that they were, of course.

A steaming plate was placed in front of her.

'Now this,' said Maria. She dipped the ladle into the saucepan. The smell was rich and pungent. Meat and tomatoes, herbs and spices. Onions? Yes. She definitely got a hint of onions.

Thelma prepared to tuck in.

'I do hope you like it, Mama.'

Maria had brought her Italian ways, as well as her cooking. She always called her Mama, and although today cooking had prevented it, she usually gave her a big hug and a kiss on each cheek.

Thelma smiled and thanked her for preparing such a delicious meal.

Maria beamed. She had a childlike innocence about her, wanted to get involved in the British way of life, to be liked and fit in.

It was impossible not to like Maria, not to be impressed by her luminous brown eyes and glossy dark hair. Her skin was like creamy coffee and she didn't wear stockings. She didn't need to. Her legs like her arms and the rest of her had been kissed by the warmth of the Italian sunshine. Everyone else looked like uncooked pastry in comparison.

'Sprinkle with *formaggio*,' said Maria, handing round a bowl.

'What's *formaggio*?' asked Alice.

It was George who answered. 'It's cheese. In Italy, they'd use a local cheese called Parmigiana, though not always. It don't matter as long as it's tasty. All we could get was Cheddar.'

With undisguised enthusiasm, George showed them how to eat what was to them an alien meal. He spun the long strands of pasta around his fork and into his mouth.

Thelma eyed him with some amusement. She'd never have thought it, his love for a foreign food. He'd always been one for roast meat, potatoes, carrots and mushy peas. The latter had to be soaked overnight or they'd be like bullets even after an hour of boiling. She wondered if part of his taste for Italian food was not so much to do with the food itself but his love for his beautiful wife, whose exuberant personality had brought sunshine into the house.

Thelma looked at the swirls of food. The fact was she needed time. She had to work up to this. Eyeing her two daughters, she spotted her chance.

'You two look as though you're enjoying this food,' she said to Mary and Alice.

Mary licked her lips and her growling stomach made her sister laugh.

'Let the pig out, Mary Dawson!'

'Come on, Mother. I've shown you how it's done. Roll it around the fork like I'm doing. Help it twine round with the spoon if you can't manage a fork.'

To his mother's ears, George sounded like a worldly-wise man with epicurean tastes.

Gales of laughter accompanied each attempt. Alice laughed so much she ended up with some of the spaghetti and sauce falling into her lap and onto the crisp white tablecloth.

Mary was less amused. Thelma had noticed her fidgeting and seemingly impatient to get up from the table.

She threw her a warning look. 'Have you got ants in your pants, young lady?'

'No.'

It was all she said.

'Why do children have to grow up,' Thelma murmured to herself. She often wished her offspring could have remained children forever.

Alice spilled a bit more of her meal. This time, the sauce landed on the tablecloth.

'Whoops!' She covered her mouth guiltily and waited to hear what her mother would say.

Thelma refrained from rolling her eyes. All she hoped was that the coppery colour would wash out and the tablecloth could be returned to its pristine whiteness.

She concentrated on following George's example and used the spoon to wind the strands of pasta around her fork. It took a few goes, but eventually she decided that the secret was to take only a small amount.

Gingerly, just in case it tasted terrible, she tucked the fork neatly into her mouth. The smell should have said it all. Now, with the taste on her tongue, she was pleasantly surprised. An infusion of spices and succulent mince suffused her senses. The spaghetti added extra substance.

The nervous expression that had tightened her face loosened. Finally, after making a few sounds of approval, she pronounced, 'It's delicious. It really is.'

George's face brightened. Up until now, he'd seemed totally in charge of the situation. But she got the distinct sense he'd been on tenterhooks as he awaited her approval. He smiled broadly. 'I told you so, didn't I?'

Thelma laughed. Faces smeared with sauce, the girls joined in – Mary less so than Alice, her amusement confined to a small chuckle.

So reserved, thought Thelma. *What is in the girl's mind?*

Cheeks red and strands of dark hair plastered to her forehead, Maria looked at each of her husband's family with outright amazement. Unable to utter a word and seeing them all staring at her, she threw her hands over her face and burst into heartrending sobs.

Mortified, Thelma drew in her chin and looked at her son. 'What have I said?'

He chuckled in a warm and approving way, almost as though

he'd expected something like this to happen. 'Nothing. You've made her extremely happy. She was worried you might not like it.' With an expression of tenderness, he reached across and affectionately cupped his wife's cheek. 'See, Maria. I told you they would all like it, didn't I?'

Thus made aware that Maria had been experiencing the same nervousness as she had, Thelma got up from the table and went round to her daughter-in-law. Leaning her chin on Maria's head, she placed her arm around the heaving shoulders and gave her a big hug. 'Come on now. There's no need to take on. Of course we like the meal. Hopefully you'll make it again for us. It's really tasty. What was it you called it?'

Maria peered out above her fingertips. 'Spaghetti Bolognese.'

Thelma went back to her chair and cleared her plate of what remained. It hadn't occurred to her that Maria too had been nervous – who wouldn't be cooking for their mother-in-law?

'It was lovely, darling.' She waved her cutlery at what remained in the bowl and the saucepan. 'Come on. Let's finish this off.' She nodded at her daughters, who were both sitting in front of empty plates. 'I bet you two would like a second helping, wouldn't you?'

Alice was full of enthusiasm. Mary, at nearly fourteen years old was more casual in her acceptance. Thelma frowned at her attitude. Where was the little girl who'd hung on every word she'd said and helped her with housework? She was acting out of character, no longer little Mary she was fast leaving her childhood behind. So many things about her were changing.

Thelma had noticed that Mary no longer gobbled her food but took her time. She even held up her pinkie finger as she'd seen one of the teachers do when supping their mid-morning cuppa. When she thought her mother wasn't looking, she went back to gobbling her food in short little spurts, satisfying her hunger whilst pretending to be aloof to such a thing.

As her time for leaving school and getting a job was not far off, Mary disliked being considered a child. A child wore ribbons in the hair, puff sleeves and played with a skipping rope. Mary no longer did those things. Thelma had even caught her applying lipstick and face powder.

'You're too young for that,' she'd declared and snatched it away.

Mary had reminded her mother of how old she was.

'You're not yet a woman,' Thelma had said as she wiped the lipstick and powder off her daughter's face with a wet flannel.

Her darling daughter was growing up. She wouldn't exactly wrap her up in cotton wool but she would need to keep an eye on her.

More of the delicious food was ladled onto their plates and generously sprinkled with grated cheese.

Thelma took it upon herself to bring in a conversation that might help fill the embarrassed silence following Maria's crying. 'This Cheddar cheese goes very well with this meal. It's melting nicely into the meat. Did you know that this cheese is made quite near to Bristol?'

Face still wet but crying over, Maria nodded and gave a weak smile.

Seeing her daughter-in-law looking happier, Thelma decided a little more general conversation would further improve her disposition. She looked directly at her when she went on to say, 'There's caves there and a gorge with cliffs on either side. I went there once on a trip with... with other kids.' She wasn't sure whether Maria knew that she'd grown up in an orphanage. It was something she mostly kept to herself. 'Our George should take you there on a day out,' she added breezily. 'You can pay to go on a charabanc outing. I think Cottles Coaches run day trips there. I think it only costs about two and six.'

George put down his fork. 'That's a nice thought, Mum.' He

looked at Maria and took hold of her hand. 'You deserve a day out, love. *We* deserve a day out.'

Thelma suggested they did it now before the baby came. 'After that, you won't get much chance. Now tuck in. Let's do this meal the justice it deserves and leave the bowl and saucepan so empty they won't need to be washed up.'

Within minutes, it was all gone and everyone was patting their bellies and saying how full they were.

Alice burped.

Seeing the chance to retaliate for her earlier comment, Mary told her she sounded like a pig.

Nobody wanted dessert. Thelma suggested they might reconsider once the dishes had been washed.

'You might find a bit more room then.' She looked pointedly at Mary and Alice. 'Are my girls going to wash the dishes for me or does their old mother have to do it?'

Alice was up in a flash. 'We'll do it.'

Mary remained seated, thoughtfully watching her finger smooth the edge of the tablecloth.

Alice had begun gathering up the dirty plates. She paused when she realised it was just her carrying out the task. A remark swiftly followed, 'Come on, our Mary.'

Mary didn't move. Her gaze was still fixed on the table, where her fingers now tapped.

Thelma noticed. 'Is there something wrong, Mary? Are you feeling all right?'

Mary didn't get chance to answer. George got there first, ruffling his sister's hair and commenting how much he'd appreciate her giving Alice a hand, but if she didn't feel up to it then he'd be obliged to step in.

'You?' She looked at him round-eyed. 'Men don't do the washing-up.'

He leaned close to her ear and said softly, 'They do if their wife is having a baby and needs to put her feet up. I was thinking you might like to come over and stay with us when the baby arrives. It'll be a great 'elp. Or I can ask our Alice, if you don't want to bother, but I reckon you'll be good at it so I thought...'

His words had the desired effect. There was barely a heartbeat between him saying it and Mary getting to her feet.

'Our Alice is too young,' she protested. 'She can't look after a baby. She still plays with dollies and prams.'

George exchanged raised eyebrows with his mother. Realising what was going on Maria looked down at the floor to hide her smile.

Quick as a flash, Mary began gathering the rest of the crockery and cutlery.

A few minutes and the sound of clattering dishes and running water came from the kitchen. So did some ribbing, accusations of being lazy, countered by those of being a baby. The comments brought smiles but were eventually subdued when George partially closed the door.

Thelma chose not to pay any great regard to the friction between her daughters. Sisters argued. It was in their nature. They'd grow out of it. Or they wouldn't. She was finding it difficult to face that her children were changing and that one day she'd look round and find them gone. Not just absent from her company but having grown into young women. Instead, she concentrated on things she'd instilled in them that formed the basis of how they behaved. Top of the list was that she'd brought them up to be polite. It was polite to wash the dishes regardless and not ask to go out to play until their visitors had gone. Play was becoming a word that didn't describe their after-school activities as it once had.

At the table, Thelma thanked Maria most profusely, then the talk turned to the expected birth of her one and only grandchild –

at least it was one only for the foreseeable future. Would it be a boy or a girl? And what about names?

Maria voiced the fact that she was keen on Giacomo for a boy, which she explained could be shortened to Jack in English. For a girl, she favoured Mariana, which was her mother's name.

'Like Marian in English?' asked Thelma.

After a little thought Maria decided that it was.

'Two good choices,' added George, who confessed that he would have quite liked his own name for a boy and Georgina for a girl. 'A father's choice should come first. After all it's 'im that does all the work.'

Maria slapped his arm.

Thelma suggested it was generally accepted that when it came to having babies the woman did most of the work. 'When the time comes, all you have to do is pace up and down outside.'

'Not just that. A little bit of effort in the first place. If you know what I mean.' His eyes twinkled suggestively, which got him another slap from Maria.

Amid the laughter, Alice came in from the kitchen with a bowl of stewed apple declaring that she was ready for a dessert. Mary followed behind her with a bowl of hot custard. It seemed that she too had a gap in her belly to fill.

Bowls and spoons were retrieved from the dresser.

George winked at the girls across the table. 'Right little housewives, you two. From pigtails to wedding veils. You two are gonna make a man very happy one day. I wonder which of you will marry first. You, Alice...'

Alice covered her giggle with both hands.

George winked again and turned to Mary. 'Or, seeing you're the eldest, it's more likely to be you. Already got a boyfriend, 'ave you?'

Mary's face turned pink. 'I might do.'

'So, what's 'is name?'

'I only said I might do. That don't mean to say I've got to tell you his name because he might not exist.' Head held high, she regarded him with challenge in her eyes. 'And it don't mean to say that I'm going to marry. I don't have to, do I?'

'Stop picking on her, George. She'll bother with boys when she's good and ready and not before,' Thelma warned.

George gave her a surprisingly knowing look. 'Mother, you're a bit of an ostrich at times.'

'I don't know what you mean,' returned Thelma, just a little wounded but unwilling to accept that secrets might be creeping into her daughters' lives. 'Now, who's for stewed apple and custard?'

Little of the stewed apple with cinnamon and custard was eaten. The girls had decided they weren't as hungry as they'd thought.

'That'll do for another time,' pronounced Thelma. 'Waste not, want not.'

With a flourish, she picked up the bowls and passed them to the girls, who usually would take them out into the kitchen without a murmur. Alice appeared willing enough. Mary looked affronted, heaving her shoulders in a heartfelt sigh.

Perhaps it's just the time of the month, thought Thelma. The sudden thought was a jolt to her system. Mary had begun her periods only two months ago. Of course she wasn't feeling her usual self. It was all new, just as new as Thelma feeling she'd lost her girls.

Forget it, she thought to herself. Dwelling on it would do no good. She followed them into the kitchen and for a while stared out of the window without seeing the hedges, the grass and the rose bushes Bert had taken to buying her. In the past, he'd bought her crockery with links to the royal family. Following her becoming disillusioned with King Edward the Eighth – the king who abdicated – he'd taken to buying rose bushes. She appreciated them, more so when he offered to do the planting. *Stop dwelling on things you can't alter!*

Taking her own advice, Thelma pushed the thoughts aside, filled her chest with air and called out, 'I'll put this apple and custard on the cold shelf in the larder. You two can have it tomorrow when you get home from school. It should keep you going until suppertime.'

She popped her head around the door and asked if anyone wanted a cup of tea.

Everyone professed they were too full.

George expressed his intention to leave. 'We need to get going, Ma. Don't want to miss the bus. And my girl and my son 'as to get their beauty sleep. So do I for that matter.'

She didn't admonish him with the suggestion that he might end up with a daughter. Whatever George and Maria ended up with would be loved and that was all that mattered.

The very air itself seemed warmed by their presence, their laughter and the love that each seemed to exchange with the other.

Thelma so wanted to say that there was plenty of time until the last bus. The evening had been so much more enjoyable than she'd thought it would be. Her son was the apple of her eye and if Maria was the apple of his then all was well with the world.

At the front door and ready to go, Maria kissed Thelma on each cheek. Dimples sat like small stars in her cheeks and her smile was bright as sunshine.

'I am so glad you liked my pasta.' Her voice was almost tearful, as though she couldn't quite believe that Thelma might really mean it.

Heart fit to burst, Thelma nodded enthusiastically. 'Of course I did, my love. But you did put in a lot of work. You must rest more now. Remember you've got my grandchild to think of.'

George took centre stage between the two women, threw an arm around each of them and hugged them close. 'And you need to rest too, Ma.' He kissed his mother in the same manner as his wife had done, though with more gusto. 'You hold down a full-time job and look after the girls. You're getting older. You need to take care of yourself. Put yur feet up. Get yourself a shawl and take up knitting.'

'Cheeky sod,' she said, giving him a cursory slap on the shoulder. She disliked being reminded that she was getting older. And he knew it!

As she saw them out, he asked her how Bert was doing. 'I thought he would 'ave been yur.'

'He would have been, but his mother's sister who lives in Cheltenham is ill. He had to drive his mother there.'

'Shame. Give 'im my regards. Tell 'im I was sorry to miss 'im. See 'im next time we pop in.'

She knew George wanted to remark that Bert's mother kept him close. She didn't need telling. Not that she didn't like his mother. She was a game old bird, but it was noticeable that either she doted on Bert or he doted on her. It was hard to tell.

Thelma and her girls stood at the gate waving off George and her daughter-in-law, not stopping until they were out of sight. She always felt sad to see them go. It hadn't been that long since George had been living under her roof. That had been before he'd joined the merchant navy, before all this talk of war, the issuing of gas masks, the threat of rations, of shortages and privation. Of battle. That was the biggest fear. In her heart of hearts, she wished fervently that he would stay in the job at the tobacco bonds and never go to sea again.

Shaking all of that from her mind, Thelma hid the tears she could so easily have shed. For goodness' sake, it wasn't as though he lived on the moon!

Finally he disappeared.

'Well,' said Thelma, feeling as though her heart was about to break, 'that was nice.' She turned to go back into the house, her hand trailing over a young climbing rose that she'd planted close to the front door. Like the one clambering over the front hedge, it was yellow. Cheerful, she thought. And happy. At this moment in time, it felt that nothing could possibly go wrong.

Alice followed her into the house, asking if she too would be allowed to look after the baby when it came. 'He asked our Mary but he didn't ask me. Do you think he will?'

'Of course he will, sweetheart.'

She gave her youngest daughter a kiss on the crown of her head accompanied by a big hug.

Mary walked slowly behind them. Her pink lips sucked on a piece of hair that had blown across her face. Her eyes were downcast.

'Are you coming in or not?' Thelma asked.

'Can I go and see the horses on the Novers?' Mary asked as she trailed after her mother back into the house.

The Novers was a wild patch of slopping waste ground stretching from Knowle down into Marksbury Road in Bedminster. Horses were still grazed there free of charge, which was why the gypsies favoured it. Mary had always liked horses, so her request didn't come as a major surprise, though Thelma had thought that both the horses and the gypsies who owned them had moved on. She mentioned this.

Mary swiftly responded. 'Yes. But there are still some horses there. Have we got any carrots left?'

'I can find a few. Getting a bit late, though. I don't like you going out this late. An hour and you're back in, my girl. Do you want me to come and fetch you?'

Mary responded hotly. 'Mother! I'm quite old enough to find my way back by myself. I'm not a child!'

Her attitude took Thelma aback. There was something about her manner that left Thelma lost for words, unable to decide whether to be upset or suspicious. Although she'd not shown any reaction, the conversation between her son and daughter rankled. Mary was still her baby, conceived in love but both mother and daughter abandoned by a man she should never have trusted. *Love is certainly blind*, she thought. And dealing with a growing girl was no easy task. Did she have the same trouble when George was growing up? She couldn't rightly recall but didn't think she did. She had heard from friends with families that the behaviour of adolescent boys did differ from that of girls. Advice would be freely available if she dared to ask. But she didn't want to ask. Partly due to pride, she didn't want to share her concerns with anyone. All she needed was time to think and to put some kind of plan of action in place. Giving Mary space might help to smooth the path from childhood into adolescence. It was hard and difficult to face but letting her go had to come eventually. Just as she'd let her son George go.

She looked down into her daughter's pleading expression. 'You go on your walk, my darling, but mind you're back before it gets dark.'

A wreath of smiles broke out on Mary's face, banishing the pleading and the dark looks that had been there. 'Thanks, Ma. I won't be late. I promise you.'

Thelma watched as she dashed off, her legs kicking out behind her. Such long legs, she thought, and for some reason the fact clutched at her heart.

A sudden thought made her shout out, 'You should take a cardigan. It might be a bit cool later.'

Her words fell on deaf ears. The hard slamming of the front door shook the house.

She grimaced in a resigned fashion. 'Oh well. Up to you.'

'Gone to see the horses, has she?'

She'd almost forgotten that Alice was still here.

Thelma studied the greenish eyes and dark hair and saw again the man who had fathered her. It saddened her to think that three men had been taken from her, leaving behind one son who was now a young man and two girls on the cusp of womanhood.

An amused smile played around Alice's mouth and she had an air of mischief about her.

'What's so funny?'

Alice shrugged but kept smiling.

Taking in that smile made Thelma aware of the truth – a truth she'd been trying so hard to avoid. 'Ah. Our Mary isn't going to see the horses, is she.' It was a statement, not a question.

Alice continued to smile but looked as if she would burst if she didn't get out what she so desperately wanted to say. Entrusting a secret to Alice was not a clever idea. She was generous in the extreme and that included the sharing of secrets.

Thelma folded her arms and fixed her younger daughter with the searching look she adopted when she wished to pry the thin line between a lie and the truth. 'Well. Go on, tell me where she's going.'

Alice's lips quivered with the effort of keeping the secret inside her. Finally, it burst out in a sing-song tone of voice. 'She's seeing Rudy.'

Thelma clenched her hand into a fist and clenched her jaw. 'I take it that Rudy is not a horse.'

Alice shook her head. How was it possible to smile and look smug at one and the same time? That's what Alice was doing.

Thelma hadn't really needed to be told that Rudy was a boy her daughter had met. The truth was there written all over Alice's face. 'Is he a gypsy?'

Alice nodded. 'And he's got a horse.'

This was the truth that Thelma had tried to avoid and not at all what she wanted. Not just that Mary had a fancy for a gypsy lad, but that she had a fancy at all. That fear of her growing up was back, let out of the box like Aladdin's genie. The big consolation was that gypsies moved on. They never did stay in the same place for long, so for now she wouldn't worry too much.

There were other questions she wanted to ask, but she decided to let it be until Mary came home and she got the truth from the horse's mouth, so to speak.

Unburdened of the secret, Alice asked if she could go and see her friend Betty in the next street.

'Of course you can go over to play, my darling.'

Alice frowned and at the same time looked quite tickled.

'Playing's for kids, Ma. Betty's got the latest *Hollywood Stars* magazine. We're going to read it together.'

Another one, thought Thelma, her heart sinking like a stone in a fast-moving brook. You couldn't hear the splash but you could feel the ripples tumbling over the stones. Her youngest daughter was also growing up. *No. Not yet, Lord, please not yet!*

She put on a brave smile in an effort to hide the consternation inside. 'I bet that Shirley Temple will be in it. I do like her. Pretty as a picture she is.'

Alice looked far from impressed, her nose wrinkling as though she could smell something bad. 'She's for babies! Betty and me like Jimmy Cagney.'

Thelma tried not to look surprised that her daughter admired James Cagney who usually played hardened criminals – gangsters in fact. What was the world coming to? What were her daughters coming to?

3

The rest of Thelma's evening might have passed doing nothing more taxing than listening to the wireless. She did attempt to hem a new dress she was making for Mary, no more than an hour's or so work. It didn't happen.

Jenny came knocking just as she put in the first stitch. Thelma remembered that there was something Jenny wanted to tell her. What it was, she hadn't a clue.

Thelma found herself saying 'spill the beans', just as James Cagney might say.

Jenny looked surprised but didn't laugh. Her smile was tight as she sat down in a chair without being asked, holding a postcard in her hand.

When Jenny continued to sit in such a distant and contemplative fashion, Thelma lost patience and jerked her chin at it. 'Either stop gripping that postcard so tightly or tear it up and throw it in the fireplace.'

Jenny jerked back from wherever she'd been. 'I received it in second post. It's knocked me sideways.'

'Bad news?' Concerned Thelma reached out her hand.

Head bowed in a rather forlorn fashion; Jenny passed her the postcard. 'It says very little really.' Her voice was little more than a whisper, one of puzzlement and perhaps a little fear.

'Judging by the look on your face, it says a great deal.'

Jenny looked down at her tangled fingers. 'Read it.'

Thelma took the post card and read it quickly.

'Oh. Well that's a turn up.'

Roy was ill though hadn't gone into great detail but it had to be serious if he'd been discharged from the army. Although she sympathised with him she was concerned for Jenny. Roy had not been the best of husbands, mostly selfish and sometimes violent and Jenny had got used to the peaceful life since he'd left for the army.

When she raised her head, their eyes met. Thelma was immediately reminded of the way Jenny used to look when she'd first arrived in Coronation Close.

'How do you feel? About him coming back?'

She shrugged. 'What choice do I have. We're still married and he's never once kept me short of money since he joined the army. It was almost as though he was willing to pay to keep me at a distance. He loved what he was doing.'

Thelma waited patiently to hear the rest. She instinctively knew there was something else that Jenny seemed to be holding tightly to her chest. It had to come out.

'I think I told you what he was like when we lived in Blue Bowl Alley.'

'Yes.' Thelma knew very well and it pained her.

Jenny looked down at her fingers which were re-entangled. 'Once we moved here, it seemed as though everything deep down inside him came to the surface. Like a volcano that's been building up pressure for a long time.'

There was courage in her eyes when she raised her head.

After taking a deep breath, Jenny came out with it. 'Roy prefers men – if you know what I mean.'

'Is that all?'

Jenny looked astounded. 'What do you mean? Is that all?'

'He wouldn't be the first and sure as Christmas pudding he won't be the last. I've met plenty like him. Most wanted to keep it under wraps and pretend to conform. Even went against their nature and got married. Anything to hide the truth. Few dared come out and say what they were.'

Jenny had been ready to feel highly embarrassed at having a husband who was different to most. Thelma had instantly put her at her ease.

'Let's have a glass of sherry, shall we?'

Suddenly feeling that it was just what she needed, Jenny nodded.

'You won't tell anyone else about Roy, will you?'

The very thought of Jenny thinking she might tell was somewhat surprising. 'Of course not.' Thelma shook her head.

Placing the needlework from her lap onto the floor, she said, 'I've not led a sheltered life, Jenny. I've known plenty of men and I'm telling you now it takes all sorts to make a world.'

She went to the sideboard, fetched out a pair of small sherry glasses and poured them both a sherry.

Jenny took it gratefully. 'Cheers.'

'Cheers.'

Both harbouring their own concerns but united in friendship, they sipped at the sweet sherry, a drink famously distilled in the city of Bristol.

'So, you stuck together for the sake of the girls? It's understandable for you to be worried about the kids and what people would say. I'd have been the same.'

Jenny nodded. Another sip of the sweet dark liquid warmed her inside and helped regain some of the contentment cut short by the receiving of the postcard from Roy. 'Yes. We didn't want gossip to affect them or us.' Her eyes fluttered at Thelma. 'Roy likes to be respected. He couldn't stand the thought of people calling him names and sniggering behind his back.'

'Or worse,' exclaimed Thelma, an all-knowing look on her face. She didn't go into detail of how some blokes took umbrage with their fists at those they considered different. Whether it was a person's nature, looks or colour of skin, the worst was brought out in some who disliked those different from them.

Without asking if she wanted any more, Thelma refilled their glasses.

'I never expected him to come back. I don't know why, but I didn't. I'm so settled here.' Jenny sighed. 'I know it sounds awful, but I'd almost begun to forget he'd ever existed.'

'You've got two kids that say he did,' Thelma remarked with a laugh. She picked up the sherry bottle and gave it a shake. 'Whoops! It's empty.'

Jenny reached up and put her glass on the mantelpiece. Thelma got to her feet. 'I'll put the kettle on.' She halted before getting to the kitchen door. 'Come to think of it, I've half a bottle of port left over from Christmas.'

'Then I think it's the port.'

A measure of dark liquid glugged thickly into each glass. Jenny drank it more quickly than she had the sherry which resulted in it going straight to her head.

'I feel so wicked.' She gave a little coy laugh before taking another sip.

Their inhibitions drowned in just a few sips they began to talk openly, about their lives as they had been, as children, as young women, as mothers.

Their conversation came full circle, back to the postcard, to Roy and what would happen next. When was he likely to come home? How ill was he?

Jenny had to admit she had no idea.

'He'll get in touch again and I should think the army will too once they know that he's well enough to travel.'

Thelma felt concern for her friend's dilemma. She'd got used to living a simple and peaceful existence. The news of Roy's return opened a jar of worms. There were questions to be asked, problems to be solved and a lifestyle to be adjusted.

'Will you tell the children soon? Before he arrives, you know, get them used to the idea? They haven't seen him for a while.'

The deep breath Jenny took was almost painful. She hadn't been prepared for any of this. 'Yes. I'll have to. I don't want whispering behind our backs once he's here.'

'You can count on me not to tell a soul.'

'I know that.' Jenny's smile lifted her expression. Thelma was one person she knew she could count on.

'I worry about what might be said – rumoured about how I behaved during the time he was away – if you get my meaning.'

Their eyes met in mutual understanding. 'They won't dare say anything in my presence, I can tell you that!'

Thelma's manner was both resolute and reassuring.

She reached across and patted Jenny's hand. 'Though some will be more interested than others – if you get my meaning.'

No words were needed. The look that passed between them was enough. Their thoughts were running along the same road and both led to the pawnbroking and second-hand furniture shop in Filwood Broadway.

The silence held until Thelma asked, 'What will you tell Robin?'

It was a question Jenny had been asking herself.

'He'll hear in time. Anyway, he's got Doreen to contend with.

And the kids. She pops in for the maintenance money and dumps the kids on him when she's off on a date with some fancy man or another.'

'He's bound to have an opinion on what you should do, to be disappointed that you'll no longer be all alone.'

'He can have an opinion if he likes, but he's got no claim on me, Thelma.'

Their eyes met. Both knew that Robin was in love with Jenny and Thelma for one was prepared to guess that Jenny had deeper feelings for him than she made out.

Jenny looked down into the small glass of ruby-coloured liquid. 'We're both married.'

'For better or worse,' proclaimed Thelma. 'In his case, definitely for worse and in your case... well... it's not exactly been a bed of roses, has it?'

Jenny drew a line under Roy. She'd would cope with it all when the time came. In the meantime mentioning the stranger she'd seen was a welcome change of subject.

'I've got something else to tell you, but I don't want you to worry. You won't worry, will you?'

Thelma drew in her chin and eyed her questioningly. 'That depends on what you're going to tell me. I always worry when someone tells me not to worry!'

Jenny took a deep breath. 'I saw a man standing outside number one eyeing your place. He looked a bit shady. Thought I'd better tell you.'

'A bit shady?'

Jenny nodded.

Thelma was straight out with a reasonable explanation.

'Our Mary's got a boyfriend. It's likely to have been him. Did he look like a gypsy – you know – all dark hair, gold ring in one ear and swarthy complexion – but handsome? The sort any young woman would fall in love with?'

Jenny shook her head as she seriously considered the question.

'Gypsy? Nowhere near so romantic-looking unless gypsies have taken to wearing a brown raincoat and hat. Plus he was definitely a bit old for her and certainly not a boy.'

Looking puzzled, Thelma asked her to describe this stranger who had been so interested in her house.

'In his forties, I think, and he was wearing a suit beneath his raincoat. A tie. Shirt. Ordinary.'

'Did you see his face?'

'He had his hat pulled down, but I got the impression that his hair was sandy-coloured perhaps even auburn – almost the same colour as your Mary's hair.'

Thelma's face went pale. 'Are you sure he was looking at my house?'

'Yes. Do you know who it is?'

The way Thelma nodded was considered and slow. Her eyes were glazed and seemingly looking far off into nowhere. 'I think so.'

The strident voice Jenny knew so well was subdued and thoughtful.

'Is it a problem?'

Thelma chewed her look, her eyebrows lowered over thoughtful eyes. 'It might be.'

'Is there anything I can do?'

'No. Leave it with me,' she said at last.

Jenny made herself comfortable in the armchair that was closest to the dresser and the shelves of coronation mugs, cups, bowls and plates. The living-room curtains remained undrawn. Beyond the window, the light of the late spring evening was fading.

Thelma frowned. 'It's getting late. My two should be home shortly. I told them not to be late.'

'Your Alice is playing hopscotch down the far end of the Close. At least you know where she is.'

'Aye,' muttered Thelma with a troubled frown. 'I know where the other is too.'

Jenny judged it unwise to pursue the subject of Alice and Mary's whereabouts. This seemed like another moment to divert their conversation to another subject. 'How was dinner?'

She was certain she saw sudden teardrops on Thelma's eyelashes.

'Oh Jenny.' Expression full of emotion, Thelma bit her bottom lip, a sure sign she was feeling embarrassed. 'Maria cooked us spaghetti Bolognese. It seemed a bit slippery at first, but once I got the hang of winding it around my fork, it was fine. The sauce – that's the Bolognese bit – was very tasty. The girls had seconds. I had a bit extra too.'

'See! I told you everything would be fine. She didn't poison you, did she – even though some mothers-in-law deserve it!'

The serious expression dropped from Thelma's face and she laughed. 'I have to say she's a nice girl.'

'Your George wouldn't have married her if she hadn't been.'

Thelma's thoughts switched back to her eldest daughter. 'I'm going to have to give our Mary a good talking-to. I'm not ready for her growing up just yet. I mean, I'm not that old myself.'

Jenny grinned.

'What?' said Thelma.

'You're about to be a grandmother.'

Thelma brushed the thought of it away with a dismissive wave of her hand. 'Hmm! No need to remind me. Is there anything on at the pictures tomorrow night?'

'You won't be too tired? After all, Saturdays at the shop are your busiest day.'

'Well, I'm going to go in as fresh as a daisy tomorrow. George insisted that Maria wanted to do everything and didn't need my help.'

'Aren't you the lucky one.'

Thelma brightened. 'Yes. I suppose I am.'

'So it's up the pictures tomorrow night?'

'That suits me. Bert will be back from Cheltenham. He'll be coming. How about you? Not working up the Broadway tomorrow?'

'Yes, but only in the afternoon. Robin's got a delivery to do, so I'm on duty. I need to be there.' Jenny caught the knowing look on Thelma's face. 'And before you ask, no, he hasn't asked me out tomorrow night. That's why I'm free to go with you.'

'And Mary. I'm bringing our Mary whether she wants to come or not!'

Jenny shook her head disapprovingly. 'Thelma, she's nearly fourteen. She might not want to come. She might want to be out with her friends.'

Thelma sighed. 'I just can't take it on board that she's growing up. First our George goes away and gets married and, who knows, another few years and Mary will be gone too – girls being the way they are, sassy and wilful.'

Jenny chortled. 'Like you. Is that what you mean?'

Thelma ignored the implication. 'You're right about one thing. I'm getting old and I don't much like it.'

Jenny eyed her with a bemused expression. 'It beats the alternative! You wouldn't want to be pushing up daisies, would you?'

'No! Of course not. It's just that... well... here's my girl likely with a sweetheart and here's me with nobody.'

'You've got Bert.'

'Not really. I ain't really got him.'

'You're close.'

Thelma gave a wry smile. 'I still think he's closer to his mother. He talks about her when he's sketching me.'

'I thought he did sculptures.'

'He still does, but of late he's taken to drawing and painting.'

Bert Throgmorton was something of a dark horse – senior rent collector by day, an artist in his spare time.

Jenny sensed that Thelma was at a kind of crossroads. Her son was married. Before long she would have a grandchild. And now her daughter was showing signs of becoming a woman.

'After the pictures we'll get some fish and chips for supper.' Jenny hoped her suggestion might take Thelma's minds off things. The response was muted. Thelma made a so-so sound.

In an effort to change the subject Jenny went back to the reason she'd come over to discuss in the first place.

'That man this morning... I wish I'd taken in more details.' She held her head to one side as if it might make her remember. 'I'm beginning to think that his hair might have been red rather than sandy. And his eyes might have been blue. A cheeky look about him, though I could be mistaken. Oh well. Time to go.'

Jenny didn't notice the sudden alarm in Thelma's expression at her mention of red hair.

No, thought Thelma as a ghost from the past came to mind and seriously made her feel as though somebody was walking over her grave. That would be too much of a longshot. Other possibilities were closer to home. Hudson for a start though she hadn't noticed him following her about of late. Though she hadn't really been looking and even if she had he was a man who hid in the shadows.

4

The man who Jenny had spotted staring at number twelve Coronation Close was now standing outside the off-licence in Melvin Square. He regretted venturing into Coronation Close. He hadn't expected anyone to be around.

The neighbour cutting flowers had bobbed up unexpectedly from behind the hedge and eyed him suspiciously, asked him if she could help. His presence was bound to be reported. It was a stupid thing to do. Had he really thought Mary would come bouncing out of the house and run straight into his arms? Of course she wouldn't. It was stupid to have thought so, but his imagination was vivid nowadays. The medicine he swigged back in bottle loads had a lot to do with it.

No matter whether it was a man or a woman, he'd never found it easy getting to know people. Even when someone he didn't know too well opened the conversation, he immediately became tongue-tied. Once he had got to know them, he could talk seventeen to the dozen. He could be warm, he could be funny and he could laugh at their jokes and let them cry on his shoulder if that was what they wanted.

He intended hanging around in Melvin Square and had braced himself with a couple of things from the off-licence to help him pass the time including a packet of five Woodbines – one of which was already dangling from the corner of his mouth. A packet of ten Woodbines three to five times a day had been the norm up until recently, but he'd cut back. He'd been warned his chest was bad but that it had nothing to do with smoking. Most medical advice had told him that cigarettes were good for clearing the chest. The one holding the opposite view had been young and idealistic. He chose to believe the former rather than the latter and suggested that he gave up smoking completely.

Whilst in the off-licence he'd also purchased a packet of Smith's crisps. Mary would like those. He'd bought them for her. Perhaps he should also have bought her a bottle of lemonade, but that might be a bit much. The bottles with their spring top were too big for one person to consume.

Nobody took much notice of him stood there outside the off-licence, the smoke from the cigarette curling up into the fresh night air. Blokes did it all the time. The odd glance came his way purely because he was an unknown in the neighbourhood.

He heard her before she stepped into a pool of light falling from a streetlight.

She came into view with dimpled cheeks and hand in hand with a swarthy-looking lad with jet-black hair. They were leading the horse this time, strolling contentedly and looking happy. Her happiness brought a smile to his face and for a moment took him back to his own youth when he'd considered himself in love on at least three occasions.

None had stood the test of time but that didn't matter. What was it they said? Better to have loved and lost rather than not loved at all. Well he'd could certainly claim that!

This was the first occasion he'd seen her without anyone of

much consequence being around, that is no adults. He'd seen her outside the school gates in the company of friends and under the supervision of a teacher. He knew from his own childhood that the teacher would be keeping an eye on things, greeting parents and saying goodbye to their charges for yet another day. He didn't want to be noticed so had to be careful. It wouldn't do for her mother to know, or any adult for that matter.

His attention was drawn to a bobby on the beat, strolling along on the other side of the square. Having no wish to arouse his suspicions he stepped back into the shadow thrown by the off-licence.

Once the bobby had gone on his way he stepped back out into the light and watched with interest.

The lad was obviously her boyfriend. She'd been with him a day or so ago when he'd first seen her. The lad had been riding bareback on a piebald horse and she'd been riding pillion behind him. Judging by the silky black hair and weather beaten complexion the boy had to be a gypsy from the encampment down on the Novers. For years, there had been an encampment there at one time or another. He remembered the painted horse-drawn caravans gleaming with brass and glass from way back, intriguing but also intimidating. The folk who lived in the caravans didn't welcome close scrutiny. They kept to themselves, lived their life in their own way and were not inclined to be friendly to outsiders. Complete with their culture and traditions, their world had changed little in centuries and they protected it.

With athletic ease the lad flung himself onto the horse's bare back. His voice carried as Mary walked away. 'See you tomorrow.'

He waved.

She waved back.

Digging his heels into the horse's sides, he trotted off into the gathering darkness, leaving Mary to brush horsehairs from her skirt before heading towards home.

'Look at the mess I'm in,' he heard her mutter smiling as she said it. In her estimation getting covered in horse hairs was most definitely worth it. Sensing the time had come for him to make her acquaintance he ventured away from the area outside off-licence and crossed the road to join her.

Her attention fixed on her skirt, she barely noticed him approaching and couldn't possibly know that he was itching to reach out and touch her, give her his name and tell her who he was. The right moment to do that would come and he had promised himself that he would tread carefully. Being too forward, giving her his name and telling her the full story might scare her.

Instead of blatantly introducing himself, he settled for something far more prosaic. He had a story ready and waiting. 'Heard what you said, love. Could be worse. Could be cats' hairs.'

Tilting her head in a lofty, defensive manner, she looked up, her face full of innocence as she flicked her fingers at what remained of the equine presence. 'What's the difference?'

'Cats' hairs make me sneeze.'

'Oh.'

She regarded him cautiously causing him to suspect that she might run away at any moment. He couldn't blame her for that. After all, she had no idea who he was and young girls were told to be wary of the over-friendliness of men they didn't know. He needed to say something that would put her at ease that would pave the way to friendship and gaining her trust.

'Is that lad a gypsy?' He didn't need to ask. He knew he was. Anybody with half a brain could see that.

Her chin thrust forward, a stubborn defiance he'd most definitely seen before in another young woman. 'What's it to you?'

She was gutsy and showed no fear, her little nose in the air, her pert chin thrust forward and a disarming look in her eyes.

'He's a handsome lad. Like an old-fashioned knight riding on that horse. Did you enjoy the ride? I saw you riding pillion the other night.'

'Yes. I like horses.' The wary look remained unabated, her head cocked to one side, eyeing him suspiciously.

He kept his smile. Kept his voice even. 'I like them too. I used to ride them when I was younger. Rode in a few horse races way back.'

'Really?' He noted her eyes widen and an expression of admiration replace the defensive glower. Horses were obviously the way to her heart. The knowledge made him quietly satisfied.

'Off riding again tomorrow?'

She shook her head. 'No. Flint is being shod. They're moving on in a week. Flint must have iron shoes, so he can pull one of the carts along the road without hurting his feet.'

'Very necessary.' He nodded solemnly.

She cocked her head a little higher as something he'd said before came back to her. 'You rode horses in races?'

'Oh yes.'

'Did you win any?'

'Only at first. After that, I put on too much weight and grew too tall.'

'That's a shame.'

'It was that.' He grimaced at the thought of it, of his own disappointment of ending up having to do the lowlier tasks around a stable instead of being high in the saddle.

He heard her stomach growl, saw her pat it as if that would quell the noise it was making.

'On yer way home fer supper?'

She nodded. 'I could do with a bit of bread and dripping right now.'

'I ain't got none of that, but I've got this.'

He pulled the packet of crisps out of his pocket. 'I bought them fer meself but decided I didn't want them. I ain't touched them. They're all yours.'

A quick glance and she was hooked. 'Ta.'

First the bag was ripped open, then the small blue package containing the salt, which she sprinkled liberally over the contents before her fingers dived in.

She turned away.

'Where are you going?'

Hand still in the bag of crisps, she came to a halt. 'Home.'

'I'll walk with you a way.'

She didn't object but glanced at him before returning to devour the rest of the crisps.

'What's the lad's name?' he asked.

She gulped back a crisp. 'Rudy Nichols.'

'I suppose he's around your age.'

'Three years older.'

'Let me guess. He's sixteen or seventeen?'

She concentrated on pulling one crisp at a time from the bag. 'Yes,' she said once she'd swallowed another crisp. 'He's sixteen.'

Only a few days ago, he'd stood outside the school just to get a glimpse of her and had seen her the night before with the lad. They'd been leaning against the fence up on the Novers shyly holding hands and exchanging a few innocent kisses. What would she think if she knew just how much he knew about her? He knew a good deal, which was very much to his advantage. She knew next to nothing about him. That was the way it would stay – at least for now.

'So what does your mother think about you 'aving a sweetheart?' He asked the question in a convivial but casual manner.

Mary's face dropped. 'Who said I did?'

'You two looked close. A bit more than friends.'

She pivoted in a shy manner. It might have had something to do with the glow of the streetlight, but a sudden pinkness suffused her cheeks. 'I haven't told her.'

'Why's that? Will she stop you seeing 'im.'

'She'll say I'm too young.'

'But you want her to know, I mean now that you're growing up?'

Mary frowned. 'I suppose I do.'

'How would you describe him to your mother?'

Mary had decided she liked this man's voice. It wasn't an accent she'd heard before, warm and lilting and similar to a song.

Mary bit her bottom lip as she thought about answering his question. 'I would tell her how marvellous he makes me feel.'

'You like talking about him?'

'Of course.'

She looked quite indignant, her small chin pulled in, her head held sideways and a challenging look in her eyes.

'Do you talk to your mother about horses?'

'Sometimes, but she's scared of horses. She doesn't understand how beautiful they are, how kind. Much kinder than people. And they're clever. They know more things than people. Have you read *Black Beauty*?'

'I've heard of it, but sadly I ain't read it. Have you?'

'Oh yes.' The pert little chin jerked up and down.

'What do you like about it?'

'About how clever and kind he is.'

'He must be a very special horse.'

'All the horses in the book are clever.'

'Is that so?'

'Yes.'

'Tell me what makes them clever.'

She looked thoughtful as she searched for a particular passage that might influence him and confirm her belief in the intelligence of animals.

'My favourite sentence is that God gave men reason but he gave horses and other animals instinct with which they have often saved the lives of men.'

He nodded in agreement. 'I can understand that. I think they're clever too and that humans are sometimes pretty stupid.' He stopped and looked as if he were considering something designed to impress – purely for her benefit; to gain her trust, to give her the sense that they had something in common. 'Tell you what, when your lad goes away you can always find me here buying a packet of cigarettes. I'll buy you some crisps and we can talk about horses. How would that be?'

For a moment, Mary eyed him suspiciously.

He judged it time to reassure. 'You don't have to, but only if you need to.'

The suspicious look was replaced by a look he could only describe as one of overflowing excitement. He'd gained her trust and it went some way to convincing him that from here on everything should be plain sailing.

'Are you married?' she asked suddenly.

He shook his head. 'No.'

'Have you got a girlfriend?'

The question took him by surprise and at the same time amused him. He thought of all the women he could have married but hadn't.

'No. I used to have girlfriends but that was a good while ago.'

There had been plenty, most of them enjoyed or endured and then forgotten. But there had been one he remembered. One that had caused him to entertain emotions he hadn't thought he had and even consider marriage.

'What's your name?'

This question he had been prepared for and had come armed with an answer. He didn't want her to repeat his name to anyone –

at least not for now. He wanted to get acquainted with her before exposing the truth and the reason he was here.

'Donald Tucker.' He said it quickly so that it sounded as though it really was his to own. The name had belonged to a stable yard manager where he'd worked back in the dizzy years of his youth.

'My name's Mary. Mary Dawson.'

'How do you do, Mary Dawson?'

He held out his hand. At first, she hesitated before wiping her salty fingers on her hips, then taking the hand that was offered.

'You said your lad, Rudy, was going away and leaving his pretty lady behind.'

Although the light was dim here, there was enough for him to see from her expression that the words 'pretty lady' had made her a bit flustered. 'Yes,' she replied hesitantly.

'How long before he goes away?'

'Three or four days.'

'Ah, you poor girl. I feel sorry for you. You're going to be lonely.'

'I might be. The horses up in the top field will be staying. I'll go and see them.'

He'd nosed about enough to know that the horses in the top field were of solid colour and privately owned. The gypsy horses would be long gone.

'That might help but you'll have no Rudy with whom to share your love of those fine animals.'

Her expression saddened. 'That's true.'

He grinned. 'I'll be around if you ever want to talk about horses. I don't know how to talk about much else. As you say, horses are better than humans. Our four-legged friends never let us down.'

She laughed.

He was transfixed by the sound of that laughter, the way she threw her head back, the soft, whiteness of her neck, the way it dipped down into the gap exposing her throat. And her hair. It was red and unruly and her eyes were blue. Just like his own.

He decided it was time for him to take his leave and for her to be home with her mother.

'Goodnight and sleep tight, Mary Dawson.'

'Goodnight.'

Then she was gone.

Up until this moment, he'd held his emotions in check. But now, left alone with the encroaching night and a whole basket of regrets, he wiped at the wetness in his eyes.

* * *

Thanks to her new friend, Mary made her way home feeling more grown-up than she ever had and she didn't need Donald Tucker to warn her not to tell her mother. Of course she wouldn't! Her mother treated her as though she were still a child.

'I'm not a child. Not now,' she muttered as she made her way home.

She'd always been responsible, always throwing herself into adult ways, which included keeping house. Alice helped of course, but she was younger. Two years made a substantial difference.

Leaving the softening night air behind her, she entered the house aware that her mother was standing in the shadow of the front door canopy, fists resting on her hips, elbows angular with intent.

'You're late.'

Mary flounced past her into the hallway. 'Don't go on at me.'

'Cut out your cheek or I'll slap your face!'

'I'm not that late. I shared a packet of crisps with Tilly on the way back.'

'Did you indeed.'

Mary swallowed. Judging by her mother's tone, she didn't believe she was telling the truth.

There was only one way out. But yawning and declaring that she was tired and needed to go to bed cut no ice.

Her mother grabbed her shoulder before she could escape up the stairs. 'I want a word with you, young lady.'

Mary's heart sank. Her first thought was that Alice had blabbed. The little mare! Once she was upstairs, she would give her sister a sharp nudge and warn her to keep her mouth shut. But before then, she would test her mother's mood.

'I'm thirsty. Can I have a cup of milk?'

'Water. And make it snappy.'

Her mother had a piercing look on her face, the one when she was weighing up whether she was going to hear lies or the truth and what her response was likely to be.

The ensuing silence was worse than an accusation. Mary felt obliged to respond and walked right into the trap as she filled the cup with water.

'I ain't done nothing wrong.'

'Who said you had?'

Thelma did not raise her voice, but it was knife-sharp, like a steel carving knife slicing through a beef joint.

Pouting and looking hard done by, Mary swilled the cup out, folded her arms and shook her head. 'I've just been out with friends. That's all.'

'School friends?'

'Just friends.'

'And Tilly.'

'Yes. Tilly.'

It wasn't a lie, but it wasn't strictly the truth.

Her mother sensed this, sighed and shook her head. 'I don't

know what's come into you of late, Mary Dawson. You're getting too big for your boots and that's a fact.'

Irritated by the comment, Mary tossed her head. 'I'm nearly grown up. I ain't a kid. I'm nearly old enough to go to work.'

If Thelma had been a kettle, there would have been steam coming out of her ears by now.

'Young lady, you will do as I say so long as you live under this roof. Now sit down!' A red fingernail flashed. A finger pointed at an armchair.

Regretting that she'd been so cocky, Mary sat down. She hadn't meant to upset her mother but at times she felt a need to stand her ground.

She sat sullenly thinking of the man who had bought her crisps and treated her like a young lady not a child. Mouth in a petulant mode, her gaze fixed on the brown and beige linoleum on the kitchen floor.

The legs of a dining chair made a scraping noise as her mother brought it closer.

'Right. Now, what's this boy's name?'

At first, Mary tried denial. Eyes round with innocence, she said, 'What boy?'

'You know what boy. The one that's got horses.'

Alice chose the wrong time to poke her nose around the door.

Mary's eyes blazed with anger. 'It was 'er, weren't it. It was our Alice that told you. Just wait till I...'

When Alice saw Mary half rise from her chair, she ducked back out again.

Her mother laid a heavy hand on her shoulder preventing her from escaping whatever questions hung in the air plus a good talking-to.

'Never mind who told me, young lady. The fact is they shouldn't have needed to tell me. You should have told me yourself!'

Mary tossed her head. 'I couldn't. You'd 'ave told me I was too young. And I'm not too young.'

'That's a matter of opinion. You still haven't told me his name.'

Mary looked down at the floor, anything other than meet her mother's angry expression. 'Rudy.'

'Rudy? Is that short for something?'

'Rudolph Nichols.'

The name was familiar, local but different to most folks.

'They're a gypsy family.'

'Does it matter?' Mary's eyes blazed with defiance.

Feeling a tad guilty for condemning the boy before she'd even met him Thelma swallowed. There was so much more she wanted to ask but Mary's outburst that she was no longer a child curbed her tongue. In growing older, her daughter had also become more stubborn.

'Mary. Now listen to me. He's not the boy for you. They travel around a lot.'

'Ma! I'm not marrying him. We're just friends and he's got a horse. His name's Flint.'

'Ah,' exclaimed Thelma. Suddenly, things were a lot clearer – and a lot less worrying. In fact, she felt like laughing. What could be more attractive in a young man than owning a horse!

'That explains it.'

She rubbed at her nose to prevent herself from laughing too loudly and upsetting her daughter's sensitivities.

'You always did like creatures with four legs and a tail.'

As her mother's cast-iron expression began to mellow and amusement danced in her eyes, Mary took advantage of the situation and decided to offer a little something to put her mother's mind at rest – and to stop her asking too many more questions. Or keeping on about it. She hated it when her mother kept on, asking questions, probing, needling her to find out what she was up to.

Well, she could soon sort that.

'He's going away soon.'

'He would be. Them folk can't stop travelling.'

Thelma knew this was true. The gypsy families had camped down at the bottom of the Novers for years. In the period between leaving the orphanage and getting a job, she too had wandered down there, listening to their music, watching them dance, smelling the smoke from their campfires. Guessing she was a runaway and hungry, they'd fed her. They'd not said much to her, but she'd been aware of the pity in their eyes. It was only once the police had come to take her away that she realised they'd sent for the authorities whilst taking care of her.

She'd liked their nut-brown faces and glossy hair. She'd even dared ask them why their skin was so brown and their hair so black and glossy.

They'd answered honestly – at least it had seemed that way at the time.

Walnut oil was smeared on their faces to protect their skin and goose fat on their hair. In later years, she'd used goose fat on her own hair when it flew dry and loose and found that it worked. Applying walnut oil made her skin smooth.

Mary began spreading dripping onto a doorstep of bread, the crusty bit from the end of the loaf. Once done, she added a generous amount of salt.

Tears stinging the backs of her eyes, Thelma watched her. She didn't want her to grow up, to leave these special years between childhood and womanhood. From dolls to boys. However would she cope.

Mother and daughter retired to the living room. Mary sat in an armchair, Thelma on the arm caressing her daughter's hair.

Feeling reassured, Mary was ready to talk. She liked these moments alone with her mother.

A bite of bread and dripping for sustenance and she was away.

'We're going to see each other when he gets back in six months' time. Just as friends. I should have a job by then.'

'Let's see what happens. With a bit of luck, you'll have more than one offer.'

She'd made enquiries at Robinsons, the paper bag factory, although Mary had expressed her desire to get a job in Woolworths where they sold cheap jewellery and make-up and other things besides. She'd have the pick of everything they had to offer at a knockdown price. She looked forward to that.

'It would be nice if I could get a job in a stable and look after horses.'

Inwardly, Thelma entertained the reality that working with horses might be nothing but a dream for a girl from Mary's background. Both the paper bag company and Woolworths were realistic options for a school leaver. So were the tobacco factories. But horses?

Her red-tipped fingers softly traced through Mary's hair, as hopes and dreams skipped through her mind. 'Let's wait and see. The future is yours to keep and who knows? If you want something that much, your dreams might come true.'

Mary grimaced then offered a smile by way of apology. 'I didn't mean to upset you.'

Thelma was touched and a bit regretful and each feeling were tempered with amusement. 'I should have known better than to get annoyed. When it comes to love, my darling girl, a horse wins every time.'

Mary felt vindicated and even more grown up because her mother seemed more approachable. She did like Rudy but she wasn't going to dwell on it or tell her mother that she was a bit fonder of him than she had admitted. Even though only on the threshold of becoming a woman, she was beginning to tell only what she had to tell. Her feelings, her emotions and some things in her life she preferred to keep to herself.

She held off mentioning Donald Tucker, the man outside the off-licence who used to be a jockey. They had horses in common and that in excited her. It didn't occur to her that he was older than her and had appeared out of the shadows to offer friendship to a girl on the cusp of being a woman. Neither did she see any harm in becoming better acquainted with him. Whilst Rudy was away, she would have someone with whom to share her interest.

5

Thelma and Jenny were enjoying a Wednesday afternoon in the kitchen of number 12 Coronation Close with a pot of tea between them. Thelma was feeding some hemming through her sewing machine with one hand and turning the handle with the other.

They were discussing the stranger who Jenny had seen eyeing up Thelma's house.

Thelma was inclined to think that it was Sam Hudson who Jenny had seen watching the house. The other possibility she kept very much to herself because it was just too far-fetched to believe.

Still, it wouldn't hurt to enquire a bit further, just in case.

Thelma pressed Jenny for more details – details that Jenny couldn't give.

'Thelma, I didn't see much. As I told you, the brim of his hat hid most of his face.'

It couldn't be anyone else but Sam Hudson. It couldn't. That's what Thelma kept telling herself.

'How about we go to the police?'

Thelma shook her head. 'I'd have to tell them about what he did. Then they would ask me why I didn't report it at the time. No matter what I said, they would say that I'd consented. The woman gets the blame. Blokes stick together, Jenny, and that's a fact.'

'I wish I had some kind of instant camera then if I see him again, I can take a picture.'

Thelma laughed. 'That's a bit far-fetched. I knew you enjoyed watching that *Flash Gordon* at the pictures! All that science-fiction nonsense. But that's all it was, Jenny – science fiction.'

Jenny agreed with her. 'Perhaps there might be something like that in a hundred years' time. In the meantime, a Kodak Brownie takes too long. He'd have run off by the time I got it set up and was about to press the shutter.'

'If he doesn't do it again, then that's fine. If he does, then I'll call at his house and warn him off. I would take George with me, but...' She shook her head and for once looked almost helpless. 'I wouldn't want him to know the reason why.'

'Then I'll come with you.'

Thelma thought about it. 'Yes. I would appreciate that.'

* * *

What with one thing and another, it was halfway through the week before Jenny and Thelma got to go to the pictures. Thelma had sat tight over the weekend to keep an eye on Mary. On Sunday, she took her girls up Cabot Tower for a picnic. Alice had enjoyed it well enough and although Mary appeared to, there were times when she seemed a bit distracted.

For a start it was Thelma's half-day. It gave her time to do a bit around the house, get ready and ensure that her girls would not stay out too late.

Bert insisted on taking them to the Broadway Picture House in his new Ford motorcar and that he would buy the tickets.

From across the road, striding through the overly long grass of the central island, Robin joined them, his hair still tousled but wearing a white shirt, a patterned tie and a smile on his face.

Jenny bit her lip. Thelma eyed him with a mix of admiration and pity. Poor man. Horrible wife and in love with Jenny.

'Will you tell him of Roy's return?' Thelma whispered.

'No,' Jenny whispered back.

He greeted each one of them in turn, but his warmest greeting was for Jenny, appreciation written all over his face.

'You're looking a picture.'

'Take a good look. Once we're inside, you won't see me once the lights go out.'

Standing in the queue for tickets, Bert considered himself in charge. 'What's it to be? Circle or stalls?'

'Don't mind as long as I've got a seat,' said Thelma. 'Me and the carpet sweeper have had quite a day upstairs and down. And I washed the curtains before I went to work this morning. Dried and ironed this afternoon. I did the lot and it's ready to go back on the beds.'

The area outside the Broadway Picture House was busier than usual. Besides the queue for the pictures, there were also men assembled around a large van displaying a notice saying, 'Mobile Enlistment Vehicle'.

The moment she caught sight of it and the crowd of men so willingly signing for yet another war with Germany, Jenny felt a cold shiver run down her spine.

'Surely not. Not again.'

Hearing her softly whispered comment and seeing her expression in the glow of the lightbulbs encircling the overhead sign, Robin squeezed her hand.

'You all right, Jen?'

Feeling slightly sick she nodded towards the van. 'Is that really necessary? We don't know for sure that there's going to be a war, do we?'

'It's just a precaution. That's all. If it's any consolation, I don't think there will be.'

He squeezed her hand again and although he wore a smile, she couldn't help but think that he looked concerned. Perhaps not so concerned as she was feeling, but it was there all the same.

Thelma put in her opinion.

'We need a woman in charge. That'll get things done,' she declared loudly.

A man in front of them in the queue rolled his eyes.

'Perish the thought.'

'It won't happen in our lifetime,' said Bert.

'Never will,' pronounced the man in front. 'Women ain't cut out to be in charge of a country. If war does break out, it's the men that will go. The women will stay in the kitchen where they belong.'

Thelma tapped him on the shoulder. 'Oi! Queen Victoria used to rule this country. And before her there was Queen Elizabeth the First. She rode into battle wearing armour. And don't forget the last war. Women were called up then to the factories, to drive buses and ambulances and God knows what else. That's how we got the vote. Because we'd stepped into men's shoes and did their jobs better than they did.'

Seeing the fury in Thelma's face and feeling the weight of her hand on his shoulder, the man's jaw sagged. When he looked as though he was about to say something else, his wife, a big woman with a fox fur resting on her broad shoulders, gave him a push.

'Shut yer mouth, Eric. You don't know what yer on about. You was working on the railways so weren't called up. Now get and buy us two seats in the one and sixpennies.'

Whatever the man might have said next was swallowed instantly. He might consider himself in charge of the world, but his wife obviously was of the opinion that she was in charge of him!

Thelma was hardly able to control her laughter.

The queue moved forward past a poster extolling the use of gas masks, warning about the possibility of bombing and what to do with your pets if war should be declared.

Jenny found it all very depressing.

On the whole, Thelma kept her concerns at bay and chose to believe it would not happen simply because she didn't want it to happen. George was her big worry. What if he was called up into the Royal Navy? Even if that didn't happen, he was likely to serve with the merchant navy on convoys bringing food into the country. Others had been called to do that back in the Great War. With increasing worry, she asked Bert if he thought there was the likelihood of another war or was this all pie in the sky.

He shrugged and shook his head. 'I don't really know.'

'I thought you would know seeing as you work for the council.'

'I oversee the collection of rent. The bigwigs in government don't defer to me for my opinion.' He looked disappointed.

'Well they should,' said Thelma in a resolute manner. 'Your opinion is as good as anybody else.'

She sounded quite put out that he hadn't been approached, which made him smile. She wasn't to know that plans had been put in place and volunteers organised for fire-watching duty. The powers that be feared the use of incendiary bombs. Although small, they were lethal. It was imperative they were snuffed out straight away. Water wouldn't do it by itself. Buckets of sand were to be made available, plus a stirrup pump and a bucket of water. To his mind, it didn't seem much in the way of equipment, but he supposed those who knew of such things had assessed everything properly. The people who worked for Bristol Corporation were good at assessing things before going into action. He just hoped they'd done it right but could say nothing about it because it was top secret and that in itself alarmed him.

Not wishing to give anything away he was careful what he said, 'I don't know about that. Anyway, Mr Chamberlain is doing all he can to stop that happening. We must trust that common sense prevails.'

'We live in hope. I for one wouldn't want to go through that lot again,' Robin added. Again, he gave Jenny's hand a squeeze. 'Still, we've got to look on the bright side. Nothing's 'appened yet, and with a bit of luck, nothing will.'

As they shuffled forward in the queue, the sight of the enlistment van was left behind. Not once did they turn round and give it another look. Like kids who don't want to face something bad. If they couldn't see it, then it wasn't there.

Thelma tucked her arm into Bert's. She too didn't want to look at it and prayed fervently that it wouldn't be there later when they came out.

Gradually, they made their way to the front of the queue and from there up into the circle, where there was a bit more legroom and being a bit more expensive – two shillings as opposed to one shilling and sixpence – a bit less crowded though not by much.

The film was *Free to Live*, starring Cary Grant and Katharine Hepburn. The picture house was full, partly down to the fact that the male lead hailed from Horfield, a suburb of Bristol, where he had been born Archibald Leach.

There was a gap between the ending of the earlier matinee and the beginning of the next one. A woman with arms like legs of ham began belting out a selection of well-known tunes on the organ, a bright gaudy thing sat like a monster between the auditorium and the screen. Someone behind them began to snore.

Thelma was becoming impatient. 'For goodness' sake, let's get the film up on screen,' she grumbled. Bert passed her a bag of chocolate caramels to help keep her impatience at bay.

Finally, the lights dimmed and the curtains swished back to either side of the screen. The performance was about to begin.

The sight of the enlistment van and all it represented might have faded from Jenny's mind and she would have settled to watch the screen if it hadn't been for Gaumont-Pathé News.

Because of the darkness, the picture on the screen made it seem as though she wasn't just watching it, she'd been transported to where it was all happening. Columns of earth, bricks, stones and dust flew up into the air and the noise of explosions thundered all around.

Men and women's worried faces, lined with grief, dirt and hopelessness stared out from the screen. There was fear on the faces of those on the screen and a deep hush came over the audience, especially women. The men seemed more reticent, even though the terrible scenes of war in China and closer to home in Spain were real and not the result of filming in a Hollywood studio. It occurred to Jenny that they were trying to hide their fear both for their own self-esteem as the stronger sex and to reassure their female relatives. Jenny was far from reassured.

She looked down at her trembling hands as the items on Spain and China were replaced by scenes of the German army marching into Austria. Was the entire world going to war?

Whether Robin felt what she was going through was hard to tell, but she suddenly became aware of his hand covering hers. No longer looking at the screen, he was studying her, trying his best to evaluate in the darkness how she was feeling. He leaned across and kissed her cheek.

She knew he was trying to reassure her that no war would come, but she didn't want to be like those people on the screen fleeing an army, an air force and the plumes of debris sent high into the atmosphere. It made her wonder whether it was happening where Roy was stationed.

At least he was coming home from there though she couldn't be sure he was happy about it. He'd fully admitted to her that he preferred the company of other men and enjoyed wearing a uniform. Words from a William Shakespeare play came to mind. 'We few, we happy few. We band of brothers.'

He'd first donned the uniform of Oswald Mosley's Fascists when they'd lived in Blue Bowl Alley and had continued to wear it when they'd moved into Coronation Close. When the uniforms were banned, he'd joined the army and almost immediately applied to be posted abroad. He'd told her that he was off to see the world and that she was unlikely to ever see him again, but he'd insisted that they remain married. Most of his army pay would be sent to keep her and the girls.

He'd changed once he'd achieved his dream, wearing a uniform and living amongst other men. He seemed happier than when he'd been married to her and they'd both admitted that marrying had been a mistake.

Still, just because they were now estranged didn't mean she didn't care that he was sick. After all, he was the father of her children and it was possible he was a changed man though for better or worse she couldn't be sure.

* * *

The film proved a thankful relief after seeing all that the shelling and aggression in the news.

At the playing of the national anthem, the audience stood up and joined in. Just for once, few had scurried for the exit before the familiar tune had struck up as they usually did.

'Cod and chips, anyone?' Bert asked as they made their exit.

'Ooow, lovely,' said Thelma. She took hold of Bert's arm.

Outside, the smell of battered cod and deep-fried chips drifted on the crisp night air.

Someone's stomach rumbled.

'I take full responsibility,' said Robin. 'I ain't ate a thing since bread and dripping for breakfast and nothing but tea for the rest of the day.'

Once they'd been served, everyone sprinkled their supper with salt from a large pot where crystals stuck to the rim. Jenny sprinkled malt vinegar from a matching bottle.

The chips were hot and needed blowing on before daring to eat them. Whilst they cooled and batter was pulled off the fish, they discussed how much they'd enjoyed the film.

'Could 'ave done without the news,' remarked Thelma. She licked her greasy fingers between words.

Jenny agreed with her. 'In future, I'm going to come late and take in the main feature. I don't think I can stand much more about fighting and killing.'

Bert lightened the mood. 'Get on with eating your supper. Nobody gets into my car until they do. I don't want it stinking of fish and chips. It's a devil of a smell to get rid of.'

Standing slightly apart from the others, Robin asked Jenny if he could walk her home. 'I've got something to tell you.'

Although he had kept his voice down, Thelma heard him.

'There's room in the car for all of us.'

'I want a word in private. It's important,' Robin responded.

Jenny presumed it was something to do with Doreen, who continually demanded more and more of his hard-earned cash but did nothing to help him out in the shop. In which case he needed a sympathetic ear.

'We'll be off then,' called Thelma as she joined Bert in the car and waved as they pulled away.

The lights outside the Broadway went out. Except for a few streetlights throwing pools into the gloom there was little to light their way home.

'I wanted to talk to you about Doreen,' said Robin as he took hold of Jenny's arm.

'I guessed that. What's she done now?' It was Jenny's opinion that Doreen had to be the most selfish woman she'd ever met.

He hung his head as they walked. 'She's moving in.'

Jenny could hardly believe her ears. 'Moving in?' There was incredulity in her tone.

'She's got nowhere else to go – her and the kids, that is.'

'How come?'

He sighed heavily, his gaze fixed on his feet. 'The landlord's told her she can't stay.'

'But I thought he was...' She held onto the word 'lover'. It seemed too inappropriate. Robin's kids used the word 'uncle' – a man a woman went to bed with who wasn't her husband. Worse still the kids referred to having had more than one uncle.

The sound of the heels of her court shoes striking the pavement graced the night with a hollow, mournful sound. The night was deep and dark. The last bus from the city centre passed them on its way to the end of the journey at Inns Court.

Surmising that Robin was gathering his thoughts, she kept quiet. He had difficulty dealing with his wife. Each meeting between the two of them, whether they were discussing the children or money – usually the latter – had ended in arguments. She braced herself for his announcement whilst still trying to analyse what must have occurred. Something distasteful must have happened for Doreen and the kids to be thrown out of the two dim rooms in a shared house in Montpelier. This was not going to be good.

'The bloke's wife came 'ome.'

She raised her eyebrows. 'A wife.'

'Yes.'

'The wife wasn't there living with him when Doreen moved in?'

'No. She'd been living with her sister. She'd taken off in a huff when she found 'im carrying on with a barmaid from The White Hart in Brislington. Divorce was mentioned, but she changed her mind. It's easy to suggest divorce but costs a bloody fortune when you go into it. Anyway, they own properties between them.'

'And now she's back.'

He nodded. 'Yep. With a vengeance. The wife's given Doreen two days to get out.' He paused. 'She had nowhere else to go. I had to do it, Jenny. For the sake of my kids.'

Jenny gritted her teeth. 'That's what she counts on. They're a weapon she'll use every time.' She felt angry that Doreen was using Robin as a convenience, but it also angered her that he was allowing himself to be used. Arms folded and jaw locked, she marched away. 'I'll find my own way home.'

'Jenny!'

She heard his footsteps running after her.

'Jenny. Stop. I had to let her move in. Her and my kids. What choice did I have?'

'You could have stood up for yourself. Told her to get her own place. Leave the kids with you if she had to. It would probably have suited her better.'

'She wouldn't do that.' His voice was raised now.

'No. Of course not. It's easier and less expensive to bully you into taking her in.'

Jenny's voice was equally strident. They stood there beneath the light of a streetlamp glaring at each other, Jenny determined to hold that stare, to not turn away.

She won the battle. He was the one who looked away first. Hands in trouser pockets, he hung his head.

'This wasn't what I wanted.'

'Are you sure?' She flung the question into his face.

He sighed, a big man heaving sigh. He sounded as though the weight of the world was on his shoulders.

But he'd given in to his wife yet again, persuading himself that it was his children's welfare he was thinking of. Jenny gritted her teeth and accepted the excuse for what it was – a way out for a man who allowed Doreen to manipulate him for the sake of the children. Even after all the years of being married, of knowing Doreen like the back of his hand and putting up with all manner of bad behaviour and infidelities, Robin gave into her.

Hesitantly, he reached for her arm. 'Please try and understand, Jenny.'

She folded her arms, her aim to present how grim she was feeling.

Robin was placating. 'Come on. Let me take you home. It's getting late. I wouldn't want anything to happen to you.'

She was about to shrug him off but changed her mind. She wanted to shout at him to stand up for himself more strongly than she already had, but a thought had occurred to her. *What would I do if I was in that situation? What would I do to keep a roof over my children's heads? I stuck with Roy for the sake of my daughters. What's the difference?*

Roy would be home soon. Following the postcard she'd received, an official letter had arrived this morning. He was on his way and should arrive sometime in July.

Whilst getting up the courage to tell Robin he was on his way, she turned to more practical issues. 'Do you have to move her furniture?'

'No. She left the furniture with me when she shot off.'

'How very generous,' Jenny said grimly. 'She got the kids and you got the furniture.'

It was hard not to sound sarcastic and Robin picked up on it, lapsing into silence and retreating into thoughts, regrets and recriminations.

When he half turned away, she touched his arm and apologised. 'I'm sorry. I didn't mean to be harsh.' Her voice was softer now.

There was helpless acceptance in the shrug of his shoulders. *What can I do?*

They faced each other and for the moment said nothing.

Robin broke the silence. 'It was a bit of bombshell, I can tell you. Things aren't going to be the same.'

'Am I getting the sack? You know how she feels about me.'

And what we once were. That was what she wanted to say, but in all honesty it had been so far in the past, when they'd been little more than children. Had there really been anything between them?

'I've told her that you'll still be working for me two or three half-days a week.'

Jenny's eyebrows arched in surprise. 'And she accepted that?'

'She had to. Otherwise I told her it's the kids with me and 'er wherever she can. Told 'er I've got a business to run and if she wants maintenance I've got to earn it before she can 'ave it. Told 'er it's either I pay 'er pennies without you or pounds with you working for me.'

'That was pretty blunt.' She chuckled. 'I bet she didn't like that.'

'You bet she didn't.' He grinned. 'I did suggest that it might be a clever idea if she did the job. You should have seen her face...'

By the light of yet another streetlamp they passed under, she saw an amused grimace clutch at his features. She wanted to ask him whether they'd be sleeping together. Was it really her business? Of course it was. She cared about him. If it wasn't for Doreen and Roy...

She forced herself to return to the subject before telling him about Roy coming home. 'Well. I bet that shocked her.' She said it blithely and followed it with a light laugh.

'She nearly choked when I wouldn't give in. The pennies and pounds bit made it clear, but I layered on another home truth so it really sank in. I put it to her that if you didn't help in the shop, then it meant she'd have to do a turn – more like every afternoon – that brought her to her senses. And I told her she can have the spare room. I've got a single bed she can sleep in.'

Well, that answered her question. It seemed Robin was finding his feet. Not only was she surprised but proud of him. He'd suffered enough and whatever happened they would remain friends.

The light from the streetlamp accentuated the dark circles beneath his eyes, the shadows beneath his cheekbones. It was logical to suppose that he'd been considering what to do for a day or two, trying to balance business demands with that of his erring wife.

'You will stay on, won't you, Jenny? I want you to. You know that, don't you?' He sounded pleading. 'I want us to...' He swallowed.

'Remain friends?'

'I wish we could be more than that, but as long as you work in the shop... it's all I can hope for.'

She choked back her own news. One shock was enough for the moment, but the rest had to come out. In the meantime, 'I'll stay as long as it's bearable.'

When they got back to Coronation Close the streetlights were off, and for the most part, the houses were in darkness. They stopped at the gate of number two, her own house, where she noted the light filtering out through the dusky pink curtains. Her girls would probably be in bed by now but had been considerate enough to leave one downstairs light lit.

Jenny rested her hand on the cold ironwork of the garden gate, tapping the top rung with her thumb as she waited for Robin to spill the rest of what was in his mind.

His words tumbled out thick and fast. 'She won't stay there forever. I know she won't.'

No, only so long as she can drain you dry. Jenny kept the thought to herself. Doreen would leech off Robin until something better came along. Then she'd be gone.

Robin's next words reflected her own thoughts. 'For better or worse – I got the worse. But there, marriage is a bit of a lottery. High hopes at first until the reality hits.'

'True.'

For a moment, they fell into awkward silence.

'You know I'd marry you if I had the choice and I like to believe that you would marry me.'

The statement went further than she'd expected.

Another awkward moment ensued.

'I've probably said too much. Hoped for too much. Goodnight.' Shoulders slumped, Robin turned away. She'd put off telling him about Roy coming home all evening and had waited for the right time. She called after him.

'Robin. There's something I've been wanting to tell you. Doreen has moved back in with you and Roy is moving back in with me. He's fallen sick. He's coming home.'

He stopped and turned, a featureless silhouette against the inky blackness.

She explained, 'Malaria and other things. That's what it said in the official letter.'

'He's been in the Far East. A soldier's maladies.'

She nodded silently and saw him shake his head in a forlorn manner.

'I wish somebody up there would get things right.' He jerked his head up at the star-filled heaven. 'You and I belong together, Jenny. And some day, perhaps we'll be favoured.'

Without another word, he strode off out of Coronation Close and home to loneliness and a troubled future.

Hardly able to breathe for stifled sobs, Jenny pushed open the gate and ran up the garden path. Her fingers fumbled with the key. Once it had turned, she almost fell into the hallway, smothering her tears against one of the coats hanging from a peg inside the hallway.

Tears stifled, she opened the door to the living room. Tilly lay fast asleep curled up on the sofa. It touched her heart that her daughter had chosen to wait up for her but had not managed to keep her eyes open.

Jenny tapped her on the shoulder. 'Come on, Tilly. Time for bed.'

Tilly half turned and blinked her eyes open. 'I wanted to wait up for you.'

'That was very kind of you.'

After rubbing the sleep from her eyes, Tilly eased herself up on her elbows. 'I wanted to tell you something so I waited up for you.'

'It must be important for you to forego your bed and wait for me.'

'I'm worried. Mary told me she's going to run away from home.'

A pang of concern grabbed at Jenny's being. 'Now, why ever would she want to do that?'

In the process of swinging her feet to the floor, Tilly held tight to her blanket. Suddenly, as though a stray thought had pricked her conscience, she bit her bottom lip. 'Oh, I forgot. It's supposed to be a secret.'

Jenny drew in her chin and regarded her daughter with both concern and slight amusement. Tilly had always taken things seriously. She was also forthright and always strived to do things right.

'Is it about a boy?' she asked.

Tilly wrinkled her nose. 'I think so. She said her mother treats her like a baby and that she's not a baby. She's almost old enough to go to work or to get married.'

'Surely she's not thinking of doing that,' Jenny exclaimed. 'And, anyway, she's not twenty-one which she has to be if she's to marry without permission and it's sixteen with parental consent.'

Tilly bit her lip again. Her blue eyes grew round. 'Rudy has a horse.'

'Is that the name of the boy?'

She nodded. 'Yes and the horse is named Flint.'

'Ah!' Jenny knew of Mary's love for horses. She liked to ride them, she liked to caress their heads and neck and she liked to draw them. There were drawings, very good drawings, on her bedroom wall – Jenny had seen them.

Tilly rubbed at her sleepy eyes before saying, 'I like Mary. I wouldn't want her to run away from home. I'll miss her.'

'Of course you will. We all would miss her, especially her mother. I don't know how she could possibly consider such a thing.'

'Rudy's gone away. Mary wants to run away and find him.'

'Does she know where he is?'

Tilly shook her head. 'Not really. She said she could ask people if they'd seen the gypsies and find him that way.'

On being told this rather naive plan, Jenny felt a deep sense of relief. Although Mary might consider herself grown-up, this sounded nothing but a childish fantasy that would soon blow over. Young girls considered themselves in love when they were just too young to know what it was. A dark thought came to her. History repeating itself. She too had thought she'd been in love. Marry in haste, repent at leisure. That's what had been pointed out to her at the time. She'd ignored the advice and married anyway. Many years had been spent regretting that action.

'She'll grow out of it,' she said with confidence. 'Now come on. Off to bed.'

It was easy enough shooing Tilly off to bed; easy enough also to take herself up the stairs, pull back the bedclothes and turn off the bedside light.

Patterns thrown by the trees on the green outside and backlit by streetlights danced over the ceiling. Jenny lay with her arms folded behind her head, her eyes following the never-ending movement of the leaves on the ceiling.

Most nights, she slept soundly, but on some, like tonight, too many things were racing round her head. Too many concerns. Too many problems that needed solving.

How would she cope working at Robin's second-hand furniture and pawn shop knowing his wife was upstairs in the apartment above? And what about Mary Dawson? Thelma would be beside herself if she knew that Mary planned to run away – and for a boy seemingly because he had a horse.

Like Thelma, she regretted that her daughters were growing up so swiftly. It seemed only yesterday, they were all pigtails and crisp gingham dresses, short socks and worthy but unglamorous sandals. Boys had been creatures to be tolerated, not liked. The girls had regarded them as rough, noisy things. Oh how she wished that was still the case. They were growing up and their attitudes were growing with them and to some extent away from those who loved them the most.

From the moment she'd moved into Coronation Close, she and Thelma Dawson had become firm friends. They shared their secrets. They shared their anxieties too. Jenny very much doubted that Mary would carry out her boast, but even so Thelma had to be told. The best time to talk things over, to discuss what was going on in their lives and in Coronation Close, was after Thelma had come home from work. A calm time when they had the house to themselves, the kettle humming on the gas stove and two cups and saucers ready and waiting on a black japanned tray.

There was also the matter of Roy coming home. So far, she'd chickened out of telling the girls. Mother and daughters had to be prepared. Roy had always been a strong man. She couldn't see him staying ill for long. And then what?

She shuddered at the thought of the old Roy, the one who'd bullied her old friend Isaac and been less than hands-off with her.

Cross that bridge when you come to it. Anyway, the army might have changed him for good. She certainly hoped so especially with regard to his temper.

In her mind, she planned how she would tell the girls – 'Your daddy is coming home.'

She envisaged telling it in a bright tone, as though she was sincerely welcoming of his shadow falling over them once again. Inside, in a dark place where all her greatest fears lurked unseen, she felt only fear and a deep wish that it were otherwise.

6

Pegs clasped between her teeth, Thelma was hanging out a line of washing when Jenny came to call.

'Thought I'd hang this out whilst I've got the chance,' said Thelma.

Although she hadn't long come home from work, she looked more presentable than any woman Jenny knew. Her hair curled around her ears. She was wearing earrings that looked to be made of marcasite with tiny stones that glittered as she dipped down for another pillowcase to peg up on the line. Jenny shook her head. 'I don't know how you do it. A full-time job and running a house.'

'I've got my girls,' returned Thelma. She sounded proud.

Jenny folded her arms. 'That's what I want to talk to you about.'

Thelma didn't seem unduly perturbed and merely asked if Jenny might kindly pop into the kitchen and put the kettle on. 'If you don't mind that is.'

Jenny said that she didn't.

Peg bag hanging from the washing line, Thelma came in just as the tea was brewing.

'Tea first,' said Thelma. 'I'm parched.'

'Have I put in enough milk?'

'Plenty. Now, what is it you want to say about my girls? Are they behaving themselves? They're the most perfect girls ever born to me, but that doesn't mean they don't misbehave when they're out of my sight. I was just the same myself. You too, I shouldn't wonder.'

'It's probably nothing, but I thought I should tell you anyway.'

'Go on.'

'Well. It's like this,' said Jenny, pushing her cup and saucer to one side and leaning her arms on the table. 'Your Mary told my Tilly that she plans to run away from home. It's all to do with some gypsy boy. He's gone off travelling for six months and she's got this crazy idea to go after him.'

'Has she now.' Looking resolute but not surprised, Thelma sat back in her chair. 'The boy's got horses. My Mary is more likely to run off and join the circus – so long as they've got horses.'

Jenny wasn't convinced that Thelma was taking this seriously and said so.

Thelma leaned across the table, the amusement on her lips shared with her eyes. 'I know my girls. They like their home. They like their home comforts and my Mary from an early age liked horses. As for the gypsy lad, he'll be forgotten once she starts work and mixes with new friends.'

'I thought you needed to know.'

'Thanks for telling me.'

They both took another sip of tea.

'Do you like horses, Thelma?'

Thelma shook her head emphatically. 'No. I do not.'

'So Mary doesn't get her interest from you?'

Thelma didn't have a ready answer. There was a moment when it seemed to Jenny that she'd been about to say something but had changed her mind.

'No. Definitely not.'

* * *

Alice looked surprised when Mary declared that she didn't want a cooked meal and that the pork dripping she was spreading on her toast would be enough. After gobbling it down in record time, she wetted a towel beneath the kitchen tap and wiped her face. The water was cold, but there was no way Mary was going to wait for a kettle to boil.

Alice looked perturbed. 'What do I tell Ma when she gets home? You know she likes to know where we're going.'

'Tell her I'm going to meet Madge. I won't be late.'

Madge was a friend from school who had left some months before and landed a job at the paper bag factory in Bedminster. Mary had used her name intentionally, knowing her mother would link their meeting with the possibility of Mary getting a job there.

'Will Madge be home from work yet?'

'Of course she will.' Mary's response was adamant and tinged with challenge.

Alice wasn't at all sure she was telling the truth. 'She might want to wash and change before meeting up with you.'

Mary grabbed her sister's shoulders and glared into her face. 'Are you calling me a liar?'

Alice winced. 'You're not running away from home are you? Only you told Tilly—'

Mary laughed. 'Tilly believes everything I say. She's a goose.'

'So you're not running away?'

'No. Not yet anyway. Not until I know where I really want to go.'

'You will tell me if you do, won't you?'

'Now you're being a silly goose. Just keep yer nose out of my business. I'm going out with Madge and that's it. Got it?'

Alice nodded mutely, her eyes big as gobstoppers.

The whole house seemed to shake as the front door slammed

shut, leaving Alice alone in the middle of the kitchen. She didn't mind having sole charge, choosing what to prepare for supper and tasting it as it cooked. In the past, the pair of them had cooked together delighting in preparing something for their mother to enjoy once she arrived home from work. It just seemed strange, almost as though a gap had opened up between her and Mary. The years between them had never seemed much of a barrier. Only of late had Mary treated her as a child whilst considering herself grown-up.

Grown-ups are difficult, Alice decided as she picked up a spoon and began stirring the supper.

* * *

Mary marched purposefully away from Coronation Close smiling to herself. She couldn't quite explain why she wanted to meet up with Donald Tucker. He was much older than her, yet she detected kindness in his eyes.

Mary saw him waiting for her. He was smoking a cigarette. On looking in her direction, he raised his hand in acknowledgement and put out his cigarette before she got to him.

She held her head to one side in a coquettish manner. 'Were you waiting for me?'

'I might have been. How are you, Mary?'

She nodded. 'Fine.'

He smiled and held out a packet of crisps and a bottle of Tizer.

Mary gobbled the crisps and glugged back the Tizer. Up until then, she hadn't been aware of just how thirsty she was. And hungry. Bread and dripping just didn't fill the gap.

'Let's walk,' Donald said.

'Where to?'

'Follow me.'

They strolled away from the off-licence and Melvin Square, heading along Leinster Avenue towards Bristol Airport, which nestled amongst the sprawling fields of Whitchurch.

'Might see a plane take off or land,' he said.

'Ain't never seen one yet,' said Mary with a sneer of derision.

* * *

The setting sun held the warmth of the day and it was pleasant to sit in the long grass. Through the feathery heads of wild grasses, they espied the airport runway. There was only one plane parked on it, and a very small one at that.

'I'd like to learn to fly.'

'Why don't you?'

'Girls aren't supposed to do things like that.'

'Girls can do anything that boys can do. Women can do the same things as men.'

'Do you think so?'

'I thought you preferred horses.'

'I like them, but I'd like to learn to fly and do loads of other things girls aren't supposed to do.'

In the absence of a cigarette, the man, her friend, chewed on a blade of grass. She thought it strange that he didn't light up or offer her a cigarette. She decided to ask him why.

'I'm trying not to. It makes my chest bad.'

'Will it make mine bad?'

'It could do. Take my advice and don't start.'

She shook her head. 'I won't. I don't like the smell.' She was telling the truth though wouldn't admit it to her schoolfriends who had all indulged. There was pressure for her to do so. She wondered if she should give it another try.

He eyed her curiously. 'You're a bright girl.'

Mary beamed at the praise.

'My teacher said that I was bright and that if I minded my p's and q's I could go far. How far do you think I could go?'

'As high as the moon if you want to.'

She frowned, not quite comprehending what he was getting at but intrigued.

'I don't mean flying to the moon but getting to be something important. Like being Prime Minister.'

Mary laughed. 'Prime Minister?'

'Yep. And why not? I sometimes think women might do better at ruling the world,' he said to her. 'Us men ain't done that good a job. Look at the war. Thousands died back in the Great War and who's to say we won't start another?'

'I don't like war.'

'Nobody does, though for a lot it was the first time they'd ever gone overseas in their lives. Some found it exciting. Foreign countries. Warm sun. Different languages, food and ways of doing things.'

Mention of excitement and experiencing different countries changed her mind.

'Could I be a soldier?' she asked.

'Well. Why not?'

The crisps were soon finished. Her mother rarely bought Smith's crisps because they were so expensive. Instead, she sliced a potato into very thin slices and fried them in the pan. It wasn't the same, of course. It just couldn't be.

Mary leaned back in the grass onto her elbows and, like him, plucked a stem of grass and held it between her lips.

The evening sun was warm on her face, but not too hot. She didn't like too much heat. Her skin was pale, as befitting a red-haired girl. Her eyes were blue. His were blue too and there was something about the way he looked at her that put her at ease. She wasn't frightened of him but couldn't explain why.

'Where do you live?'

The question seemed to take him by surprise. He recovered quickly.

'Here and there.'

Confused at what he might mean, she studied his face for a clue to his meaning.

'Do you live in a house?'

He wasn't looking at her, didn't really seem to be concentrating on her question but was staring into the distance. An evening mist hung over the fields that stretched up to Dundry Ridge. The branches of trees waved around, the taller ones looking as though they were scratching the sky.

'Not exactly.' He got to his feet. 'How about we walk a bit further. I want to show you something.'

He stretched out his hand to help her up. At first, she hesitated to take it.

'Well, come on. I ain't got all night.'

His palm was warm and reassuring. The track he led her along veered away from the aerodrome and narrowed as it wound between tangled blackberry bushes. The first few flowers that would eventually turn into fruit shone like stars amongst the purplish green leaves and prickly thorns.

They came to a stop at the top of a hill. The trees she'd seen in the distance seemed much nearer now but did nothing to inhibit the view of the city. There it was spread out in front of her, tinted with the colours of twilight, gold, purple and orange.

'Can you see it?'

He pointed. She wasn't quite sure what at.

'Ummm. See what?'

'There.' He pointed to the far left where the Clifton Suspension

Bridge hung above the deep ravine that was the Avon Gorge.

'It's the suspension bridge.'

'And beyond that?'

She shrugged. All she could see were the cliffs on either side. The Royal Observatory stood on the left-hand side – the Abbots Leigh side – terraces of Georgian houses on the other.

He rested his hand on her shoulder and spoke softly into her ear. 'Beyond that is the world. Beyond that is adventure. That's where the river Avon goes. Out into the sea and from there... well, you can go wherever you like. It's the open sea.'

'My brother George used to go to sea. He works at the tobacco bonds now.'

The comment seemed to take him up short. 'Ah yes. Older than you of course.'

She pulled back the hair that was whipping across her face and looked at him. 'Yes. He is. Do you know my brother?'

'I knew him a long time ago when he was little.'

'Are you a sailor? As well as riding horses, have you sailed on boats?'

At first, he said nothing, then, taking a deep breath, fists on waist he looked out over the city. 'I wanted to travel and I did. But there's a price to pay for excitement and adventure. That's how it is when you're young. Things change as you get older.'

Mary frowned. 'But you had adventures. What could be better than that?'

He took off his hat to brush off stray leaves. What was left of the sun formed a halo behind his head. His hair was almost as red as hers. In the halo of light, it looked as though it was on fire. 'Family. That's what matters, Mary. Family.'

For a moment, it seemed as though he was going to say something else but changed his mind.

'Come on. I'll tell you when I see you again. Time to go home.'

She didn't argue. She couldn't explain why, but there was something about his tone that made her wary.

Once she'd regained her confidence, she asked what she'd thought about asking earlier.

'Can I have a fag?'

'A cigarette?' His eyebrows rose in surprise but there was also condemnation.

'Yeah.'

'I told you that I was trying to give up.'

'I only want to know if I like it.' She had her peer group to impress. The last time she'd tried, she'd coughed so much it had felt as though she would choke.

He shook his head, then seeming to give it second thoughts delved into his pocket and brought out the packet of five cigarettes. He used a lighter that shone like silver. The flame ignited a red glow.

She did what she'd seen others do and breathed in the smoke. It came back out with a series of splutters.

Finally, she said, 'It tastes vile.'

He took it from her, stubbed it out between finger and thumb and suggested she went home.

'Will you walk me home?'

It was difficult to read the look in his eyes. 'No. I have things to do. I'll see you tomorrow.'

She looked disappointed but nodded her agreement.

He watched her walk away. She still wasn't much more than a child and yet he could see traces of the woman she would become. At present, she was like a young filly, leggy as a colt and inquisitive as you like. There would be many more things she would want to learn as she got older. He only hoped he would have some input into her learning, though was unsure just how to get involved without Thelma finding out and telling him to get lost.

7

Thelma had just got home from work. It had been a long day and her new court shoes were pinching.

She stopped by the front gate, aching to get indoors but on seeing neighbour Cath Lockhart stopped to call out to her.

'My feet are killing me. Lend us yer slippers, Cath!'

Cath Lockhart lived at the far end of Coronation Close. By day she wore a pair of oversize slippers that flapped on her feet and metal curlers hidden beneath a headscarf.

Cath scurried on by. 'Got to get to the chemist before they close. Steep yer feet in a mustard bath.'

Thelma didn't ask what for but guessed it was something personal like a packet of Doctor Whites. It wasn't something you'd shout out across the street.

In the street, Thelma's voice, good humour rippling through it, rang out like a bell. The front gate clanged as it shut behind her and she headed for the front door.

Cath wasn't the only one who'd seen her. Jenny was in the living room and also saw her.

Opening the window, she called out, 'Thelma. I'll be over once you've had a bite to eat.'

Thelma acknowledged her with a curt wave.

Jenny went out into the kitchen where the remains of a cheese and potato pie sat cooling on the window ledge before she put it away in the larder.

Taking a pair of shears, she headed out into the garden and began trimming a particularly straggly bit of hedge. Whilst doing so, she couldn't help her attention straying to the kids from number five and the Arkle kids from next door. Both sets of kids were ill-dressed, tousle-haired and not particularly clean. They were what her mother would have called rough-and-ready. What they were ready for, she'd never been quite sure.

The eldest Arkle boy stepped from out of the line of siblings and their friends. The eldest kid from the other lot – the Stenners and their mates – also stepped forward. She recalled her name being Rosie and she looked as aggressive as her male counterpart in the Arkle family.

Perhaps they were going to fight. She'd seen them do so before. Sometimes the boy had won, sometimes the girl. Both were around thirteen years old. On this occasion, it seemed a discussion was going on. The words were muted, but she just about caught what they were saying – something about a bat and a ball.

Her heart lurched when she saw the Arkle boy swing a cricket bat above his head. For a moment, Jenny feared the crack of bat on bone. Fortunately it didn't happen.

'We bat first.'

'I've got the ball.'

'Can't 'ave a game of cricket without the bat. Can use any old ball if we 'ave to.'

Rosie Stenner and her supporters went into a huddle. Once an agreement had been reached, Rosie nodded though petulant still. 'All right. You can bat first.'

Breathing a sigh of relief that there would be no fighting today, Jenny sank down behind the hedge and began snipping.

A door slammed from across the street, followed by the clicking of heels. A face popped over the hedge above her. Jenny got to her feet. 'I've made a fruit cake. Fancy a slice with a cuppa?'

Thelma threw a worried look at the kids playing cricket before saying that she would love some. 'Just so long as them kids don't put a ball through my window.'

'It'll be dark before too long. Too dark for cricket!'

The sound of a ball thwacking against a bat sounded as they went down the side path and into the back garden, which was more sheltered than out front.

There were two steps to the backdoor. Cups of tea grasped in their hands, they sat on the top step sipped tea, nibbled at fruit cake on the tea plate that sat on the step between them and watched the moon come up.

Jenny sensed Thelma's air of tension. Perhaps taking her thoughts into the past might help. 'It's been only a couple of years since I moved in. Nineteen thirty-six. It seems a lifetime away. It's amazing what a difference two years can make.'

Thelma laughed. 'I could say that it's more peaceful since then. Old Mrs Partridge had it in for me and that's a fact.'

'And her poor husband passing himself off as her sister for all those years.'

Thelma nodded, a curl of smoke rising from one of the cigarettes she'd taken to smoking of late.

'For my nerves,' she said in response to Jenny's tiny frown. 'I've never worried about my girls until now. My Mary is becoming more and more awkward to deal with. I tell myself that it's all down to her growing up. She's bound to change.' She shook her head. 'I can't help thinking it's more than that, though what, I haven't a clue.'

Conversation ceased as each entertained their own personal thoughts.

The rising moon was liquid silver and drew their attention. The sound from the cricket game out on the green had ceased. It had gone oddly quiet.

A thoughtful frown creased Thelma's forehead. 'I think I need to pop along to Rigby's sometime this week for some wool.'

'Gracious, Thelma, that grandchild of yours already has enough matinee jackets and bootees to clothe triplets.'

'That babe will want for nothing,' Thelma pronounced, a short burst of jollity coming to her face. It didn't last, replaced by a darker more thoughtful expression. 'I was thinking of Beryl. She's probably right out of wool. It's all she's got to do all day stuck there by herself. I'll get her some.'

'Oh, Thelma, you're not going to that house again. What if he catches you?'

'I feel sorry for her, I really do, him locking her up in the front bedroom.'

Knitting was how Beryl had spent her days and when Thelma had first met her, she'd run out of wool. That's when she'd begun buying wool for her. If nothing else, it had helped fill her days. Nevertheless, to Jenny's mind, it all seemed a bit dangerous. She couldn't help but issue a warning. 'I really don't think you should. It's dangerous.'

Thelma was determined. 'Now look! Beryl might be able to tell me if he's been following me. You know he did before when I was working late at Bertrams. Luckily your mate Charlie Talbot came to the rescue. There are times when you must bite the bullet, Jenny, and this is one of those times.'

It stung hearing Charlie's name. Jenny had entertained strong feelings for Charlie, but they'd come to nothing. Thelma's determination to find out if Sam Hudson was indeed the man watching her house took priority.

Jenny adopted a resolute stance, arms folded, jawline straight and firm. 'I'll come with you. And I'm not taking no for an answer. I've got some spare wool we can take. Four-ply blue and double knit dark green.'

'Good. That'll save us some time.'

Their mood lifted. 'My Tilly needs a new jumper for school. It must be blue. It's her favourite colour. When she was younger, it was pink.'

'Funny how they grow out of one thing and into another.'

'And think they know more than we do. All their big plans...'

'Oh yes. They certainly have plenty of those,' said Thelma. 'My God, Jenny, but I wish I could turn back the clock and have back the little girl Mary used to be. Yours don't seem to be giving you much trouble.'

'So far,' said Jenny with a wry smile. 'But we both have to accept that they're growing up and we're getting older.'

Thelma tossed the remains of her tea onto the garden. 'We're getting older all right.' Her tone was resentful.

Jenny wanted to erase the pessimism from Thelma's voice. Best to say something cheerful. 'At least you've got something fantastic to look forward to. You're going to be a grandmother.'

She'd expected Thelma to smile with pleasure at the thought of it. Instead she looked wistful, her dark penetrating eyes gazing into the blackness now descending at the bottom of the garden. 'They're a lucky pair, George and his Maria. They've got each other. For better or worse. But what if they go to live in Italy.'

'I don't think that's likely. They wouldn't have come back if that was the case. They might get a council house close by.'

'They might.' Thelma's face clouded. 'But I don't want them to think of me as the interfering mother-in-law. I don't want to live in their pockets. They're due their own life, as are my girls. But on the other hand...' When Thelma turned her head to face Jenny, her eyes were luminous with unshed tears. 'I don't want them to grow up, Jenny. I would prefer that things were as they used to be. And I feel...' Her breast heaved with her deep intake of breath. 'Alone. I see a future of me all alone...'

Surprised by the heartfelt emotion in Thelma's voice, it took some time before Jenny spoke.

'You mean you want a man? A husband?'

Thelma nodded. She swiped at a tear-filled eye before turning back to gaze unseeing at the darkening garden.

Jenny had long admired Thelma's independence. It had always seemed as though her children were everything and she had no need of a man.

'What about Bert? Has he never mentioned marriage?'

'He's got a comfortable home and his sculpting and painting in that studio of his.'

'He's never given you one of his paintings or anything?'

Thelma shook her head. 'No.'

'Not to hang up on your wall?'

'No.'

Jenny couldn't help asking why that should be.

'He says he won't move anything out of the studio – well, barn would be a better description – until his mother is gone.'

Jenny judged it time to change the subject. 'Are you going to mention anything to Mary about running away?'

Thelma shook her head. 'No. I wouldn't write anything serious into it. It's all part of growing up.'

'I suppose you're right.'

'How about you and Robin? When does Doreen the Shrew move in?'

'Tomorrow.'

'Be careful. Being in the shop at the same time as her is like swimming in shark-infested waters.'

'I know.' Jenny heaved a huge sigh. 'I'm nervous about it of course, but I can't leave Robin in the lurch. And he couldn't leave his kids homeless. The trouble is, giving them a roof over their heads means having her there too.'

'He's a bit of a softy that bloke of yours.'

'He's not my bloke,' Jenny snapped. 'Might I remind you that Roy is on his way home.'

'That being as it may, Robin wants to be your bloke. Might be at some time in the future, if anything should happen...' She shook her head. 'Sorry. I shouldn't say things like that. Roy's still alive, and though I don't like him, I don't wish him dead.'

'Never mind that. When are we going to ask questions of this Mrs Hudson?'

They planned for Jenny to meet her at the bus stop on Wednesday.

'Then that's settled,' exclaimed Thelma.

'That's settled,' Jenny repeated. She fervently hoped that Mr Hudson wouldn't be there.

8

It was ten in the morning when Jenny arrived at the second-hand furniture and pawn shop in Filwood Broadway. Robin had already opened and dealt with the first pledges of the day. There was always a queue first thing Monday morning – half a dozen or more in desperate need after a heavy drinking weekend. Most of the drinking was done by the menfolk, though not all. There would be less customers as the day wore on.

The brass bell hanging above the door jangled its usual welcome. The smell of wax polish pleased her. She'd taken to polishing at least once a week to hide the occasional whiff of mothballs. The smell mostly came from Edwardian wardrobes, but so long as she polished the exterior, it was enough to keep the worst of it at bay.

She stopped by the door and listened. Here on the ground floor, she was met with the sound of wall clocks, their pendulums ticking backwards and forwards, though not necessarily in time with each other. There was no sign of Robin.

Voices raised in argument sounded from upstairs. Although it was early morning, it seemed Doreen had already found something to argue about. Jenny presumed the two children were at school.

She made her way to the small vestibule that served as the accounts office at the back of the building. Until today she'd been happy in her work, humble though it might be. Today she felt a distinct change in the atmosphere.

Resigning herself to changed circumstances, she took off her coat and prepared to engross herself in some work. Hopefully entering and adding up figures should dull her senses to what was happening above her head.

Should I be here at all? she wondered. She was in two minds. Robin had faith in it working out, Jenny wasn't so sure, and what with Roy coming home... things could get difficult.

The raised voices subsided into an uneasy silence and Jenny too was beginning to feel uneasy.

Her attention was drawn to the jangling of the brass bell above the front door.

A voice shouted, 'Shop!'

A customer.

Plastering a smile on her face, she left the figures and went out into the shop.

The man was wearing a gaberdine raincoat and a brown trilby hat. He turned to face her. 'Good morning.'

He seemed familiar.

'Can I help you?'

'I want to pawn this.'

He handed her a brown carrier bag. Inside was a silver cup. Well-polished. Well looked after.

She took it out and examined it closely. 'It's solid silver.'

'Yes. It's engraved with the name of a horse race I won. Years ago now, but it is still solid silver so that makes it valuable?'

'Oh yes. Of course it does.'

She looked at him, taking her time to register his features. The blue eyes were familiar but she couldn't quite pin down where she'd seen them before.

'I'd like to pledge it. For twenty pounds if possible.'

'Twenty?'

'I know it's a lot of money, but it is valuable.'

Judging by the weight of it, she would estimate it at much more. 'If you would like to come into the back, we can tackle the paperwork and I can give you a receipt.'

He followed her into the back room, where she entered the details into the pledge book.

She indicated the inscription on the cup. 'And this is your name?'

'Yes.'

She read the name. Stuart Brodie. 'Address?'

He gave her the address of a boarding house on the Wells Road at the top of Broad Walk. She couldn't recall ever seeing it but took it as read that he was telling the truth. A few imposing Victorian villas had been turned into boarding houses catering to itinerant salesmen and those seeking work in any city that had jobs to offer.

'How long would you like to pledge it?'

The twinkle she'd perceived in his eyes died as he thought about it. One finger traced a line along his top lip. Finally, he produced a response.

'I'll come back in when the time is ripe. I'll tell you then. I find meself temporarily out of funds. But only temporarily.' He emphasised the last word as though suspecting she didn't believe him.

Only notes of lesser denominations were kept in the day-to-day cash drawer. Five-pound notes were kept in the safe. To her surprise, it was already open. It was her guess that Doreen had demanded money and Robin had given her some.

Jenny counted out four crisp five-pound notes which he took from her, folded and tucked into his inside pocket.

'Much obliged,' he said and touched the brim of his hat before making his way to the shop door. The brass bell sounded as he exited.

For a while, Jenny stood there trying hard to understand why he seemed so familiar. She didn't get chance to consider too much. First, there was the sound of thudding heels coming downstairs. Next, the door dividing the rear of the premises from the stairwell opened with a flourish. Like the leading lady on the first night, Doreen stood there in a cloud of face powder and cheap perfume. She was wearing a fox fur and a dark blue velvet hat with a black veil. If she was going shopping, she was overdressed. If she was out on the town, it was far too early in the day.

There was a hard squareness to her jaw as she looked Jenny up and down. 'Is that outfit handmade?'

Jenny was wearing a navy-blue dress she'd made from an item Thelma had given her. 'Yes.'

The shrew-like eyes were accompanied with a scathing smile. 'It looks it.'

'It's clean and paid for,' Jenny retorted. 'And it is a work dress.'

The dress was simply cut and flattering. Its simplicity was offset by a brooch in the shape of a butterfly pinned to her shoulder. The contrast between it and Doreen's flashy outfit was marked. Doreen liked glitter. She liked furs. She liked make-up.

Doreen sniffed and gave her another once-over. 'You're right. It's definitely a work dress.'

'And you would know that?' Jenny retorted.

Doreen winced at the obvious barb, recovered and began pulling on a pair of raspberry-coloured kid gloves. Her gaze locked on the open safe before declaring, 'I'm going out.'

'I thought you might be.' It was hard not to sound sarcastic. Doreen brought out the worst in her.

Jenny's attention turned to the small pile of paperwork in front of her, dividing it into three piles, though there was no reason to do so. There was nothing much that needed to be done with it. The action was purely a diversion, an attempt to convey to Doreen that paperwork was far more important than she was.

Triggered perhaps by Jenny's offhanded manner, Doreen sauntered purposefully over to the desk. Her eyes narrowed with glittering contempt and she worked her jaw as though she was chewing on gravel. A painted finger jabbed at Jenny's shoulder. 'Let's get this straight from the start. No funny business. I've made the bed upstairs, so I'll know if anyone's been in it. That means you, lady. When the cat's away...'

Jenny glared at her defiantly and, getting to her feet, determined to fight her corner. 'Now, you get this straight. Describe yourself as a cat if you like. I won't argue with that. But don't refer to me as a mouse. I'm not a mouse, as you may soon find out! As for going to bed with your husband when you're not around, well, think again. I certainly don't want your left-offs. My one and only reason for working here is to earn enough so that I can properly look after my children. Some other people couldn't care less about their children. They still think they can go out at night and act the same as when they were single. Well, I don't think that and I care for my children, Doreen Hubert. So stick that in your pipe and smoke it!' As a finale, she slammed down the stapler, a large cast-iron thing. She'd remarked to Robin that it vaguely resembled an item of medieval torture. He'd laughed at that. He'd also mentioned who he'd like to use it on.

The outburst had come like a tidal wave. It was more than she'd meant to say and certainly more than Doreen had expected if her indignant expression was anything to go by. Twin dots of colour seeped through the peachy face powder. Doreen resembled a Roman candle about to explode.

'Robin!'

Her shout was ear-splitting.

Jenny clenched her jaw, which helped her keep calm.

'Robin,' Doreen shouted again with as much ear-splitting volume as before.

Footsteps raced down the stairs until Robin was standing there behind his wife, his eyebrows heavy over his eyes.

'You don't 'ave to shout,' he grumbled. His face was as crumpled as his clothes.

'She's insulted me. I want her out of yur.'

'I've already told you that's not possible – unless you work in the shop.'

'I've already told you—'

'I know,' he said with a heavy series of nods. 'You married me so you could give up work and become a housewife.'

'And have children.'

'Yes,' he said with a sigh. 'And have children. The offer's still open for you to work in the shop, though seeing as you're me wife, I won't be paying you any wages.'

Doreen made grumpy noises whilst glaring at Jenny with pure hatred. 'Well, you can keep things as they are. I'm better than a lowly shop girl. Give me ten bob.' She glanced at the safe. 'Or a fiver.'

Robin purposefully slammed the door to the safe. 'Ten bob. That's yur lot!'

There was pure malice on his wife's face. She clicked her fingers at shoulder height. The vile look was fixed on Jenny, although Doreen's clicking fingers were directed at her husband.

The ten bob was snatched and secreted inside a crocodile

handbag and the clasp snapped shut like a pair of reptile jaws. With a toss of her head, Doreen was gone.

'Jesus,' Robin muttered under his breath.

'I take it she came early this morning.'

He shook his head. 'Last night. Wanted to get the kids in school. Said she was meeting friends.'

He looked tired and it occurred to her that he hadn't slept in his own bed, most likely the sofa. His crumpled clothes were evidence of that.

Jenny sighed and sat in the chair behind the desk. Eyes brimming with pity, she looked up at him. 'You had faith this would work – me still working here. I did have reservations and now, what with Doreen and Roy coming home...'

Robin perched on the corner of the desk, arms folded and trouble etched all over his face. She felt a great urge to reach out and tell him that everything would be all right, but there was no point. As expected, Doreen had shown her true colours. She felt angry towards Doreen but also sad for the hurt Robin was going through. 'Jenny.' There was both hurt and fear in the look he gave her. 'I had no right asking you to stay on with her moving in.'

'We both have commitments. This cannot work.'

His eyes met hers. He shook his head. 'You're right. I wouldn't want to cause any trouble.'

Trouble was the right word. There was trouble with Doreen and there could easily be trouble with Roy. She might find out how much trouble once he was home.

'I could have a word with Percy Black. He used to help me shift furniture back when my old ma used to run the business. He's too old for that now but fit enough to run the shop.'

'I might as well go now. There's no point hanging around, is there.'

'Stay for the rest of the day.' There was pleading in his voice and in his eyes.

'No. We know it's for the best.'

She grabbed her coat and bag, pulled her hat onto her head a little too firmly. Leaving saddened her, but they'd been foolish to ever think it might work. Doreen wouldn't let it work.

Jenny squeezed past, heard him suck in his breath, then felt his fingers grip around her wrist.

'I don't want to do this, Jenny. You must believe that.' There was an urgency in his tone of voice that was both regretful and hopeless.

Not bearing to see the look in his eyes and for him to see her own sadness, she turned away. She would miss her job, miss the bit of money too, though was confident she could get by. The fact was she had got used to his cheerful welcome on those days she did work. She'd also got used to him coming to the pictures with her, Thelma and Bert. Surely that too would cease.

In the next breath, it seemed he had read her mind. 'I can still come to the pictures with you.'

'Doreen won't like that!'

'I don't care whether she likes it.'

Jenny looked at him and shook her head. 'Robin, she'll give you hell if you do.'

'Give it a few months, even a few weeks and she'll 'ave found a new fancy man and be off.'

'And take the kids with her? Surely not. How could she be so cruel.'

Robin looked crestfallen. 'I won't let it happen this time.'

He looked forlorn.

'You may not be able to prevent it.' It came out too quickly and she sorely wished she hadn't said it. She wished she could say something more positive but knew what Doreen was like.

Although she hated doing it, Jenny loosened his hand and

headed for the shop door. Tears of anger stung her eyes. Fate had not been kind to them.

He followed her, his words stilling her. 'When she deserts me this time, I'll divorce her on the grounds of adultery.'

'You don't know what you're saying, Robin. Divorce is shameful and proving adultery is never easy. She's not going to admit what she's done.'

He looked aggrieved. 'We'll talk about it – sometime.'

She shook her head. 'No, Robin. We won't.'

'You can't stop me going to the pictures on the same night as you three do.'

'Goodbye, Robin.'

She knew his eyes were following her as she walked away, and although it was difficult, she didn't look back. Her relationship with him would never be over as such. They'd known each other for most of their lives, but he had to understand that carrying on seeing each other – however innocent it might be – would not do any good. Doreen had always been the sort to spread malicious gossip and was vindicative in the extreme. Jenny didn't want Gloria and Tilly to suffer. There was also Roy to consider. He used to have a temper and there was no reason to suppose that anything had changed. The nastiness had to be kept at bay.

She'd written to him to say that the girls were looking forward to seeing their father again. This much was true but as for herself... that was a different matter.

9

It was Wednesday half closing for most shops and Bertrams Modes where Thelma worked was no exception. As agreed, Jenny met her at the bus stop before the one she usually got off at.

Jenny had been to the wool shop that morning and bought a few skeins for the unfortunate Beryl Hudson, which she now handed over to Thelma to put with the ones she'd already bought.

Although Jenny had never met Sam Hudson or his wife Beryl, she knew enough to be wary.

The heels of their court shoes tapped in unison as they made their way down Donegal Road and turned into the small cul-de-sac of houses.

Although she had a touch of the collywobbles inside, Thelma was most definitely putting her best foot forward.

'What if he's there?'

Jenny's question was met with a grim set of Thelma's mouth and a muttered, 'I'll cross that bridge when I come to it. I'm not having him stalking me.' Ever since Jenny had mentioned a stranger coming to the Close and looking across at her house, Thelma had simmered with indignation. How dare he? How bloody dare he?

It wasn't just a case of him hounding her now, she feared for the safety of her children. Her girls were growing up and she feared the likes of Sam Hudson, a man who seemed to think that the female of the species were there for his pleasure.

'Thelma. What will you do if it was him? Surely, you'll have to go to the police?'

In her heart of hearts, Thelma was in two minds about the man Jenny had seen in Coronation Close. For the first time since embarking on this mission, she found herself face to face with a predicament she might not be able to handle. A ghost from the past. Her face darkened along with the thoughts in her mind.

Thelma took a deep breath. 'This is it.'

She stopped at the gate of the garden. The familiar stone gnomes were still there, cheery and smiling despite the bird splashes on their pointed caps and crusting over their eyes.

'What now?' Jenny was feeling apprehensive, unsure of what to expect once the front door was opened.

'We go in.' Thelma gave the garden gate a determined push.

Halfway along the path, Thelma stopped and looked up at the bedroom window.

'I can't see any sign of her and the curtains downstairs are drawn.'

'Are you going to knock?'

Thelma nodded. She reached the front door, took hold of the knocker and gave three sharp raps. The sound echoed between the houses.

Jenny looked at the downstairs front window. 'Thelma. Stop.'

Thelma looked disinclined to do so, until Jenny pointed.

'Look.'

Thelma stared at the card stuck in the window. It was edged in black. She didn't need to peer closer to know that it announced a death, though whether in the street or the house wasn't obvious.

Jenny had walked back to the garden gate. From there, she could see that every house in the street had their curtains drawn and most displayed a death card.

They would have gone there and then, except that a neighbour popped out from the house next door. 'If yur relatives, you've come too late,' she proclaimed. She wore a black scarf over her head, but her clothes were a motley collection of assorted colours and patterns.

'I'm sorry,' said Thelma. 'When did it happen?'

'A week ago. Didn't you read about it in the papers?'

Thelma's finely plucked eyebrows creased into a frown. Poor Beryl. It seemed her twisted body had finally given up.

'When did she die?' Thelma asked her.

The neighbour looked a little perplexed. '*Her*? No. Not her. Him.'

Thelma and Jenny exchanged looks of outright surprise. Thelma asked what had happened.

'Seems he fell down the stairs. Beryl was in her bedroom – she spent a lot of time in her bedroom. From the looks of it, he'd just come out of there carrying the gazunder. She couldn't get up and down the stairs to the bathroom, so she had to use the chamber pot. He was on his way to empty it when it happened. None of us knew until the next day. Beryl shouted at us from out of her bedroom window. She was locked in, you see. Somebody got a ladder and went in there. The bedroom door was locked and Sam had the key – that's what Beryl said. Must 'ave locked her in by mistake.'

'No mistake,' Thelma whispered under her breath. 'So where's Beryl now?'

As the woman's voice dropped, her eyes shifted from side to side as though she was about to impart a great secret.

'Gone to live with relatives. Don't know who. If you ask me, the family might 'ave 'ad her put away. She was a bit disabled.'

'That's awful,' muttered Thelma, kneading the bag of wool with both hands, finding it hard to take in what had happened.

Jenny took the view that the woman was merely surmising. 'But you don't know for sure.'

'No.'

After taking leave of the neighbour, they walked away in stunned silence.

Thelma shook her head in disbelief. 'I can't believe it.'

'Poor woman.'

'I feel guilty that I didn't drop by sooner – for her sake, not to confront him.'

'Well, he certainly won't be bothering you again or putting his poor wife through hell.'

'That's true.'

There was a certain sense of relief. Sam Hudson was gone. But so was Beryl. Thelma voiced the fact that she felt sorry for her.

'I shouldn't have abandoned her.' She shook her head.

'From what you've told me about her, she needed someone to care for her properly and show her some kindness. Let's hope she's found that now.'

Thelma had to hope that Beryl's life might have changed for the better.

'I wish I could say the same for Robin,' said Jenny as they walked away. 'Doreen and Sam might have suited each other. Both cruel. Both selfish.'

'I don't know the woman but already I don't like her.'

'She went out on the day I left dressed up like a dog's dinner. Robin reckons it won't be long before she latches on to another fancy man.'

'Fur coat and no knickers!'

Jenny laughed. 'That describes her exactly.'

Thelma eyed her tellingly as they made their way back to Coronation Close. 'That might leave the door open for you.' She dug Jenny with her elbow. 'You know he's in love with you. And aren't you a tiny bit in love with him?'

'You forget one thing, Thelma. Roy is on his way home.' She shook her head and looked Thema fully in the face. 'I don't want any tongues wagging. Roy never was very forgiving.'

* * *

Stuart Brodie known to young Mary Dawson as Donald Tucker, sat bare-chested on a medical couch.

Doctor MacGregor had been recommended to him by the landlady at the Rhubarb Tavern in Barton Hill when she'd heard him cough. She was a good sort and had taken to him.

'I don't want to know who you're running from and what you're doing in Bristol, but I would advise you to get that cough sorted.'

He hadn't needed her to tell him. It had been getting worse over the past few years. Sometimes he could barely catch his breath and coughing up blood had been a warning sign that his illness could no longer be ignored.

The prognosis was not good. He'd known that for a long time. A feeling of profundity had infused his soul. Things he'd thought of no great significance in his life were now of immense importance. The most important of all was Mary.

The stethoscope was cold on his back. Again and again, he was commanded to cough.

When the stethoscope moved to his chest, he kept his eyes lowered. A silver watch chain dangled from Doctor MacGregor's tight-fitting waistcoat.

Finally, it was over.

'You've a bad rattle there, Mr Brodie,' the doctor pronounced as he placed the instrument back around his neck.

Stuart Brodie concentrated on doing up his shirt buttons, straightening the detachable collar, sliding his silver horse-head cufflinks into place. 'How long do I have?'

The doctor looked up abruptly from writing something on a notepad – a prescription perhaps. 'Do you really want to know?'

'If I've only got a year, I want to know. I've got things to do.'

White bushy eyebrows lowered over a pair of washed-out blue eyes. 'I'm afraid I can't give you that long. I give you five months at the most.'

Stuart slid his arms into the sleeves of his jacket and then into those of his khaki mac. He nodded as he took in what he had been told. A shock. He knew he was dying but hadn't expected it to be that imminent. 'Thanks for telling me.'

He reached inside his pocket for one of the four five-pound notes and held it out. He wasn't sure what the going rate was for a consultation. He'd been away from England for quite a while.

The doctor's lowered brows became raised. 'Do you have five shillings?'

'I was hoping you might know of a specialist that might keep me going a bit longer. I've a reason, you see. I've only just caught up with my daughter. I'd like to spend some time with her before I meet up with St Peter.' He raised his eyes skywards, which brought a smile to the doctor's ruddy face. 'I've got twenty pounds that might go some way to getting a bit of extra help.' He held up the four white notes.

Doctor MacGregor fixed him with a pitying look. 'You'd be wasting your money. Put it back in your pocket. There's a good fellow.'

Stuart looked down at the money. He'd thought the silver cup the most precious thing he owned. Becoming ill had soon taught him there were far more important things in his life – or could be. He wanted to get close to Mary and the most effective way of doing that was through her mother. But there, he'd let out on her when Thelma had told him she was pregnant. He'd done wrong. Left her high and dry. And now, it seemed, there was a price to pay. He had this great longing to have his daughter close for the last months of his life. But how to go about it? Somehow or other, he had to find a way.

10

Saturday night at the pictures. Thelma and Bert were taking with them a bag of chocolate caramels, seconds from Fry's chocolate factory. Bert's mother had worked there in her youth and still had friends there. It was them who went to the factory shop and bought her the brown paper bags of misshapes.

Jenny had declined to come. 'I've got things to do. I was daft enough to do a load of washing so I've now got a load of ironing.'

Thelma wouldn't let her be but kept on and on until she gave in.

She finally agreed to forego the ironing and everything else she had to do except for one particular thing. She'd penned a letter to Roy. This was only the second time she'd written to him. As per the first one she made it light hearted and chatty keeping to home life in general and their daughters in particular.

Our Tilly is doing very well at school. She enjoys reading and writing stories. Gloria prefers needlework, cooking and drawing. Another two years and Tilly will be leaving school. Gloria not far behind. I can't believe how quickly they're growing up. You won't recognise them when you see them...

And how would he be? she wondered. She'd been informed by the War Office that he'd contracted several tropical diseases that had left his body in a very weak condition. It would be a while yet before he returned home. Apparently ships travelling under the flag of Empire called in at various ports to pick up other passengers and mail for the folk and government back home.

Thelma glanced over towards Hubert's second-hand and pawn shop across the road. Lights shone from above the shop but none from the picture windows downstairs. It might have been only a glance, but Thelma, who had informed Bert of what was going on, noticed.

All the same, she had to make comment. 'I wouldn't fancy his Saturday night, poor chap.'

'You make your bed and you lie on it,' stated Bert. He took hold of her arm and guided her into the entrance of the picture house. 'There's nothing we can do. Let's get in and forget about it. He's old enough to sort things out for himself.'

Thelma had to agree and, following his lead, began to shuffle forwards in the queue for tickets. 'Anyway, I'm looking forward to this film. Been looking forward to it all week.'

'Blimey. You sound as though you've won the pools.'

'I wish,' said Thelma, guffawing with unabated laughter. 'But overall I'm happy. What with thinking about the baby and all that.'

Her exuberant explanation seemed to satisfy him, though it was far from the truth. The death of Sam Hudson had lifted her spirits no end. Death shouldn't have such an effect on her, but for him she'd make an exception. He could so very easily have ruined her life, but now he was out of the picture. No more spying on her! For that, she was extremely grateful.

Although they were a bit later than usual, the news feature was there before their eyes, though, thankfully, it seemed they might have missed the pictures of explosions and tired-looking soldiers.

Politicians and international diplomacy took the place of fighting, although the two were tightly linked. Neville Chamberlain lifted his top hat and smiled at the camera. Men in uniforms goose-stepped and saluted beneath fluttering flags. The next item was about the distribution of gas masks, which was presented in a much more light-hearted manner. But Thelma recalled what gas could do. She'd seen the evidence many years ago. Tension stiffened her body.

Sensing her disquiet, Bert squeezed her hand.

She looked at him. They exchanged smiles – slightly nervous smiles. The future was becoming an uncertain place.

The black and white reality of life was replaced by the colour and sheer fairy tale of *Snow White and the Seven Dwarfs.*

A tide of relief swept over Thelma.

For a while, she forgot both the world's troubles and her own. Someone had once said that only a fool worries about what he cannot alter. That's how she felt. She sincerely hoped that Beryl was having a better life without a husband who imposed such abject cruelties on her. In future, Sam Hudson would not be troubling either of them.

With that in mind, she settled down to enjoy the film.

Mary too had wanted to see the big new Disney feature-length cartoon and mentioned it to Donald Tucker. He had instantly obliged and taken her to see the earlier matinee.

They'd exited about a quarter of the way through the news, dark figures making their way between the seats and up the ramp to the outside.

A line of people were queueing at the ticket office booth buying tickets for the next performance. With a start of recognition, she set eyes on Bert and then her mother.

'Quick. In here.'

She'd dragged Donald into the small alcove where a curtain cloaked the door to the manager's office.

Without saying a word, he did as she directed. From their small hideout, she jerked her chin towards Bert and her mother.

'My mother.'

It seemed odd that he expressed no surprise, made no comment but stared so hard she wanted to drag him back into the depths of the alcove and explain just how dangerous this could be. Her mother would explode with anger and certainly forbid her to ever go near this man again.

There was something about the awestruck intensity of his gaze. It was, she thought, as if a film star had left the screen and was there amongst the audience.

'Don't stare at her like that. It's creepy!'

With a sudden jolt, he turned his attention away from Thelma Dawson and back to the young girl, who had, up until now, been the centre of his plan. To some extent, she still was, but seeing Thelma again had knocked him sideways.

Coming to, he grabbed hold of Mary's arm and dragged her towards the entrance. 'Let's get you home.'

By then Thelma and the man she was with had disappeared into the dark interior of the picture house. But still he hurried her along. He needed to think about what he was doing.

* * *

On the other side of Filwood Broadway, the tip of a lit cigarette glowed in the darkness. It was the only other light beside the streetlamps and the endless lines of lightbulbs shining from the canopy above the entrance to the Broadway Picture House.

Robin felt sad seeing Jenny, Thelma and Bert joining the queue for tonight's performance wishing that he could have gone with Jenny. Instead, Doreen had insisted on going out, leaving him to take care of the kids.

'I'm going dancing with Mabel. Don't wait up.'

He'd never heard of her having a friend called Mabel and doubted she really existed. Even if she did, it was likely they were two of a kind, out to have a fun time. Not that he cared much about that. He liked having the old place to himself. The less time Doreen spent under his roof the better.

It was too early for the kids to be in bed and he had no qualms about them staying out to play until darkness fell. Inside or outside, he would be waiting for them. In fact, he'd promised them chips and scrumps from the fish and chip shop. Until then, he would occupy himself, dealing with the paperwork Jenny had so efficiently taken care of, coming out here to have a smoke and see what the rest of the world was doing.

He saw people he knew coming and going across the road at the Broadway. Seeing Jenny, Bert and Thelma had tugged at his heartstrings. He might have continued dwelling on his disappointment if he hadn't seen Thelma's daughter, Mary, almost crossing paths with her mother and Bert.

Mary's male companion was dragging her along so fast it seemed she was having trouble keeping up.

Flicking his cigarette onto the pavement, Robin narrowed his eyes and straightened. Mary was a few of years older than his own daughter but still far too young to be in the company of a man who, even from this distance, looked old enough to be her father.

Deciding that something wasn't quite right, Robin crossed the pavement, onto the grass, which was damp and springy underfoot.

'Dad. I'm hungry!'

'Can we go to the chip shop now?'

Games and running around playing tag had finished. His kids were home. Robin's steps slowed, but his eyes watched the older man and young Mary Dawson disappear into the darkness. Did Thelma know who she was with?

It crossed his mind to stand outside the Broadway until Bert and Thelma emerged, but his kids were tugging at his arms, whinging and whining that they were starving.

'All right, all right!'

Wednesday afternoon the shop would be closed and both the kids would be at school. Doreen would make herself scarce. It had become obvious that she had no intention of being alone with him in the house – and for his part he wasn't keen on leaving her there. The fact was he didn't trust her to break into the cashbox or choose a pledged item of jewellery. It would be OK if Percy was there to mind things whilst he made his excuses to deliver or collect items of furniture. She wouldn't turn a hair at him doing that and whilst doing that, he would call in on Jenny and tell her what he'd seen. Her being Thelma's best friend she might know what was going on.

11

It was Wednesday half-day closing. Thelma was home and waiting for Bert to arrive at teatime with his drawing book. She'd got used to him drawing pictures of her as she went about her household tasks and found herself liking those more than the ones he did in the disused garage that he called a studio. Some he turned into paintings and some he sculpted likenesses from clay. There were several reasons she enjoyed him doing this, not least because it made her feel beautiful. Here she was, a middle-aged woman that he found interesting enough to use as a model.

For now, Thelma had time to kill and where better to kill it than having a chat with Jenny across at number two.

Jenny was on her hands and knees cutting the front lawn with a pair of sharp shears. 'I'll take a break,' she said on seeing Thelma.

She was just about to lean on the gate, prior to inviting her in, when all hell seemed to be let loose.

First there were two tousle-haired kids, recognisable by their dirty faces and scruffy clothes as two of the Stenner children from number five. Behind them, slippers flapping as she ran and face red with fury, Cath came flying down the pavement from her end of the close shouting at the top of her voice, 'You bloody perishers. Just wait till I get me 'ands on you!'

It was hard to see what the two kids were carrying except that it was pink and white and they hugged it close to their chest.

Like magpies seeking sanctuary in the nest, they flew to their garden gate, which was opened and closed sharp as a rat trap.

Their mother, a clay pipe hanging from the corner of her mouth and hair bundled on top of her head like a bunch of barbed wire, was leaning over the front gate. Her stance was rigid and defiant, giving every indication that there was no chance of anyone being let in.

'Them little sods…' Cath shouted between gasped breaths, waving her fist at the woman.

'They're my little sods!' Ida Stenner shouted back through a gaping mouth of few teeth and a filthy tongue.

'I want my things back. They've stole stuff from my washing line and I want them back.'

'Don't come yer with yer moaning. Clear off.'

'Them little guttersnipes are thieves.'

'Shove off.'

After gobbing a mouthful of phlegm into the bushes, a broad back was turned. Big hips wobbling beneath shapeless clothes, Mrs Stenner waddled to the front door and slammed it shut.

Cath was in no mood to be fobbed off. She reached for the gate catch. 'I ain't having this!'

Just as she was about to give the gate a shove, a big hairy dog came barking and bounding around from the back of the house.

Cath slammed the gate shut and stepped back. 'Bloody hell!'

She stood disconsolate, some metal curlers made loose from running flopped on her forehead.

'Out with it,' said Thelma as a breathless Cath made her way across the road. 'What have them kids been up to.'

'Them little sods pinched some of me underwear off the line.'

'Are you sure?'

''Course I am,' said Cath somewhat testily. 'Four pairs of knickers. Two pairs were mine and the others were our Mavis's.'

Jenny's eyebrows rose in surprise. 'They must be desperate.'

'And what's that supposed to mean?' Pulling an indignant expression, Cath began to tighten the metal curlers.

Jenny hesitated before saying, 'I meant that perhaps they've got none of their own?'

Cath scowled. 'Bloody cheek. I've got a good mind...' It seemed she was reconsidering marching over there and demanding her underwear back. One look at the huge dog that had chased around the side of the house was enough to change her mind. It was standing on its hind legs at the gate, its paws resting on the top cross bar, slavering and barking as if challenging anyone to dare approach.

Cath looked from Jenny to Thelma. 'Have you 'ad any laundry nicked from your line?'

Thelma shook her head. 'No. I can't say I have.'

'Me neither,' said Jenny.

Cath frowned. 'So why me?'

'Are you going to call the police?'

Cath blushed. 'I couldn't. I just couldn't. They'd want me to describe it all.'

'They would go over there and ask. They might even search the place.'

Cath hissed between gritted teeth. 'I'd go over and pinch theirs when they're not looking, but what with that dog... Besides which, I shouldn't think their stuff is worth pinching – not if their outer clothes are anything to go by.'

Jenny was inclined to agree. The family in number five were

scruffy as well as numerous. Nobody, Jenny included, could be certain of exactly how many people lived there. There were the parents, of course, a man and a woman, but it was nigh on impossible to tell how many children lived there. It had to be seven at least, running in age from three to thirteen. None of them went out to work, though somehow managed to pay their rent. Plus the school inspector was always calling round to demand why the kids had missed so much school. Like them, he'd backed off when the dog appeared.

Cuthbert Throgmorton, senior rent collector and Thelma's very good friend, had some knowledge of the problem. 'I believe he deals in scrap metal,' he'd told them.

'So I noticed,' Thelma had scoffed. 'Their front garden is a right mess. The council should point out to them that it's a garden, not a scrapyard.'

Bert had to agree. The front garden of number five was a right mess and full of junk. A zinc bath, a mangle with cast-iron frame, bits of brass, copper and old flat irons, all scattered over what had once been a lawn. In times past, the council had inspected the houses, checking to see if the tenants were keeping both inside and outside in good order. Of late, the inspections had lapsed. Bert had said it was down to worrying about other things.

'Gas masks,' he'd stated with an air of authority. 'We're organising the distribution of gas masks and making lists of those likely to be sent to safety if we do end up at war with Germany.'

Jenny and Thelma had flinched at his pronouncement and exchanged worried looks.

'What's that supposed to mean?' Thelma had asked in her forthright, no-nonsense way. She suspected she wasn't going to like the answer but preferred to know.

'We've been briefed that if war is declared, there's a plan being drawn up for children to be sent to the country. Expectant ladies too.' The last comment was made after a polite cough. Bert was old-fashioned in that respect.

'Children sent away from their parents? That's terrible.' Jenny couldn't imagine being separated from her children.

Bert had sighed. 'Let's hope war is avoided.'

'With a bit of luck, it won't come here. It'll be in France like the last war – poor French,' Thelma had added.

'They'll bomb us,' Jenny had declared. 'Like in Spain.' She'd been horrified by the scenes from Spain at the picture house.

Thelma had muttered, 'Oh God,' beneath her breath. 'I'd forgotten about that.'

In the absence of any action regarding the mess across the road, they put up with it because they had to.

Thelma offered to make Cath a few new pairs of knickers. 'I've got some nice bits of material I can use. Pink, white and pale blue.'

After accepting Thelma's offer, the three of them stood eyeing the straggly privet hedges that helped hide the junk in number five, though not completely.

Thelma shook her head. 'I hate to think what lurks under all that rubbish.'

'Long as it ain't rats,' added Jenny. She'd had enough close brushes with such loathsome vermin back in Blue Bowl Alley. Not a sign of them here – at least up until now.

Curlers rattling with indignation, Cath shook her head and made her way back to her house at the far end of Coronation Close.

Thelma also made her excuses. 'Bert's coming. We'll have the house to ourselves. He wants to do some more drawings,' she added swiftly on seeing Jenny raise one eyebrow.

Jenny rubbed at the small of her back before returning to the job in hand.

It was with surprise that she espied Robin Hubert's van turning in at the end of the Close. A few reasons for his visit sprang to mind. Top of the list was that Doreen might have moved onto pastures new and she could have her old job back. Anything was possible where Doreen was concerned. Move in one minute and out the next.

He held up a hand in friendly acknowledgement as he got out of the driver's side. 'Any chance of a cuppa?' He looked happy. Had Doreen moved on?

She cheerfully answered his enquiry. 'So long as there's water in the tap and tea in the caddy.'

For some unfathomable reason, the dog over the road stopped barking – not that Robin had been giving it any attention. Perhaps the creature was just curious about this man in a van.

In the cosy comfort of the kitchen, Jenny eyed Robin speculatively as she filled the kettle and put it on the gas ring. 'To what do I owe the pleasure of this visit?'

'A pleasure?' A saucy grin was followed by a mischievous grin. 'That's nice.'

'You know what I mean.' There was a lot of meaning and affection in the way her eyes met his. She set out the cups, saucers, sugar and milk jug. 'Are things a bit better?'

'That isn't what I came here to talk about.'

His cheerfulness was diminished.

He stood, looking down at the floor, his hands buried in the pockets of his trousers.

She tried to make light of it. 'You look to me as though you've got the worries of the world upon your shoulders. Care to sit and talk?'

'This is difficult,' he said once he had accepted her invitation to sit down and the teacups were full.

'Just tell me,' Jenny urged.

Another sip of tea was followed by a deep sigh.

'How old is Thelma's eldest girl?'

She frowned. 'She leaves school soon. Are you thinking of offering her a job?'

'That isn't what I'm here to say.' He waved a hand dismissively. 'Truth is, I didn't know what to think, but seeing as you and Thelma are friends...'

'Robin, for goodness' sake! Spit it out. What is it you want to tell me?'

He took a cigarette from a packet, then thinking better of it slid it back in again.

'I saw her the other night. She was with a bloke old enough to be her father.'

Jenny sat upright in her chair; teacup clasped with both hands. 'Are you sure?'

He nodded. 'I watched you go into the Broadway with Thelma and Bert. The moment you disappeared, I saw this bloke and young Mary. They came rushing out hand in hand and ran off towards Kenmare Road.'

Shocked by what he'd said, Jenny sat there ashen and rigid. She couldn't believe what she was hearing.

Finally she found her voice. 'Are you sure?'

He nodded.

It was difficult to know what best to ask next – after telling herself it just couldn't be true. 'Did she look her age?'

At first Robin frowned, unsure of what she was getting at. He fought to find the right words – the ones that would answer what she was asking. 'She looked her age. I don't think she was wearing make-up or high-heeled shoes or anything like that.' He shrugged. 'She just looked as I would expect her to.'

The sound of a teaspoon clinking against a cup irritated. Then it surprised her to see that it was her the teaspoon against the saucer.

He nodded. 'I mean, I've heard of blokes like that.'

'So have I.'

He shook his head disconsolately. 'If I thought a bloke my age was after my girl...'

Jenny met the dark look in his eyes with one of her own. She knew instinctively why Robin was here. 'You want me to tell Thelma.'

He nodded. 'I know it's a bit of a nerve, but...'

'Leave it with me. Bert's coming over for tea, so I won't have much chance today to have a word. But I will. You can be sure of that.'

'Thanks.'

'No need to thank me. I'd want to know if somebody was showing an unhealthy interest in my daughter.'

He nodded. 'Of course you would.' He swallowed the rest of his tea and got to his feet, leaving her disappointed that he was not staying longer. 'I have to get back.' Regret twitched a smile onto his face but failed to mask the disappointment in his eyes.

'I know you do.'

She walked him to the front door.

He nodded at the dog across the road which still stood on its hind legs, gazing across at them as though spellbound, jaws open and slaver dripping from its mouth.

'What's he guarding?'

'A load of junk in the front garden. Bert tells us he's a scrap metal merchant. We want the rubbish removed, but nobody seems able to do anything about it.'

'So the bloke wants money for it?'

'I suppose so.' Jenny shrugged. 'It doesn't look to be worth much to me. Old iron bedsteads and brass curtain rails mostly. It's just rubbish.'

'Leave me to be the judge of that. Anyway, it'll give me a good excuse to come calling 'ere – when I can, that is.'

They looked sheepishly away from each other, Jenny brushing

an imagined windblown tress away from her face, Robin unable to curb the look of awkward longing on his face.

The moment passed as both watched Bert drive up in his little Ford. It was hardly the most attractive of vehicles and reminded Jenny of a box on wheels – a shapeless thing with little wire-spoked wheels.

'Thanks for the tea.'

She watched as he passed a quick word with Bert. She waved to both men, then retreated inside her own front door, even though she'd left the pair of shears outside.

Robin had left her with two predicaments. Number one was that she and Robin were very attracted to each other. Number two was the worrying prospect of having to tell Thelma that her daughter had been seen at the picture house with an older man. The very thought of it sent a shiver down her spine.

In the morning, she told herself. *I'll tell Thelma in the morning*. Or when it was the most convenient. Or when she felt the bravest. Thelma was likely to be devastated.

12

Something woke Thelma from sleep and the very nice dream she was having. She couldn't quite work out what it was that had disturbed her. A scurrying of feet, a few muted bumps and bangs and a creaking sound, like something that needed oiling.

The dream enticed her back into its fuzzy world, where she was waltzing down the aisle in a cream dress and wearing flowers in her hair. Bert was standing in his best suit at the altar waiting for her.

A sudden thought brought her up short. What if somebody had broken into the house?

Her eyes flicked open. The dream vanished.

Rubbing the sleep from her eyes, she pulled aside the bedroom curtains and looked out. The streetlamps went out before midnight; Coronation Close was in darkness relieved only by shades of grey cloud beyond the rooftops.

A dark shape loped past her garden and out of the close, its shape resembling the dog from number five. Someone must have left the gate open and the creature had escaped.

Assuming that was the noise she had heard, she went back to bed. Hopefully, the animal would be in its own garden by the time everyone was up and about. She certainly didn't want to come face to face with it in the morning, and neither would anyone else.

Snuggling down under the bedclothes and into the pillow, she closed her eyes and attempted to retrieve the wonderful dream she'd been having.

By the time she woke up and made herself ready for work she couldn't recall whether she got back into that wedding scene or not.

Looking out of the bedroom window at a day that promised a mixture of cloud and sunshine, she recalled the noises in the night and the dog she'd thought she'd seen. It wouldn't hurt to check if it was safely back in its own territory. There were children to consider.

'I'll just have a slice of toast,' she replied when Alice asked her whether she'd like a slice of back bacon and a fried egg.

Mary was silently preparing her own.

'I'll be right back,' said Thelma. 'There's something I've got to check on. Now promise me not to go out of the garden gate until I get back.'

The girls, both wrapped up in what they were doing, agreed they would stay put.

Resting her hands on the top bar of the front gate, Thelma looked up and down the Close, then set her gaze on number five. There was no sign of the dog. No sign of anyone above the straggly untrimmed privet hedges.

Well, it is early, she thought to herself.

Taking her courage in both hands, she stepped outside her own garden gate. Before going through it, she once again looked up and down just to ensure the big brute of a dog wasn't wandering loose.

Satisfied that all was well, she was about to go back into the house when Maude from number seven came out of her gate waving and shouting, 'Thelma. Thelma.'

Maude had obviously only just got out of bed. Her hair was still tucked into a hairnet and the man's dressing gown she wore was flapping around varicose veins which clung like grapes to her snow-white legs.

Maude patted her chest in an effort to catch her breath. 'They're gone,' she said. 'That lot in number five. They've done a midnight flit. I'm sure they 'ave.'

Thelma frowned in the direction of the house in question. 'I thought I heard something.'

'I was sure I did, too, but Jack told me to shut up and go back to sleep. That I was dreamin'. That's what he said. I said to 'im this morning, "You 'ad a skinful up the pub. What would you know?"'

Maude still in her nightwear and Thelma dressed for work took it upon themselves to peer over the hedge into the garden of number five. The mangle, the old iron bedsteads and zinc baths were still there. Amidst the pile of tangled grey metal, bits of brass shone through. Curtain rails, warming pans and other old stuff difficult to identify.

'They've done a runner,' said Maude.

Thelma knew it was true. Bert had hinted that the Stenners were behind with their rent.

'Won't be long before they're thrown out,' he'd said to her. On realising what he'd told her was private he'd had her swear not to tell a soul. 'My job would be on the line if you did.'

She had no time to stay in conversation with Maude. Dressed in a smart dark green jacket and skirt, the seams of her stockings straight as they could be, court shoes brushed free of marks, she was ready for work. All she had to do now was wash her slice of toast down with a cup of tea and apply her make-up.

* * *

Jenny knew she had no chance of speaking to Thelma about Mary this morning and was glad that it was so. In her mind, she tossed around the way she might approach the subject and even thought about questioning her own girls on the subject. Or tackling Mary herself? No matter which way she turned, she didn't relish the thought of bracing the subject at all. Out of friendship she would do it, but in private, she decided. The best approach would be in private, but, goodness, life in Coronation Close could be busy at times.

Looking out of the window made her mind up to meet Thelma outside Bertrams Modes at lunchtime. The sunshine was intermittent between clouds. Today was a day for wearing a cotton dress and sandals, a small straw hat and white gloves.

Without forewarning Thelma, she planned to catch the mid-morning bus so she would get into the city centre, leaving enough time to do some shopping before heading for Bertrams. She wouldn't buy anything in there. The prices were high and the money in her purse wouldn't go far at all.

It was on the bus going into the city centre Jenny wondered at the possibility that the man she'd seen staring at Thelma's house was the same man Robin had seen with Mary.

The shops at the bottom of Park Street drew her attention, though she frequently looked at the watch Robin had given her. Someone had long ago pledged it for the princely sum of ten shillings but had never come back.

'I can't even remember who it was, except that she was wearing a leopard-skin coat.'

Her attire was enough to convince both that the watch had a decent heritage. Even so, Jenny had insisted that she would only accept it in lieu of wages – or part wages. Robin had countered that it should be regarded as a Christmas bonus. She'd promised him that the next Christmas, she would cook him Christmas dinner.

Whether that would happen now Doreen had reappeared and Roy was on his way home from the colonies was debateable. In the meantime, the watch had proved invaluable – doubly so today.

She knew from Thelma that Bertrams closed for lunch for an hour from one o'clock. At the stroke of one, she was waiting outside, admiring the ornate walnut window frames and the curved glass windows themselves. Elegant plaster models, their poises frozen in time, eyes glassy and unseeing, stared out at her.

'What are you doing here?'

Thelma's crisp voice interrupted Jenny's many thoughts.

'I wanted to talk to you.'

No excuses, no saying that she'd fancied a day in town. A serious conversation was in order.

'About that lot from number five? I heard something during the night, but you could have knocked me down with a feather when I heard they'd done a moonlight flit. Bert will know all about it, of course.'

'They didn't pay the rent, did they?'

Thelma shook her head. 'I couldn't possibly comment. You know, seeing as Bert will be involved in all of it.'

'Fish and chips?' Jenny suggested.

'Lovely.'

They made their way to Lintons, an upmarket fish and chip restaurant at the top of the Christmas Steps. There was no queuing here and newspaper was not used to wrap up customers' purchases. Waitresses wearing black and white slid like velvet between the tables and the customers kept their hats on as they placed their orders in rounded vowels.

Thelma stated how glad she was to see the back of both the family and their dreadful dog at number five. 'Hopefully the council won't be long clearing up all that rubbish. It does look like a scrapyard.'

Jenny agreed with her before admitting that there was something else she wanted to talk about.

Thelma frowned. 'You look like you've been slapped with a wet kipper.'

'This is difficult for me to say.'

'Well, get on with it. I'm starving.'

Jenny poured the tea that had just arrived. Thelma was her best friend, but she couldn't help procrastinating. 'You know the other night when you went to the pictures?'

Thelma replied slowly. 'Yes.'

'Well...' Jenny cleared her throat. She put it as delicately as she could. 'Someone noticed your Mary in the company of a man, charging out of the picture house as you went in.'

Thelma's face crumpled. She shook her head. 'What man? What are you implying about my Mary?'

She said it almost accusingly, as though Jenny was being insulting, when in fact she was only trying to be helpful.

'Thelma, she's only a child still, but you know how it is at that age. You think you know it all. We did – I suppose.'

Thelma didn't respond. Old memories had come to mind that were best never voiced and she certainly wasn't going there now. 'What was he like? This bloke. What did he look like?'

Her tone of voice gave Jenny the impression that Thelma half expected what her answer would be.

'Robin didn't see him too clearly but...' She took a deep breath and voiced her uppermost suspicion. 'I was wondering whether it was the same man who I saw staring across at your place. Remember he ran off when I asked him what he was up to.'

Thelma looked strangely thoughtful. Even once her fish and chips arrived, she was slow setting into it with knife and fork.

Jenny asked her what the matter was.

'You thought the man watching my house might have had sandy-coloured hair. And blue eyes.'

Jenny covered her mouth with one hand. The description could easily have applied to the man who had brought the silver cup into the shop. 'A man came into the shop on Monday with a cup. He looked like that. Reddish hair and blue eyes. I thought I'd seen him somewhere before. Perhaps it was the same man.'

Thelma's complexion visibly paled. 'What kind of cup?'

Jenny flinched. 'A silver cup. Won in a horse race. There was a name on it... Brodie, I think.'

Suddenly, Thelma grabbed the salt pot, then the bottle of malt vinegar and gave her meal a good sprinkling of both. The smell of hot fat, fish and chips was soon overcome with that of vinegar.

'Just wait till I get home. I'll be having a word with that young lady!'

Jenny was aware of the change in her own daughters. When younger, it had been easier to cajole them, to be let in on their secrets, to be almost accepted as a child herself. Their attitudes and behaviour had changed now they were older. No longer children, they were swiftly growing into adults with their own opinions.

'If I don't get answers, I'll insist on meeting this man.'

'Let me know if you want me to tag along with you.'

Thelma's eyes flashed. One brightly painted fingernail tapped compulsively on her teacup. 'No need.'

Jenny fell to silence. She had the distinct impression that Thelma knew more about this man than she was letting on.

This, Jenny decided, was one of those moments when a change of subject was called for. On finishing most of her meal and laying aside the cutlery, she asked Thelma if she'd heard anything from Beryl Hudson.

'She's written to me. It appears she's moved in with a relative but isn't staying with that one. She's been offered a place with another relative – a cousin, I think. I hope it all works out for her. I just need to write back. I'm not a great one for writing, but I really should. The poor woman needs a friend.' She sipped the last of her tea. The imprint of her lipstick was left red and perfectly formed on her teacup. 'And how about Robin? Is he coping with that cow Doreen?'

'As best he can, though he won't let go of turning a shilling. Don't be surprised if he accosts you on Filwood Broadway and asks if you can approach Bert regarding the rubbish in number five's front garden.'

For the first time that day, Thelma's ruby red lips flickered with the hint of a smile. 'He's welcome to it. I'm sure Bert will think so too.'

Jenny glanced at her watch. 'It's two o'clock.'

After paying the bill, they left together, Jenny wondering about Thelma's response to what she'd been told. It had been far more subdued than expected. If either Tilly or Gloria was seen in the company of an older man, she'd be furious, but Thelma was strangely contrite.

She asked Thelma whether she would see her later.

'You might do. First off, I'll be putting some questions to my daughter. At some point, I'll let you know how I get on.'

13

Apprehensive and barely controlling the sharpness threatening in her voice, Thelma tackled Mary.

'I want a word with you, young lady.'

'I'm going out.'

Mary folded her arms, her little chin thrust forward.

The stance touched Thelma's heart. She recalled with a pang of nostalgic regret that she too used to adopt a stance like that, defiant no matter what anyone told her to do. Of course, back then, she'd been just one of many children in an orphanage. Such a lot had happened once she'd been released into the world. Some of it good. Some bad.

Knowing that Alice had gone out to play, she closed the door so it was just them talking.

Thelma looked her daughter up and down. 'Mary, you're becoming a woman. You've got curves where you used to be straight as a candle. You're not exactly pretty, but you are handsome.'

'What's that supposed to mean?' Mary asked indignantly.

'You're good-looking but defiant. That scowl you often wear lets you down.'

Mary tossed her head and squared her shoulders.

Thelma was having none of it. Leaning forward, she gripped her daughter's shoulders to ensure Mary's full attention. 'You were seen with a man coming out of the pictures.'

Mary's face reddened, a sure sign of guilt as far as her mother was concerned.

'He's just a friend.'

Thelma's apprehension became anxiety. 'Did he tell you his name?'

For a moment, it looked as if no reply would be forthcoming. Finally, she pronounced his name.

'Donald Tucker. And he was nice to me. He didn't touch me or anything,' she declared whilst shaking her head, eyes round and compliant. 'We talked about horses. He used to be a jockey.'

Mother and daughter held each other's gaze. On seeing the look on her mother's face, Mary's eyelids flickered.

Thelma made a concerted effort not to convey the concern that had erupted inside. 'Are you meeting him tonight?' she asked.

Mary nodded mutely.

'Where?'

'Up the Novers to see the horses.'

'What time?'

At first, Mary was reluctant to answer, but a sudden increase in her mother's grip on her shoulders coupled with a swift shake persuaded her to comply.

'Seven.'

Anger creased Thelma's face. 'Right. Let's put a stop to this once and for all.'

'No! Please don't. I know what you're thinking.'

Thelma's eyebrows rose. She shook her head so vehemently that a few tresses fluttered free from her carefully coiffed hairstyle. 'No, my girl! You know nothing.'

Her tone was angry and sent Mary into a stony silence, her young eyes glaring. She knew when her mother was really mad, knew when to back down and retreat into childlike comfort.

'Right, young lady,' said Thelma, finally letting go of her daughter's arms. 'You're staying in tonight.'

'No!' That one small word was hot with defiance. Dismay contorted her features.

'No arguments.'

Mary scowled.

* * *

Stuart Brodie was in his shirtsleeves, his jacket thrown over the fence, his hat perched at a jaunty angle on his head. As he relished the breeze and fed clumps of fresh grass to the chestnut mare and the dapple-grey gelding, his thoughts were with Mary.

The doctor had been honest about his chances and he believed him. There was no medicine that might help. These precious moments with a daughter he'd abandoned – even before she was born – meant so much to him. When he looked at her, he imagined her at various ages in her life: baby, toddler, little girl – ribbons in her hair.

She'd told him how she felt about horses. To his mind, her love of horses superseded any feelings for the gypsy lad.

The muzzle of the chestnut mare nuzzled against his hand.

'Cupboard love,' he said to the friendly animal. The mare went on munching, her attention fixed on the grass rather than on him.

* * *

The scent of blackthorn blossom was strong. There had been more than enough rain a while back to turn the grass green. The recent sunshine had brought the buds into flower.

Thelma cussed and swore as she made her way up the rough track that led to the Novers. If she hadn't been so shocked, so determined to sort this, she would have changed her shoes and left her stockings behind. Three-inch court shoes did not suit the stony ground.

The track widened at the top where a dirt path intersected. It ran parallel with the fence straight across in front of her. She stopped there, caught her breath and checked on the state of her shoes. Thankfully, the heels were still in place, though dusty.

Placing her hand on her chest, she felt the thudding of her heart. She took three deep breaths. She needed to be in control of herself and thus of the situation.

Looking left proved to be the right direction. There he was leaning over the fence feeding clumps of grass to a pair of horses. His shirtsleeves were rolled up. He looked nonchalant, as though he had not a care in the world.

On seeing her, he stopped feeding the horses, stood upright and straightened his hat.

He smiled. 'I had a feeling you'd catch up with me.'

'I want you to leave Mary alone.'

He turned to face her full on. His tie hung loose around his neck. His smile was as she remembered it. Mary had inherited his blue eyes.

'I'm her father. I got rights.'

Her guts twisted like tangled wire getting tauter by the minute. 'You gave up those rights when I told you I was expecting a baby and you left me high and dry!'

With what seemed casual indifference, he took off his hat and set it on a fence post. His hair was still auburn – very much like

Mary's, though softened to a sandier shade thanks to the advancing years.

No matter that the years had flown by, she still felt her heart flutter and her knees go weak.

'I was young. You were young,' he said it nonchalantly. He'd always had that air about him, as though nothing really mattered in the great scheme of things.

'Yes, but I faced up to my responsibility. You ran away!'

He shook his head, regretful. 'You were always more responsible than I was. I was naive enough to think you would either get rid of the kid or put her up for adoption.' He shook his head again. 'Stupid me. I should have realised you'd grab the nettle and do what had to be done. You'd been married. I take it you passed Mary off as your husband's and rearranged the telling of his story to compensate. In other words, you lied. Am I right?'

Thelma's jaw locked. Her eyes blazed. 'So did you! You told Mary that your name was Donald Tucker. Your mate's name!'

For a split second, he held her angry gaze, then he threw back his head and laughed. The sinews of his neck stood prominent. 'I'm surprised you remembered.'

'He was a gambler. Like you.'

The same old boyish amusement flickered around his lips when he shrugged his shoulders. 'I'm cured now.' His look darkened. 'Nobody likes going inside.'

'I guessed that must have happened at some point, but not when I got up the duff with Mary. You were still free then. You just ran away. Where did you go?'

'Skipped on a ship. What with you and the coppers after me... what else could I do?'

This time, there was helplessness in his shrug. His beaming expression remained and she knew that whatever he said, Stuart Brodie could never be trusted.

She rested her arms on the fence rail and feebly patted the muzzle of the dapple-grey creature that had stood back, dominated and pushed out by the chestnut mare – just as she had been dominated by the man she'd thought had loved her. 'So why now?'

He too leaned his arms on the fence next to hers. She felt their warmth. Felt the soft touch of the hairs stretching from his wrist to his elbow.

'I wanted to see her. No matter what, she is my daughter.'

'You never sent a penny towards her keep.'

'How could I? I was on the other side of the world. Been everywhere, I have.'

Thelma frowned. 'I bet you have!'

'I ain't been in prison if that's what you mean. Not since back then. A long while ago.'

Thelma wasn't so sure and didn't care. This was all about Mary.

'But why now? And why didn't you come to me first before making contact with her?'

His eyes narrowed behind a lock of hair tossed by a puff of breeze. 'It wasn't you I wanted to see. It was her and anyway you'd likely have told me to get lost.'

'Too right I would.'

She smouldered inside and was also hurt. Her relationship with Stuart had happened a long time ago, but still she could see why she'd been attracted to him. He'd been dangerous to know back then and likely as not was still the same now. Bad boys were exciting when she was younger, but now she had Bert, quiet, gentle Bert – Stuart's complete opposite.

'Thing is,' he said. 'I've come into a tidy sum of money. I can give her a better life than you ever could. Working in a frock shop, are you?'

His tone was sarcastic.

'It's an upmarket shop for well-off ladies,' she replied hotly.

The sneer that wiped the smile from his mouth reflected the darker side of him, the one she remembered and had chosen to ignore when she'd been with him. After the sneer and the sarcasm, the smile would return. My word, how she'd loved that smile, the mellow warmth of his words, the charm he could turn on and off like a tap.

'You didn't tell Mary you were her father. You could have done.'

'I could. I chose not to.'

'Any particular reason for that?'

'She would have come running to you directly and you'd have told me to shove off right from the start. I didn't want that. I would have done eventually. Now it looks like I don't need to. You'll tell her; won't you? Invite me for tea. You can do it then.' Dark eyebrows creased into a vee shape above his nose, a devilish look, just like the smile that wasn't a smile but almost a smirk as he outlined how it would be: '*Mary darling, this is your daddy.* That would be good enough.'

Thanks to that one comment, the affection of their past acquaintance that had threatened to surface vanished.

He blanched when one of her red-tipped fingernails pointed to within an inch of his face.

'I'm warning you right now, Stuart Brodie. Keep away from my daughter or I'll report you to the police!'

She bristled with anger, so much so that she almost choked when she tried to say anything else.

Face red and fists clenched, she marched off as best she could along the uneven path with tears stinging her eyes. The tears were not just of anger but also of fear.

As her heels stuck and wobbled on the downhill track, she tried hard to get her thoughts in some order. There was no doubt in her mind that she was facing a demanding situation. Mary becoming of a rebellious age was bad enough, but Stuart Brodie, her natural father, coming on the scene could only make things worse.

By the time she got home, any thought about supper had been and gone. The only hope she had was that Mary's father would fall in with her wishes – though she doubted it.

She'd been a young widow with a son when she'd met him. There had been nothing stable about his disposition. He'd been an out-and-out charmer. If his effect on her daughter was anything to go by, he still was. But what to do?

Alice had taken herself off to bed. Mary was still up sitting in an armchair, hands clasped and a morose expression on her face. With her head lowered, eyes that so resembled her father's looked up from beneath a thick wedge of dark hair. In a certain light, it held the same auburn persuasion as Stuart's did.

Thelma stood in front of the fireplace eyeing her reflection in the mirror as she unclipped her earrings and wiped the lipstick from her mouth. 'You might as well go to bed. School in the morning.'

'Not for much longer,' Mary returned sourly. 'Then I'll have a job. And any boyfriend I want. And I'll marry anyone I want.'

'No you will not. You need my permission until you turn twenty-one.'

'Then I'll run away.'

'With the gypsy boy?'

'With anyone.' She paused as though searching for a further response that would anger her mother the most. 'With Donald. I'll marry Donald.'

Thelma flicked at what remained of the lipstick in the corners of her mouth. 'No you won't.'

'Yes I will.'

Thelma took in the anxious look of her reflection. First it was as if a dam had burst inside. Resignation and calm followed just as flat water comes after a thrusting tide. 'You can't marry the man you know as Donald Tucker. His real name is Stuart Brodie.'

'I don't care what his name is. I'll still marry him.'

Keeping her eyes fixed on her reflection, Thelma thought how old she looked, how tired from fighting against the ebb and flow of life. She'd come so far and had truly thought she'd reached a sunlit upland where everything was wonderful – or as wonderful as it could be.

Weariness descended on her shoulders and ran through every muscle and nerve in her body. She could fight no more. The truth would out.

'No matter whether he calls himself Donald Tucker or Stuart Brodie. You can't marry him. He's your father.'

A stunned silence followed. Thelma couldn't tell how long it lasted, but Mary's shock was obvious from the expression on her face. Her eyes were on stalks, her face pale, as though all the blood had drained from her upper body and flowed away.

Her back to the fireplace, Thelma reached out her arms. 'Darling, I'm sorry you had to find out like this...'

The moment her mother's hands touched her, Mary was up from the chair. There was hatred in her eyes. 'It's not true.'

'It is true,' said Thelma in as calm a voice as possible. 'He left me high and dry before you were born.'

Eyes wide with disbelief, Mary shook her head. 'I don't believe you.'

Undeterred by her daughter's anticipated response, Thelma reached out one arm. 'Mary, I wanted you. He didn't want you.'

Mary looked at the floor, the walls, even the drawn curtains as though somehow the truth she wanted to hear was there for her to read.

A thought seemed suddenly to take hold of her that made her jerk her head up. 'Then why has he come to see me now?'

It was the one question Thelma couldn't answer. Why had he sought out his daughter now? She recalled he'd said something about having a good deal of money and wanting it to benefit his daughter. Based on past performance, she didn't believe him. There had to be another reason.

She sighed. 'I'm too tired to think about it now. You go on up to bed, Mary. I'm going to make myself a cup of cocoa. Are there any biscuits left?'

Mary nodded.

'Then I'll bid you goodnight, sweetheart. Try to get some sleep.'

'What about Alice? Is she…?'

Much as it grieved her to do it, there seemed no longer any point in telling a lie – except for one small lie that didn't really matter. Thelma shook her head. 'No. Her father died.'

'If Donald… Stuart… is my father, will I see him again?'

'Let's see, Mary. Let's think about it and do what's for the best. Goodnight.'

Memories flooded back as Thelma sat there alone drinking her cocoa and blaming herself for making a mess of her life. She recounted the men who'd been part of that life: George's father who had died during the Great War, Stuart who had been fun whilst it lasted and Archie. If he hadn't already been married, perhaps they might still be together and blessed with more children. But he'd chosen his wife. She was an invalid and although there had been no physical relationship to their marriage, he'd loved her and stood by her when Thelma had told him she was expecting a baby.

The tears were flowing freely when she whispered to herself, 'Oh why do I always choose the wrong man?'

And if Stuart did come knocking at the door, how would she explain him to Bert?

Life was difficult in youth and in later life it didn't become any easier.

14

It came as something of a surprise for Jenny to find Bert Throgmorton standing at her front door.

'Bert. To what do I owe this pleasure?' she asked brightly.

Gentlemanly as ever, Bert swept his hat from his head and smoothed back the slick band of dark hair on the right side of his head.

'I've just inspected number five.' He shook his head. 'What a terrible mess it's in. Inside it smells of dog and dirt and outside it looks like a scrapyard.'

'So we've all noticed. Is there anything I can do to help?'

'There is indeed.'

Jenny opened the door that bit wider. 'Then you'd better come in. Fancy a cuppa?'

He declined the offer but gratefully sunk into an armchair.

'I've got much of what's to be done arranged. The decorators will paint it all inside first. There's not much furniture left and what's there isn't much good. I should think most of it will go for firewood.' He shook his head. 'I dislike seeing a perfectly good, clean house treated like that.'

Jenny agreed with him. The council house she was lucky enough to live in was a big step up from the two rooms she'd lived in with Roy and the kids in Blue Bowl Alley. She very much appreciated the three bedrooms, the separate kitchen and living room, the downstairs bathroom and the gardens front and rear. Plus the plumbing, of course. It was an absolute luxury to have a cold-water tap in the kitchen. The same applied to the bathroom, though the water for bathing was heated by the zinc laundry boiler in the kitchen. She truly felt she was living in luxury compared to what had gone before.

'Is there any way I can help?'

'Yes, there is,' said Bert as he shifted in the chair and passed his hat from one hand to the other. 'I was wondering whether your friend Robin could clear away what's been left. He might be able to sell some of it to someone in need – or give it away for that matter. We're willing to pay an uplift fee. On top of that, I wonder if I could impose on him to clear away the mess in the front garden. From what I can see, it's mostly metal – old bedsteads and such like. Do you think he might oblige?'

'I think he'd jump at it. Unfortunately, I can't ask him myself. You see...' It occurred to her that Thelma might already have hinted at the details to Bert of why she was no longer working for Robin. Bert was a stickler for detail when it came to Bristol's stock of council houses. Details of personal matters and gossip just flew over his head, even when he was close to them.

Just as expected, he looked a bit puzzled at first until Jenny explained a bit further.

'Robin's estranged wife has moved back in. She's a very jealous woman, so it's best I don't show my face.'

'Ah!' Although he appeared to understand, he chewed it over before coming to the obvious decision. 'Then I'll pop in myself.' He chuckled. 'I warrant she won't be jealous of me.'

'Let's hope not,' said Jenny with a light laugh. The truth was that she would love to oblige, but Robin deserved a quiet life and her turning up would most certainly set the cat among the pigeons.

* * *

By the weekend, yet another trip to the picture house had been arranged and Bert took the opportunity to tell Jenny that Robin had accepted the job the council had given him. She didn't ask how Doreen had received him as it seemed he'd survived unscathed.

Whereas Bert seemed as happy as one could tell, Thelma was a little distracted. She frequently swept her gaze around Filwood Broadway, across the expanse of green, past Robin's shop to the Venture Inn.

That was where Mary had met the stranger who had turned out to be her father. He'd seemed determined to see his daughter again, but thankfully had not yet turned up on the doorstep. Her stomach quaked at the thought of it. What would she say? What could she say and what would Bert think?

Tonight, although it was still light, Thelma could see no sign of Stuart Brodie. As her nerves settled, she determined to settle down and see the film.

The lights went down. The theatre darkened. At first, the black and white picture was mutated by the curtains. Once they were pulled back, up came Gaumont News.

'*Her Majesty the Queen inspects soldiers wearing gas masks and capes, the latest fashion in the event of an air raid...*'

Whoever had written the script might have thought it amusing, but its humour was lost on the audience. It seemed to Thelma that everyone had drawn in their breath. Please. Not again. Not another war.

The queen appeared for a second time in another context; her and Princesses Elizabeth and Margaret visiting a horse show. Thelma breathed a sigh of relief. This was normality as far as she was concerned. Ordinary living without the shadow of war.

The reel for the featured film hadn't turned up. Tonight's main feature turned out to be one she had seen before – *Dandy Dick* starring Will Hay.

Thelma couldn't help but grimace when she recalled that it was about doping horses, which immediately brought Stuart to mind.

She couldn't help feeling relieved when the film was over and they could queue for fish and chips. There was no recruiting van outside on this occasion, but posters were being pasted onto advertisements for Bisto Gravy or Cherry Blossom Shoe polish. The innocuous posters extolling the benefits of everyday products were being replaced by ones encouraging women to join the auxiliary fire service and for men to join the Territorial Army.

Thelma shivered and looked away. 'I've got a bit of a headache. I don't fancy any fish and chips. I'd prefer to go home.'

Bert was full of sympathy. 'Oh my poor darling.' Gently, he rubbed at her shoulder. 'I'll take you home. You could probably do with an early night. Are you coming too, Jenny?'

'I might as well.'

Somehow, Jenny knew there was more than one reason for Thelma wanting to go home. When they got there, number twelve was in darkness.

'Now you go on in, darling, and get yourself to bed,' Bert insisted.

Thelma told him to stop fussing.

'I'll make sure she does as she's told,' said Jenny.

'Goodnight, my love.' Bert planted a kiss on Thelma's cheek before heading back to the car.

Once inside the house, Thelma bolted up the stairs.

Jenny stood at the bottom. Thelma's action hadn't surprised her and she thought she knew what she was up to.

Just as expected, Thelma reappeared and came swiftly back down the stairs.

'I take it Mary is safely tucked in bed.'

'Yes,' said Thelma, the word delivered within a breathless sigh. She opened the door to the living room, went into the kitchen and put the kettle on. 'I'm making cocoa. It might help me sleep. Will you join me?'

'You bet I will. You're aching to tell me something and guess what? I'm a good listener.'

Two mugs of hot chocolate were duly made. They both took a sip, Jenny not letting her eyes drop from Thelma's downcast eyes and thoughtful expression.

She waited patiently, took another sip.

'You know the man's identity. Are you going to tell me what you've found out?'

Thelma's chest rose in what Jenny could only describe as an act of determination. 'Right. I made Mary stay at home and I went to meet him.' She raised her eyes. 'The moment she spoke his name – or what she thought was his name – I guessed who it was. So off I went to where my girl was supposed to meet him.'

Jenny nodded mutely.

Cocoa slopped from the mug when Thelma banged it down on the table. 'Stuart. Stuart Brodie. Mary's father.'

'Wh-at?' The word was strung out.

Thelma shook her head and looked exasperated. 'Don't ask me why he's turned up now. He tried to say that he had at last become responsible, that he now had the money to make good things happen in her life. But...' she spat the last word as though there was poison in her mouth '...I don't believe a word of it.'

'What does Mary think now that she knows?'

'She's hurt. And confused. She can't understand why he left. He always did run from responsibility. He was a gambler, Jenny. He lived in the moment and would do anything to earn an extra shilling – by fair means or foul. It was exciting at the time, before I came to realise that he was stealing to feed his habit. He stole from his employers.' She grimaced. 'That's how he ended up in jail. It was a long time ago. I don't know whether he's done anything wrong since and I'm not going to ask.'

Having sipped at her drink whilst listening, Jenny finally finished it and returned the mug to its place on the big square dining table that dominated the room. 'Do you think he'll hang around?'

Thelma placed her palms together, almost like an angel in prayer – though Jenny knew from the bits of history she'd been told that Thelma was no angel. She shrugged. 'I don't know. I hope he'll go away. Mary is very upset. I've always told her that her father was dead – she assumed that George's father and hers and Alice's were one and the same. But it isn't true.' She turned her dark eyes onto Jenny. 'My three children had three different fathers.'

'You told me when we first met.'

Thelma gave a lopsided grin. 'You're a mate.'

It was true that Jenny had known from the beginning not long after they'd first become friends. It made no difference. She would do all she could to support her through this dire time.

Thelma looked forlorn. It was rare to see her so confused. She didn't usually take too long to fight her way through a problem. The return of Mary's father had thrown her.

'What are your plans?' Jenny asked.

Thelma snorted, a sure sign that she was working through things. 'Well, if he thinks he can just walk into my life and take over my daughter, he's got another think coming! He wasn't there to change and feed her when she was a baby. He wasn't sitting by her bed all night when she had whooping cough, and he's never provided a penny towards anything. He can sod off!'

Her last outburst made Jenny jump.

On seeing the effect, there was first a smile, then an outburst of laughter from both of them.

'Bloody men!' exclaimed Thelma.

Humour turned out to be the best antidote to Thelma's mood.

Her back straightened against the back of the dining chair and there was a loud slapping sound as she brought her palms down on the table. 'He's not welcome here and that's it!'

* * *

On hearing voices, Mary had crept down the stairs. She'd had a dream that her father had come to the house, that he wanted to tell her all the reasons why he'd never been in touch before. She warmed to anyone who liked horses just as she did. The man who'd introduced himself as Donald Tucker – who she now knew was Stuart Brodie – liked horses.

Halfway down the stairs brought the voices she'd heard only a little clearer. She recognised Jenny Crawford's voice. Disappointment replaced the anticipation that it might be her father.

Head resting on clenched fists, she sat at that halfway point, her elbows resting on her knees. The voices became clearer as the living-room door opened.

'Thanks for listening.' Her mother's voice.

'What are friends for? Thanks for the cocoa.'

Fresh air and light from a lamppost came in. Mary didn't move.

The last goodnights were said. The front door was closed.

It was when Thelma flicked the light switch on that she saw her daughter.

'Mary. You should be in bed. Get your sleep over the weekend so you're fresh for school on Monday.'

'Not for much longer,' Mary snapped, got up and raced back up to bed.

Thelma stood immovable. As she gazed into the dark abyss at the top of the stairs, she remembered giving birth to Mary. The night of her conception was still clear – a beautiful bed in an old and very grand house. Stuart had told her that the house had belonged to his uncle. She'd been impressed. Any woman would be. Only some time later had she found out the truth. The house had belonged to his employer – a racehorse owner who had made the mistake of trusting Stuart Brodie, just as she had.

Not only had he left her high and dry once he'd discovered she was in the family way, but he'd also gone back and burgled the house before leaving the country.

She'd been mortified when the police had questioned her, though once it became obvious that she too was a victim, they let her go. She vividly remembered going back to her lodgings and finding little George sound asleep in his bed. Exhausted and close to despair, she'd broken down and had barely stopped crying all night.

So there she'd been, left a widow with one child and expecting another. It had been close to being the worst time in her life, but she'd pushed it all behind her, rebuilt her life and was happy.

Stuart had come back and ruined it.

15

It had rained overnight, but daytime brought scudding clouds and the promise of periods of sunshine.

Before the girls left for school, Jenny took them aside and asked them to keep an eye on Mary Dawson.

'She's a bit unsettled at present.'

'She's being a misery,' Gloria countered.

Tilly frowned at her sister. 'She's got rights to be a misery if she's upset.'

'Well, I don't want anything to do with anyone who looks miserable all the time. It's because of the gypsy boy. He's taken the horses with him.'

Jenny sighed. 'That was a while ago.'

'So why is she—'

'Never mind. Get to school.'

Waving them off at the front door, she watched as they joined up with Alice, all chattering gamely. Mary dragged behind them, looking down at her feet as though wondering why they were taking such slow steps.

The sight of a van turning into the Close stopped Jenny from closing the door and her heart leapt.

It has no rights to, she told herself, but the sight of Robin getting out lifted her spirits.

As per usual, he waved one hand before using both to set his cap more firmly back on his head. In an act of sheer bravado, he swung his legs over the closed garden gate. He looked pleased that he'd achieved it.

Jenny eyed him with bemusement. 'Very impressive. Why don't you join the circus?'

He grinned as he walked up the path towards her, rolling his shoulders as if to loosen up his muscles. His grin widened. 'If it weren't for the kids, I would, though on second thoughts, the best option is for my old woman to join – preferably on a trapeze with rotten ropes.'

Jenny didn't suggest that he didn't really mean that. She knew he did.

'I take it you're here to clear out number five.'

'Yep.' He flung a quick glance in that direction. 'It might take two or three trips depending on what's there and where I take it – the tip or the scrapyard. The Red Cow Yard is giving a decent price for metals. Reckon it's gone up of late, thanks to all this talk of war.'

Jenny felt a shiver wash over her like a sudden shower of rain. 'Let's not talk about that, shall we?'

A curt nod, then, 'I'll go and start to sort things out, then I could do with a cuppa.'

'You don't want one now? Before you begin?'

He thought about it, then jerked his head sideways. 'Go on then.'

In the coolness of the kitchen, the gas jets hissed and the kettle began to whistle.

'I wanted to ask you something,' he said as he set his cap on the table and sat down.

Not anything to do with Doreen, she hoped. Although she would have liked to tell him to stand up to his wife and her demands, she held back. It wasn't her business. Robin was only a friend. That's what she kept telling herself.

'Go ahead and ask.'

After he'd helped himself to two sugar lumps, Jenny added milk to his cup.

He took a sip, looked thoughtful and a little worried. 'It's about an item of silver that was pledged and you signed for. The signature of whoever brought it in is a bit smudged and I'm not sure about the address.'

She frowned. 'A cup. An engraved cup.'

'That's the one.'

'What did I do wrong?'

'I don't think you did anything wrong except that you gave 'im twenty quid.'

'I gave him too much?' She was mortified to think she might have injured Robin's takings.

He shook his head. 'On the contrary, you could 'ave given 'im a lot more than that. Fifty quid at least. It's valuable. Very valuable. Do you recall what the bloke looked like?'

'It was him,' she exclaimed.

'Him?'

'The man I saw staring across at Thelma's house. I thought I'd seen him before when he came into the shop. I just couldn't place him at the time.'

'It's a nice cup. Can't say for sure, but if he don't put in an appearance and redeem it...'

'You think it might be stolen?'

He reached for his cap and began shaking his head. 'I could be wrong. It might be wise to speak to the police. They might know something and at least then I would 'ave done what was right and not get done for receiving goods that might 'ave been stolen.' He rolled his shoulders as he got to his feet. 'Now I'd better get on. Thanks for the tea.'

She watched as he got into the van and parked it outside number five. Was it really possible that the piece of silver was stolen? If so then it seemed likely that Mary's father was a thief. She hoped it wasn't so.

Cath from up the road waved at her.

Jenny waved back, then went swiftly indoors. She had a lot to do and Cath did tend to hang around for a chat. What were the chances of avoiding her?

The answer came about thirty minutes later.

'Can I borrow a cup of sugar?' Cath asked brightly.

'I can't. I need some myself. I could lend you some after I get back from the shops.'

She had no real need to go to the shops. She had enough sugar to last until the morning. Her prime objective was to avoid gossiping. Cath must have seen Robin and his van, noticed him popping into the house and was bound to be curious.

Jenny's suspicion proved to be right. Instead of leaving once she'd been told there was no sugar to lend, Cath jerked her chin at number five from whence came the sound of things being shifted around, sorted into heaps and finally loaded onto the van. The rear doors were open and the day being warm, Robin's shirt was open to the waist and his sleeves were rolled up above his elbows.

'I see your friend Robin's got the job of clearing the rubbish out. Been in to see you first, I notice.'

'Bert asked him to clear the front garden. They did leave a bit of a mess. He did pop in just to let me know he was here, so I could tell Bert.'

The day and time of Robin doing the job had no doubt already been agreed between him and Bert but was a suitable excuse to give Cath. Sometimes Jenny had the distinct impression that Cath could go beyond general tittle-tattle and descend into outright mischief-making. Lurking in the background was the fact that before Jenny had arrived Cath had regarded herself as Thelma's best friend. So far, Cath had been accepting, but there was no guarantee things would continue that way.

'You puttin' the kettle on then?' asked Cath.

'I'm sorry, Cath, but I'm just about to put a load of laundry through the mangle.' She looked purposefully at the fluffy clouds bounding like sheep across the sky. 'Looks like a good drying day.'

Cath grunted what seemed more like disappointment than agreement.

Jenny felt obliged to go some way to repairing the moment. 'Got anything planned for the weekend?'

Face brightening, Cath said that indeed she did. 'Our Cyril's coming to visit. He's bringing Marion and the kids with him. They want to take a look at number five before applying for it – when it's cleaned up and the corporation's decorated it, that is.' She wrinkled her nose. 'It must stink to high heaven what with that scruffy lot and their dirty great dog.'

A policeman living in Coronation Close! Such a thing wouldn't go down well with some of the neighbours – those that didn't always stick to the straight and narrow. But this was no time to voice any misgiving. Cath was fond of her brother, even though it meant that Bill, who worked down at the docks, might have to be careful what went out of the dock gates and into their house.

'That's nice for you.'

A broad smile spread brightened Cath's face. 'Someone respectable. And clean!'

It crossed Jenny's mind that Cath might tidy herself up during the day. She might even forego wearing curlers in her hair, plus her oversize slippers slapping along the pavement.

She said nothing more as Cath made her way back up the road to her own house at the head of the close.

Jenny went out of the back door, where a pile of folded sheets was waiting to be put through the cast-iron mangle. The rollers were big and the handle took some turning. The job was best done by two people; usually Tilly or Gloria would take turns on the handle whilst Jenny fed through clothing, bedding or towels. It struck her that she could have asked Cath to do a few turns, but she would manage, and besides, wasn't that bending and stretching good for the figure?

As each piece came through, Jenny placed it in the wicker laundry basket. Once it was full, she headed for the washing line and the bag of pegs hanging from the end post nearest to the house.

A mouthful of pegs clutched between her teeth, she readied each item to hang out, flicking sheets and pillowcases like a matador would his cape. Knocking the dolly pegs onto each piece made her hands sore but helped her stop thinking of Robin across the road. There'd been little chance to talk more of what was happening at his shop with regards to Doreen. Their conversation had concentrated on the piece of silver – expensive as it turned out. She hadn't mention what Thelma had told her about her suspicion that the stranger was Mary's father. It had been a private conversation and not for his ears.

Leaving the bedsheets to crack like sails in the breeze, Jenny took one step back into the house and before taking further steps heard the blowing of a whistle. A policeman's whistle. That's what it sounded like. On top of that, she became aware of shouting and running feet.

Doorknockers were being banged at every front door by the sound of it.

The sound of her own doorknocker reverberated through the house. Robin's voice accompanied it. 'Jenny! Jenny!'

There was an urgency to his voice that hadn't been there earlier. When she opened the front door, ready laughingly to ask if there was a fire, Robin was standing there looking breathless and worried. One look at his expression and the smile was wiped from her face.

'You need to get out of the street.'

Without explanation and still exhibiting the same air of urgency, he grabbed her arm and began to pull her from the house so forcefully that she stumbled down the front steps.

'Robin! For goodness' sake, what's the matter.'

Over his head, she could see PC Pyke, their local beat constable, with his arms outstretched, accompanied by two or three other men who worked nightshifts or didn't work at all, shepherding a group of neighbours along. Another police constable came running to assist.

'I heard yer whistle,' the lately arrived constable explained.

Coronation Close looked to be a flurry of motion, women and small children looking confused and lost, heading for the end of the street.

'What's going on?'

Pushed through the garden gate, she almost collided with Cath.

'Blimey,' cried Cath. 'Not only did they leave rent arrears, but they also left a bloody live shell as well.'

Only once Jenny and her neighbours were on the main road at the end of Coronation Close did Robin get the chance to explain.

'I was sorting out the metal. Got a fair bit of cast iron and lead piping out and into the van. I could see there was brass stuff beneath it. Plant pots, curtain rails and copper kettle I thought – until I saw it. Artillery shell. In perfect condition. Never ever got to be used on the Western Front by the looks of it.' His face was pale, as though his blood had fallen to his feet.

'A shell? From the Great War?'

'Unexploded. Luckily, I saw Pyke on his beat. He sent somebody along to the police box to report it.'

'Now what?'

'Up to St Barnabas on Broad Walk until the Territorials come and take it as far away from the houses as possible and blow it up.' He shook his head. 'Bloody idiots! What the 'ell were they thinking?'

Jenny thought of the children coming home from school. 'Do we know how long they'll take?'

A look of relief softened his face. 'I'm no expert, but Pyke reckons it shouldn't take too long.'

PC Pyke interrupted their conversation. 'All right. Everyone to the church hall. The vicar's wife is providing tea and cakes.'

'Sorry I was so rough,' said Robin as he caressed Jenny's arm. 'You go on to the church hall whilst I go and fetch my van. Don't want anything happening to that.'

He'd barely gone half a dozen steps when one of the police constables sent to assist PC Pyke stopped him.

'And where do you think you're going?'

Robin gestured to the black van parked halfway along the close outside number five. 'I was going to move my van.'

Whilst adjusting his chin strap, the policeman proclaimed in no uncertain terms that he couldn't possibly allow that. 'Sorry, sir. Off to the church with everyone else.'

'But I don't live here,' Robin protested.

The police constable was firm but polite. 'I'm sorry. You can come back for your van when the Territorials have been and gone.'

Robin recognised that there was no point protesting.

Once he'd arrived at the church hall, he confided in Jenny he'd wished he'd loaded it onto the van with the rest and said nothing.

She pointed out that it might have gone off. 'And then where would you be?'

He flicked a dirty thumb to the corner of his lips and grinned. 'Then I might well be up on the church steeple rather than in the church hall.'

She eyed him ruefully. 'That's not funny.'

'I suppose not.' But still he grinned.

Full of the self-importance usually confined to more selective and smaller events, the vicar's wife demanded of women who enjoyed doing good for the church, she put herself in charge of one of the very large teapots. 'Do let me fill you up. You most certainly must need it.'

She said the same to everyone. A small, mouselike woman scurried along behind her carrying a plate of biscuits.

Jenny took a bite of one. It was a bit soft. She concluded the biscuits had been hanging around for a while – perhaps stored for such an occasion. An emergency that might never happen, but one for which the likes of her would always rise to the occasion and perhaps even enjoy.

Robin had made the mistake of dunking his biscuit into his tea. Being stale and thus a bit soft, the biscuit had disappeared.

'Serves you right,' said Jenny.

'Never mind. It makes it a bit stronger. How long do you think she's 'ad these biscuits?'

Jenny gave him a look of reprimand. 'She's doing her best in difficult circumstances. I expect she had a very different day planned. I bet she saw the weather and planned to put some laundry out on the line.'

'At least the tea's wet and warm, though a bit too like gnat's... if you know what I mean.'

'I know what you mean.'

Cath spotted them and came over with her youngest clinging to her skirt. She smiled pointedly at Robin. 'Well, you got well and truly caught out, didn't you.'

'I don't know what you mean, missus. I was asked to come yer and get rid of a load of scrap metal. Didn't expect there to be an unexploded shell amongst it.'

Maude came butting in to say that it was all very inconvenient. 'All I 'ope is that they take care of our 'ouses whilst they're empty.'

She swiped at a trickle of snuff trickling from her nose. Robin offered her a cigarette.

In consequence, Maude looked horrified. 'Don't touch tobacco. Disgusting stuff it is.'

Jenny exchanged an amused look with Robin. Maude was something of a champion of snuff and opposed to the smoking of tobacco. The fact that snuff was derived from tobacco seemed totally lost on her.

Maude declared her intention to ask the vicar's wife if she'd baked one of her famous cakes of late. 'Fruit cake usually. And I reckon she puts a tot of brandy to give it a bit of flavour.'

The feather in Maude's hat fluttered determinedly as she followed the vicar's wife out into the kitchen.

'I bet a tanner she gets a piece,' said Robin and laughed.

'If there is a cake,' Jenny added.

Cath was easily forgotten in the moment of shared humour and it came as a surprise when she suddenly asked Robin, 'How's your wife? I used to go to school with 'er you know. Her mother used rags to tie up 'er hair at night. She 'ad ringlets down to her waist. We was all jealous of them. Nobody else 'ad ringlets like she did. I thought I might call in when I'm next up at the Broadway. P'raps you could let 'er know that Cath Routledge – that was my name at school – will call in when she's next up that way.'

'To check if she still has ringlets?' Jenny asked, her smile tight enough to make her face crack.

Robin's eyes met hers. She could tell from his expression that he'd perceived a hidden meaning beneath Cath's comment just as she had.

'She used to be something of a friend, did Doris. Back when we were kids.'

'Doreen,' said Jenny after exchanging yet another glance with Robin. 'Her name's Doreen.'

The sudden fiddling with one of the metal curlers that covered her head like slivers of armour was a sure sign that Cath realised that she'd been mistaken. 'I wonder if Maude 'as got a slice of cake yet,' she muttered in an offhand fashion. 'I'm going to see if I can get one.' Cath was gone.

Taking a sip of tea, Jenny smiled at Robin. 'You know what she was up to, saying she'd call in the next time she's up your way. She thinks we're having an affair and wants to make us feel uncomfortable.'

'She was halfway there.'

'We're not having an affair.'

'No. We're not. More's the pity.'

Heat rose onto Jenny's cheeks as she looked into his face and saw the truth written there in large letters in his twinkling eyes.

Somebody came tumbling through the door shouting that an army lorry had pulled up outside number five and that several soldiers had alighted and placed the unexploded shell into an iron receptacle for the onwards journey to where it would finally be exploded.

'Let's hope they get there all right.'

Jenny congregated with her neighbours in the doorway of the church hall, keen to hear the lorry start up and drive away with its frightening load. Robin stood next to her.

The breeze she'd trusted to dry her laundry was blusterier now. She looked up at the sky. Several dark clouds hung like dishcloths beneath the fluffy white ones that had predominated earlier.

'Are you up with them clouds?' asked Robin.

She shook her head, suddenly craving a few raindrops on her face, even though that same rain would fall on her nicely drying laundry. 'I was feeling glad that that shell was here and didn't get used back in the Great War. And that you noticed it.'

There was understanding in his expression and the gentle way he looked at her. He voiced what he was thinking. 'Because if it had exploded back then it would have taken a lot of young men with it.'

Jenny murmured a wordless response. The two of them were not touching each other physically but their thoughts appeared to be travelling the same path. They were grateful it had ended up here today and nobody would be hurt. Thanks to Robin's careful dismantling of the heap of scrap, the people of Coronation Close had also survived.

16

They were inside number twelve, sitting at the table, George on one side, Bert on the other. Thelma was pouring the tea.

George looked and sounded puzzled. 'Why now? Why does 'e want to take our Mary away now? If he was any sort of father he'd have shown his face long before now.'

Thelma tugged the tea cosy over the teapot somewhat forcefully.

'He's got a bloody nerve, that's all I know,' Thelma replied.

'Are his intentions...' Bert looked embarrassed as he sought the right word. 'Honourable?'

Instantly recognising where this question was going, Thelma grabbed his hand and gave it a squeeze. 'I wouldn't marry him if he was hanging in diamonds.'

Face brightening, Bert smiled.

George sat frowning on the other side of the table. 'I think I'm going to 'ave a word with 'im.'

'Me too,' said Bert.

Thelma pointed out the one thing that might prevent them doing that. 'We don't know where he lives. He did leave a nice little piece at Hubert's pawn shop. Jenny said there was an address, but it was a bit blurred. Also...' Her voice trailed off. She glanced at each of them, Bert looking worried and George looking angry, before saying, 'Nobody's heard of the address. Not even the police.'

George's jaw dropped. 'The police?'

'What's he done?' asked Bert. He looked quite shocked.

Dear Bert, thought Thelma. He'd led such a sheltered life. Even during the war, he hadn't joined up but had been given a job overseeing the creation and printing of railway timetables. 'So the troops can move about smoothly,' he'd told her, not without an element of pride. She'd agreed that it was an important job.

Thelma passed on the information about the silver goblet as it had been told her by Jenny Crawford. 'One look at it and Robin knew it was valuable. Jenny had thought it was lovely, but that's as far as her knowledge went.'

Bert shook his head and tutted. 'This is certainly a bit of a do, Thelma.'

She eyed him anxiously. From the very start of their relationship she'd been in no doubt of their differences, but then didn't opposites attract? She'd lived and loved in the moment – lived life to the full.

'What did the police say?'

Bert's question jolted her from regrets and reminiscences.

'That they'd check their records and see what they could find out. Not that they held out much luck, seeing as they had no idea of his address.'

Bert grunted and looked weighed down with thought.

Glumly preoccupied with what seemed a mountain of problems, Thelma looked at her interlaced fingers. If she clasped them much more tightly, she was in danger of breaking the bones.

On the other side of the table, George's fingers were beating a constant rhythm. His eyes were downcast and his brow furrowed.

She worried about his thoughts most of all. She loved her son and badly wanted to ask him if she'd been a bad mother – despite everything. Despite the men. Despite giving birth to his half-sisters.

He went on tapping. The same rhythm repeatedly, one finger on the table, the next finger on the table, then the next, the next, and the next, again and again and again.

The repeated tapping was joined by the sound of a bluebottle buzzing as it beat against the window, trying to get out, to be free to buzz around and do what it liked. She opened the window and let it out.

George was still tapping the table with his fingers. It was still irritating.

Finally, she'd had enough. She brought her clenched fist down onto the table. 'Stop that, George.' Crockery rattled. The loudness of her shout assaulted their ears.

George huffed something about not being a child any longer.

Thelma unfurled her fist, rested both hands in her lap and sat back in her chair and mumbled sorry.

She would have liked to know more of what George was thinking, what he was remembering. Although only a toddler at the time, he recalled Stuart calling on her. She herself recalled the happiness she'd felt then, going out with a dashing, devil-may-care type of man. He'd been far from a saint but she'd only been a young widow unwilling to wear black for the rest of her life. He'd been lively, out for a good time and had seemed to have a never-ending stream of money for gambling, drinking and generally having fun. She'd never questioned where that money had come from. He'd made her happy and that was all that had mattered.

Recalling that time didn't just bring back happy memories. It also brought regrets and a sudden heavy dose of guilt. How could she have been so carefree when she'd had a young lad to look after?

Bert made his excuses to leave before George did. He looked

thoughtful as he stood on the doorstep twirling his hat in his hand. He gave her a perfunctory kiss on the cheek and never once raised his eyes or smiled into her face as he usually did.

'I won't be around tomorrow. I've got something on that might take some time.'

Bert had never come across as a keeper of secrets, but he did now.

She refrained from asking him what it might be. She was feeling unnerved by recent events.

You've got through worse than this, she told herself whilst trying not to think the worst. *You've had more than one man let you down.*

'That's fine. I'll expect you when I see you.'

George said that he too was off home. 'I promised Maria I wouldn't be long. She's beginning to get nervous about giving birth to this baby. She wants me there when she does.'

'Men aren't allowed in at the birth,' Thelma said tersely. 'Don't you worry,' she said, patting his shoulder, her red lips smiling. 'She'll be in good hands. Oh goodness,' she said suddenly, her hand flying to her mouth. 'I'm not long off becoming a grandmother.'

It was good to hear him laugh. It made her think that everything in the garden was rosy and reaffirmed his opinion of her as a mother.

She patted his arm and knew for sure that her eyes were filling with tears. 'I did my best, George – you know – bringing you up. I did my best.'

He enfolded his mother in his arms and patted her back. 'I know you did, Mum. I know you did. Do you know what, Mum? I'm glad I weren't born a woman. It's too hard what with babies and all that.'

He kissed her as Bert had done, a brief kiss, then he was gone.

He'd disappeared by the time a distraught-looking Alice came racing along the road. Her face was smudged with what looked to be a mixture of dirt and tears.

Coming to an abrupt halt in front of her mother, she looked up and asked, 'Why haven't I got a daddy? Why has Mary got one and not me?'

The question was totally unexpected and caught Thelma off guard.

'Oh, my sweet girl,' she said softly, her hand resting on her heart. 'What is this all about?'

'Mary said that she's got a daddy. I asked if we could share him but she said that he wasn't mine. That I'd had a different daddy and so had George. She said that hers belonged to just her and that I couldn't have him!'

'Oh, Lord,' Thelma muttered. As if she hadn't had enough to deal with today now there was this. 'Look my darling girl,' she said, placing her hands on her daughter's shoulders. 'Darling, your dad's name was Archie. He's with Jesus now. He got sick and died. If he hadn't, we were going to get married. We both knew that you were on the way, a little sister for Mary and George. We'd even discussed naming you after the sister of King Edward the Seventh. Alice. The Princess Royal. And that was what you were going to be. Our little princess.'

It was an outright lie but more acceptable than the truth. Archie hadn't been free to marry.

'He's in heaven?'

'Yes. He is. He was a good man. I've no doubt that he's in heaven.'

It seemed to Thelma that her elaborate explanation was not quite enough. Alice hung her head and leaned into her mother's body. Thelma stroked her daughter's hair, thinking how the colour matched that of her father.

'Mary said that her father's moving in with us. Will he want to be my father too?'

Thelma stopped stroking. 'Moving in with us? Mary told you that?'

'Yes. She said he'd come back to be with her.'

Thelma's eyes darkened as she looked from her daughter to some place where her anger could be given full rein. Her first plan was to go to the far end of the garden and scream. On reflection, it made more sense to have a word with Mary, to explain that there was no chance whatsoever of her father moving in. Damn Stuart. Damn him to hell!

17

'There are still several unfilled vacancies in the newly formed Air Raid Precaution units. Supervisors and organisers are also required, preferably those from a professional background. A spokesman in Whitehall was adamant that there was no need for panic but that if war does happen, Britain will be prepared...'

'Shut up! Shut up about war.' Jenny sighed. She flicked at the top of the now silent wireless with a duster, a cream-coloured one she'd cut down from a worn-out pair of cotton knickers. There was no dust there. The act was by way of admonishment. She didn't want to hear talk of war.

Satisfied that her living room was clean and tidy – and silent without the wireless – she made her way into the kitchen. Even though the day was overcast, the kitchen looked sunny thanks to the yellow check curtains and the honey-coloured wooden table and chairs. She sniffed the air and immediately wrinkled her nose. What looked good wasn't smelling so good.

The pig bin – the small round bin reserved for food scraps – was due to be put out for collection. Orders of what should be placed in there were very specific. Food. Any type of food, all to be forwarded on to pig farms. Pigs would eat anything, including gristle and fat. Bones would be placed to one side and sent to the boneyards to be rendered down into bone meal for use as fertiliser.

Holding the bin by the ring that connected lid to bin, Jenny carried it out of the back door and around the side of the house. One or two others in the Close were bringing theirs out. A wave here, a nod of acknowledgement there, then hanging around on the gate. Gossip was the usual reason for lingering, catching up on whose kids were playing truant from school, the price of sausages at the butcher's up in Filwood Broadway and who'd got a job on the docks purely because of their face fitting.

Today none of that happened because something else was happening: there was movement at number five. A representative from the council was showing a family around. The family of four were currently in the front garden looking up at the front of the house.

Mrs Arkle was leaning on her gate at number one.

Jenny smiled and wished her good morning.

Mrs Arkle smiled back and said, 'New neighbours.' She looked very happy about it, understandable seeing as the Arkle and Stenner kids had not got on. It was also rumoured that a drunken Mr Stenner had threatened Mr Arkle. Apparently, Mr Stenner had come off worse.

'It would seem that way.'

Mrs Arkle grunted a wordless agreement, coupled with a quick jerk of her chin before almost dancing up her garden path and into the house.

Cath arrived from the other end of the Close looking pleased with herself. She was wearing a dusky pink dress and an apron which was a mass of roses. Jenny recognised it as her best apron. That was shock enough, but to cap it all, Cath's hair, usually studded with curlers at this time of day and covered with a headscarf, was styled into thick waves, preened and pertly resting on her shoulders.

Trying to see something when you don't want another party to see you watching was difficult. Jenny's curiosity was rewarded with sight of a smart pair of brown leather shoes not the oversize slippers that Cath usually slopped around in all day.

Her face was wreathed in smiles.

'That's my brother and 'is family,' she said with obvious pride. 'He's put in fer number five. The Housing Department jumped at the chance to show 'im around. That last lot owed a fortune and made a right mess of the place.'

Jenny was about to add that the last family could have blown them all to smithereens, but Cath didn't give her chance. Off she went, listing all the reasons why her brother Percy should be given the house.

'He's a policeman, he goes to church and his wife, Margaret, does housework every day. Their oldest is going to grammar school. The girl's doing well enough at school, but 'er doing well at school don't matter much, do it. A girl don't need to get a decent job. All she'll do is get married and look after babies. Ain't that right?'

Jenny almost choked. She'd always held that girls should be as well educated as boys. She'd failed in that regard herself but had no intention of her girls not being given the chance to better themselves. 'Girls can be as clever as boys, women as clever as men.'

Cath sniffed. 'I'm 'appy being a housewife and mother. It's the greatest thing a woman can be – a mother. Making sure the old man and the kids are well fed and clothed and the 'ouse spick and span.'

'Keeping a house clean and tidy does not take much intelligence.'

Jenny met Cath's puzzled expression then wished she hadn't said it.

Cath retaliated. 'So why ain't you got a job?'

'I did have and I will again.'

'In Robin Hubert's shop?' She gave a disbelieving snort. 'Not while Doreen is there, you won't.'

'You're right there!'

'I did 'ear she's in the family way.'

The comment was alarming. 'Who told you that?'

Cath shrugged. 'Can't remember.'

Across the road, the man from the housing department was taking his leave, a plump leg thrown over the saddle of a bicycle. Cath's brother waved him off.

'Percy! Percy! Come on over yer. My brother,' said Cath to Jenny, her face glowing with pride, her grin wider than a Cheshire cat. 'You've got to meet him,' she said, the excitement of an awestruck child in her eyes. 'He's done so well. Best in our family so far.'

Percy Routledge sauntered across the road, hands clasped behind his back. His son stalked beside him. His hands too were clasped behind his back. Nobody could possibly deny these two being father and son, one was a shorter version of the other, both hewed from the same stone but at different dates.

Head bowed and without a glance to right or left, his wife followed on behind clutching the hand of a skinny little girl. Like her mother, the child kept her head down, her braids sticking out like sticks on either side.

Cath bubbled with excitement. 'Well. How did it go, Percy?'

He nodded. 'It's in the bag.'

'This is my neighbour, Jenny Crawford.'

Greetings were exchanged, hands were shaken.

'This is my son, Howard. Shake hands, Howard.'

The boy duly obeyed, bending slightly from the waist and lifting his cap from his head. 'Good day, ma'am.'

Unsure how to respond to Percy's scathing opinion, Jenny

looked tellingly at his wife and daughter.

'That's my wife, Margaret, and Judith, our daughter.' He spoke dismissively and neither mother nor daughter were brought forward to shake hands. They stood somewhat timidly just behind him, not saying a single word.

Cath's brother was just above the legal height requirement for a policeman. Jenny's main impression was of a man who thought very highly of himself. As if to compensate for his lack of height, he held his head high, his pale eyes viewing her from either side of a snub nose. His pursed lips failed to make her think them ready for a kiss. More as if they'd recently tasted something sour or bitter – a lemon, a strong onion. They gave the impression of meanness above his receding chin.

Shaken but not entirely believing Cath's comment about Doreen being in the family way, Jenny felt obliged to say something, 'So, how do you like the house?'

He made a snorting sound, like a pig about to have a ring put through its nose. 'There's a few things I want done. Cleaned from top to bottom. Painted throughout. Locks changed. Can't be too careful.'

'I'm sure they'll oblige.'

Percy's nostrils flared big and filled with black hairs. 'They must. I'm being transferred to Bedminster police station. There's talk of there being a new station built on the estate, but what with a war in the offing, then Bedminster police station it is.'

'Will they give you a car?' asked Cath, whilst Jenny tried to blank the word war from their conversation.

Judging by the sudden and barely perceptible bristle of indignation, the question was not welcome. 'Don't be so stupid. Not every day of the week anyway. I'll have a bicycle. A new one, all being well. I've got my eye on a little Ford Prefect I saw for sale. I might buy my own. It would be most convenient.'

Jenny was under the distinct impression that Percy thought he deserved a car but his pride wouldn't let him admit it.

Cath asked her brother whether he was stopping for tea. 'I've got your favourite. lardy cake from Rudy Gregg. And plenty of butter.'

Percy made a grandiose gesture of pulling up the cuff of his jacket to expose a mighty fine wristwatch complete with alligator strap. 'By the time we get home, it'll be bedtime for our children. We keep to a strict schedule,' he said. Keen to have it admired, he was slow letting his cuff drop, to show off the watch's shiny face and alligator strap. 'Breakfast eight o'clock, lunch at twelve thirty, tea at four, tea at seven, bed at nine. I run a tight ship.'

In a way, he made Jenny feel careless with her children. Time to do anything wasn't a fixed thing in their house. In his, it seemed as though everyone ran like his wristwatch, strictly to time no matter what. 'That must be a bit difficult when you're working shifts – I mean like when you're plodding the beat at night.'

He gave her a condescending look. 'Of course. When I'm not there, Margaret runs the house as though I was there.'

She wasn't sure, but Jenny thought she saw a slight twitch at the corner of Howard's mouth which did not mimic the meanness of his father's. When the cat's away…

Percy Routledge and family said their goodbyes and marched off to the end of the road, leaving Cath looking disappointed.

Jenny had the feeling he would have preferred to have left the Close by motorcar, a further emphasis on his status. Her heartfelt sympathy lay with Cath, who was still standing looking down in the mouth.

Two of Cath's boys came racing into view around the corner. As always, they were hungry.

'What's for tea, Ma?'

Their mother's face brightened. 'You're in luck. You can 'ave the lardy cake I got for your uncle Percy. He couldn't stop,' she said. 'It's a busy life being a policeman.'

'Great.'

They were gone, racing off at speed, arms flailing at their sides.

'I'd better go,' said Cath, moving off in unaccustomed court shoes, sideways at first. 'Otherwise they'll gobble the lot.'

Jenny reached out to grab her arm and ask what to her was a pertinent question. 'I wanted to ask you...'

Despite her court shoes, Cath was already out of reach. Despite her disbelief Jenny had wanted to ask if she was sure about Doreen being in the family way. She couldn't believe it to be true. Robin would have said so. And who was it had told Cath in the first place?

Thelma would have mentioned it, but being at work she wasn't party to as much gossip as those who were housewives and mothers. Gossip was the preferred entertainment to some women who collected rumours like kids collected cigarette cards, stamps or marbles. Gossip was their lifeblood, exchanged when out shopping or over a pot of tea and never when men were around.

Back inside, Jenny picked up a piece of knitting she'd been doing, a navy-blue man's jumper she'd picked up at a jumble sale. Unpicking it had been a chore but would be worth it. It would make a lovely winter cardigan for Gloria or Tilly to wear to school.

The stitches were nice and even and it was beginning to take shape. She had toyed with the idea of interspersing the navy blue with a stripe of another colour – orange or red. With a bit of luck, Rigby's might have a single skein or ball of wool sat alone on the shelf just waiting for her.

Her head shot up. A thought had occurred, something obvious that she should have thought of earlier. Rigby's was on the other side of the expanse of grass to Robin's shop and was a hotbed of gossip. That, she decided, was where she might find something out.

18

Not for Percy Routledge a handcart or a horse-drawn cart to move his family's belongings into number five Coronation Close. A green removals van, the company name emblazoned in mustard and outlined in red, pulled up, almost blocking the road.

Percy himself, complete with family, had arrived there first in a little black Austin 7. Neighbours watched from their garden gates and Percy preened at the sight of them. Nobody else in the Close owned a car and it made him feel special – which, of course, he was, being a policeman. If his father-in-law had lent him some money, he would have bought a nice little house with a bay window and an arched front door. Four hundred pounds was the asking price, but he hadn't had enough for the deposit.

'I need it for my old age,' his wife's father had said. 'Mable and I intend selling up and buying a little bungalow on a clifftop in Norfolk overlooking the sea.'

It had been a great disappointment. Not wishing to move into a police house next door to another police family, his wife, a little sensitive at the best of times, had burst into tears.

When his sister Cath had told him about the semi-detached in

Coronation Close, he had made a slightly different approach. Working in the local police station was good enough for now, but Percy had ambition. If he were to get speedy promotion, he needed a car. Police headquarters were in the heart of Bristol and it was below his dignity to get there on the bus.

He'd tackled his father-in-law on the subject. 'I'll need a car.'

There were guffaws and grunts of disapproval but his wife bursting into tears on cue had convinced the old man to dip into his pocket and given him the money for the car.

It sat there now in front of the pantechnicon, glossy black with shiny radiator, headlamps perched on each side and wire wheels gleaming as though every spoke had been polished.

He'd planned to make sure that his darling little car would make heads turn. To that end, he had got both children and wife out of bed early to apply themselves to the task of cleaning and polishing the car inside and out.

Now he stood there, eyeing the house that was to become their home, in front of his car smart and spruce in his best suit, his shirt bright and white.

He felt the neighbours eyeing him as he instructed the removal men to be careful with the piano, in which room to place which bed and to ask his wife where exactly to place all the crockery, saucepans, kettle and cutlery.

'How would I know,' he responded when asked. 'That's a woman's department.'

Like the ringmaster at the circus, the array of family and removal men responded to his orders and the advice that they should go careful with that chair – his favourite. That clock – it had once belonged to his wife's father who'd been a Methodist minister and in time had become a city alderman.

'A very important man,' he proclaimed whilst drawing himself up on tiptoe.

'Yoohoo! Perceeee...'

Percy set himself back on his heels. His love for his sister was tempered with toleration for her dull lifestyle, her six children and the casual way she dressed that owed nothing to fashion but to a Scouts jumble sale.

'Hello, everyone!'

She was carrying a large tea tray, on which were cups, saucers and a plate of cakes.

'Tea and rock cakes,' she announced with great gusto.

She sounded exuberant, more so when she called out to the neighbours, looking as proud as Punch.

'That's my brother Percy and his family,' she said, jerking her chin towards her smartly dressed brother and his family, the latter all scurrying around like ants. 'They're moving in. He's a policeman.'

Wariness replaced expressions of welcome. Her beaming countenance burst like a balloon as one by one the neighbours watching from their garden gates turned away and went indoors.

'Oh. They're gone.'

Cath looked contrite, unable to comprehend that a number of local families were not always law-abiding. Things dropped off the lorry down in the docks, men got drunk and disorderly on a Saturday night, petty crime was not really considered that serious – just little bits and pieces that helped keep heads above water. There were plenty roundabout who had sometimes drifted to the wrong side of the law – the side that had led them to at least a night or two in the cells – or a longer sojourn at His Majesty's Pleasure. A police constable moving into Coronation Close was disconcerting.

A solitary voice called out to ask if everything was going well.

Cath's countenance brightened on seeing Jenny. Cath liked friends and liked to be liked. Seeing that all the other neighbours had gone indoors on hearing that her brother was a police constable, Jenny Crawford from number two was the only person she had to impress.

'Very well. My brother Percy 'as everything under control, don't you, Percy?'

She beamed at her brother. His response was less amenable, perhaps because he disliked the insinuation that things might not be.

'I've brought tea and rock cakes. Judith and Howard must be hungry. And little Albert.'

'I heard you the first time. Let's get our priorities right. Then we'll take a break.'

Little Albert, who looked in imminent danger of dropping the enamel jug he was carrying, gazed at the tea tray with round-eyed appreciation. His father's sharply delivered order stayed his hand.

'Take that jug in first before thinking of yourself.'

The little lad's expression dropped to his boots. They were pristine boots. So were his grey flannel trousers that ended just above a pair of very clean knees – unusual in any boy. Like his father and older brother, he was also wearing a shirt and tie. A green knitted sleeveless pullover finished the overly tidy ensemble. To Jenny's eye, he looked kitted out for Sunday school, not the laborious task of carrying domestic items from one point to another.

Cath, her arms stretched to either side of the tea tray, looked abashed and disappointed. Giving her brother a warm welcome had been on her mind all night. She was so proud of him and so pleased that he was moving into number five.

'He'll be a credit to the neighbourhood,' she'd confided to anyone that stopped long enough to listen. 'He's a policeman. A member of 'is Majesty's constabulary,' she'd declared with immense pride.

Jenny eased the enamel jug from out of the hands of Albert Routledge who didn't look much beyond five years old. 'Why don't you go and say hello to your Auntie Cath. She's got a rock cake waiting for you.'

With total disregard for the disapproving look on Percy Routledge's face, she headed into the house.

Percy's disapproval and weak-chinned countenance had turned darker by the time she came back out. The weak chin, which he must wish was at least square if not lantern shaped, was thrust forward. 'Excuse me. Just so you know. This is my family. I'm head of the house. Albert is my son. He does what I say.' His voice was sharp and he stood with legs akimbo and fists clenched at his side. Like a cowboy about to reach for his Colt 45s.

Albert's eyes were round as glass marbles above the almost eaten rock cake. He looked nervous. So did Cath.

How to get them out of this?

'How about we take the tea and cakes into my house until your brother and his family are ready for it?' Jenny took the tray from a surprised-looking Cath. At the same time, she purposely let a pair of silver sugar tongs fall off into the road. 'Oh sorry. Can you pick those up, Albert, and bring them for me. There's a good boy.'

It was perfectly feasible for Cath to pick them up but Jenny angled herself so that Cath was between her and the garden gate. Albert, bringing up the rear, was the only one who could retrieve them.

Sugar tongs! Had she really seen such a thing? It had never occurred to her that Cath owned a pair of sugar tongs. Obviously they were only brought out for the most important people in her life – such as her brother.

They ended up in the kitchen, where the yellow gingham curtains and painted walls made it seem as if the room was made of sunshine.

Cath set the tea tray on the table.

Albert shoved what remained of the rock cake into his mouth

before legging it out of the door, his little body and kicking legs urgent with intent.

'Might as well pour ourselves a cup,' said Jenny, taking charge of the pot. 'We can always make more here when your brother's ready for it.'

Cath looked doubtful whether her brother would ever be ready for it.

Judging by Cath's pensive look, Jenny took it as read that Percy was a difficult man. Difficult in that he was the sort who liked to have things his own way. Difficult also that his opinion and way of doing things were always the right way.

Coronation Close had always been a friendly place. Even the rougher element had not caused that much consternation – apart from the monster dog and the storing of an unexploded shell amongst scrap metal in the front garden.

Cath was not usually as quiet as she presently was. She always had something to say. Today she seemed not so much thoughtful as disappointed. Jenny concluded that if there was to be any conversation at all, then it was up to her to instigate it.

'Albert's a nice little lad. Willing too for a boy of his age. How old is he?'

Cath took her first sip of tea. 'Five.'

'So he'll be going to Inns Court Junior School?'

'For now.'

'And the others to Connaught Road seniors?'

'That depends.'

It was a rare occasion indeed when you couldn't get a conversation out of her neighbour from along the far end of the cul-de-sac. Today was that occasion.

One more push, thought Jenny, *and then I'm finished.*

'Depending on what?'

'Percy believes in scholarships. I believe I told you 'e wants both 'is boys to go to grammar school.'

'Let's hope they get in.'

'Oh, Percy will make sure they do.' Cath was adamant and suddenly recovered from her brooding silence. 'He's a stickler for 'omework. If the school don't give them 'omework he gives them some. Percy's got a blackboard. He gives them lessons before they go to bed.'

Jenny frowned. To her mind, this all seemed a bit too intense. In fact, she was reminded of the school in *Tom Brown's School Days*, *Jane Eyre* or even a Dickens novel.

'Well. So long as they get to go out and play with their school-friends.'

She feared the worst the moment she espied the expression on Cath's face.

'Surely they're allowed to go out to play?'

Cath was slow to respond as someone is who doesn't think something is right but feels powerless to do anything about it. 'Percy believes that free time should be spent in study or prayer. He likes them to go to Sunday school,' she added brightly, as though somehow that would counterbalance his rigidity on their socialising.

No longer could Jenny countenance continuing this conversation just to fill the awkwardness of Cath's silence. Percy was her brother but they were chalk and cheese. Jenny had never met him before excepting the rare occasions when he'd visited his sister. Now, faced with him and fully expecting a nice family to replace those that had lived there before, she found herself feeling apprehensive.

The silence was broken by sounds from outside; Mrs Arkle singing something in Spanish as she hung her washing out on the line. Someone else a few doors up shouting at her small children to stop trampling across the potato patch. 'We've got to eat them, you scruffy little tykes!'

'Your hair looks nice.' It was the only thing Jenny could think of to say. Today Cath had made the effort to take her curlers out and style her hair. There was a reason of course. Jenny surmised that Percy would have disowned his sister if she'd appeared in her usual guise.

'Percy has standards,' Cath suddenly exclaimed.

'Yes. I guessed he did.'

First impressions never lie, thought Jenny reflectively. She'd assessed Percy correctly but it gave her no satisfaction. On the contrary it seemed that the neighbours about to make a home in Coronation Close might seem at first sight to be respectable and upright. But that didn't mean they might not cause a whirlpool in a place that had once been just a tranquil pond.

19

The Rhubarb Tavern was situated in an area of Bristol Thelma had never frequented before.

Not wanting to be seen in Coronation Close, Stuart had left a note at Bertrams suggesting they could meet up and discuss him having access to Mary.

Thelma had been uncomfortable with the idea. 'I don't want to meet you in a place I might be recognised.'

That was when he'd suggested this rambling old place set amongst dingy terraced houses and close to the main railway line into Bristol.

She got the bus to Temple Meads and walked from there. A light drizzle was falling, the kind that settles in your hair and on your clothes without running off. Like sequins. Shiny and immovable.

He'd given her directions scribbled on a scrap of paper torn from a pad. The road from the station went around the back of the building. From there, she went under a railway arch and across the Feeder Canal. Once that was crossed, she slipped and slithered on a damp pavement that ran alongside a cobbled road. A train thundered overhead dislodging dirt and grime from the interior of the arch.

Stuart was waiting for her. 'Nice to see you, Thelma darling.'

She turned her head when he attempted to kiss her cheek. She also brushed away the arms threatening to hug her. 'I'm here to talk, Stuart. Nothing else.'

He shrugged it off. 'I thought you might still have some affection for me.'

She looked at him as though he was mad. 'Are you kidding? You left me high and dry. You're a rotten, dishonest sod, Stuart Brodie. Now come on. Oh, and by the way, the drinks are on you.'

Copper-framed gas lanterns hanging from wall brackets set in the dark grey stone fell in silvery pools. The cobbles gave out to patches of tarmac. Light from the interior of the pub seeped through the leaded patterns of old Victorian windows.

'In yer,' he said, pushing against the etched glass of the upper half of the door rather than the brass handles. His sweaty palm print disappeared into the fancy glass.

The inside of the pub was divided into small snugs. The middle one formed the off-licence. He guided her into the one to the left. Coloured glass set in lead formed the word 'saloon'. He pushed that door open.

The saloon bar wasn't exactly luxurious, but it was fairly large and in the past might have been considered opulent. Plasterwork swirls and swags writhed across the ceiling in an unending pattern. When new, the plasterwork would have been white. Nicotine from thousands of pipes and cigarettes had turned it a mellow shade of burnt sienna.

Apart from the two of them, it was empty.

'Port and lemon?'

'Half a shandy.'

He looked bemused. 'I recall port and lemon being your favourite tipple.'

'That was a long time ago. I've changed since then.'

She still did like a port and lemon, but this was an occasion for keeping a cool head. She didn't want to agree to anything she might regret. She wasn't the woman she used to be.

There was a damp smell to the red velvet upholstery of the bench seating she was sitting on. The floor was bare boards. Behind her, she could feel a draught. The building was old and the windows ill fitting.

'So,' Stuart said as he set down the drinks. 'Half a shandy for you. A pint of bitter for me.'

The top layer of foam on the pint of bitter disappeared in the first gulp.

Thelma took only a very small sip. She locked her fingers across her handbag and said in a no-nonsense manner, 'So what is it you want?' The sooner she got away from him and this place, the better.

'I want us to be friends. After all, we do 'ave something in common.'

'Really?'

'Our daughter.'

'You weren't around. When she needed a father you weren't around. I brought her up by myself.'

He shrugged. 'I was off to make me fortune.'

'And did you?' she demanded, her temper rising despite promising herself that she wouldn't do that.

He looked at her as though he was in two minds what to say next. Finally, 'Yeah. I did make me fortune. That's why I'm back now. I want to share it around. I want to give it to Mary.'

'Ha!' Thelma threw back her head and laughed. 'You! Make a fortune? I don't believe it. You've been a loser all your life. Full of promises that were never kept and plans that never worked out. I'm going...'

'You can't go. What about Mary? I want her to know who I am.'

Thelma glared at him. What right did this man have to come back into her life and demand anything?

That's what she said to him, plus a bit more. Years ago, she'd sworn a lot. Nowadays, seeing as she worked in such an upmarket shop, she'd got out of the habit, just as she'd made the effort to lose her Bristolian accent.

After she'd had her say, she left him sitting there. Even after all that she'd snarled at him, he looked disbelieving, a quirk of a smile lifting one side of his mouth.

The night was drawing in and the cobbles beneath her feet were slippery. But she kept going, tears stinging her eyes and wishing the impossible wish that he'd never entered her life. But she reminded herself that Mary would never have existed if she'd not met him.

By the time Thelma arrived at the bus stop, she was hot and unhappy. To make her even more unhappy, she spotted the rear end of the bus disappearing towards Bedminster Bridge. 'Damn!'

She apologised for saying it, even though there wasn't a soul at the bus stop. Ten minutes or so and another bus would be along. In the meantime, a flood of light poured from the showroom of the big motor dealer that had set up on the corner close to Bath Road. It was getting on for nine o'clock but it was still open and perhaps like many shops would stay open until ten for the benefit of those who worked long hours or by dint of wealth expected to be served no matter what the time.

A lone figure moving inside the showroom drew her attention. She knew the set of his head, the crop of dark blonde hair, the expensive cut of his suit and the casual elegance of the way he moved.

The lights within the showroom began to diminish, as he switched them off one by one.

As he neared the door, their eyes met.

'Thelma isn't it?'

'Yes.' She searched for his name and finally found it. 'Charlie?'

'That's right. Charlie Talbot.' He shook her hand.

Even in the diminished light, she could see why Jenny had fallen for him. Not that she'd ever admitted it; Jenny was the sort who couldn't easily forget that she was married. Thelma wasn't so rigid – or hadn't been. She reminded herself that she'd just left a man she'd fallen for hook, line and sinker. And he'd turned out a stinker!

'You've missed the bus,' he commented.

'Yes. But only just.'

'On your way home?'

'Yes. I had to meet someone. Purely business,' she added with a broad smile. Hopefully his questions would end there. She didn't want to talk about who she'd been with or the reason why.

He offered her a cigarette from a silver cigarette case, then a light from a silver lighter.

She wasn't that regular a smoker, but on this occasion she accepted, taking a deep draught and, with her head back, blew the smoke into the fresh night air.

'Can I give you a lift?' He nodded to a sleek black car parked beneath an overhead streetlight. Like the cigarette case and the lighter, it looked expensive.

'Are you going my way?'

She thought quickly. Accepting a lift would get her home in good time and there'd be less risk of Stuart catching up with her.

'I've got time to kill.'

The interior of the car smelled of sun-baked leather and

newness. It impressed her when he pressed a switch and the engine sprang into life.

'No handle?'

It was usual to use a starting handle pushed in below the radiator at the front of the car. Bert's car had to be started that way. Most vehicles did.

'The Americans use an electrical switch and so do the Germans.'

'Well, that's something good to come out of Germany.'

The silvery glow of the elegantly arched lights above Bedminster Bridge was left behind.

Charlie asked her how her job was going before moving on to a more pertinent subject. 'No more problems from anyone following you?'

The memory of Sam Hudson following her in the gloomy passage beneath Park Street sent a shiver down her spine. On that occasion it was Charlie who had come to her rescue.

'I'd rather you didn't remind me. Anyway, he's dead. Fell down the stairs, so I hear.'

'Or did someone push him? Not you, surely, Thelma.' He said it laughingly.

'I'd rather not talk about Sam bloody Hudson. He's gone and that's that.'

She clenched her jaw. There was nothing more she wanted to say, though she could have asked about the car showroom back on the Bath Road.

'How's Jenny?'

Her response was clipped and to the point. 'Very well.'

'How about that husband of hers – has she heard anything from him?'

'He joined the army.'

'He's still in it then, though I suppose he would be if a war's about to happen. Thought he might not be sure which side he's on – if you get my drift.'

Thelma wound down the window. The stub of cigarette she threw out flew past in a shower of red sparks. 'That's unfair. He's no longer a Blackshirt. And he's ill.'

'Sorry he's ill. I suppose his experiences as a fighting man might have affected his behaviour. Hopefully.'

Charlie didn't sound convinced. It wasn't so long ago that Jenny had fallen for him, even though he'd been of a different class and she was a married woman with two children. Charlie Talbot was an easy man to fall in love with. His dashing appearance was coupled with lashings of charm and a belief in the rights of man. He had appeared to be on a crusade to help those less fortunate than him.

'Are you still a communist?' she asked.

He didn't hesitate to answer that he was sometimes. 'The rest of the time I'm a car salesman. I own the place back there. Talbot Luxury Car Sales.'

'You own it?'

'That's what I said.'

'So your politics have changed?'

'No. My way of raising money for the cause has changed.'

'Ah!'

He laughed. 'Thelma, my darling, I find it amazing that you portray incredible eloquence in one tiny word. You disapproved of my former way of raising money.'

'Those women...'

She remembered him coming into Bertrams with middle-aged and very wealthy women on his arm. Like Jenny, they adored him, but differently to her, they gifted him valuables that he immediately sold on. Or sometimes they just gave him money – 'for your services'.

She felt him looking at her. 'How about you, Thelma? Have you never given gifts in exchange for favours? Many women marry men for their money. Many landed gentry with titles marry a rich heiress – even if she has the face of an elephant's rear end! We all do what we have to do to get what we want. I want to change the world. The end justifies the means.'

What he was saying made sense, but deep down she wasn't decrying him for that. Her concern was for Jenny. He'd fled without a word on the night when Jenny had gone out with him and came home to find there'd been a gas explosion.

Thelma eyed him wryly. 'You saw me that night of the gas explosion and disappeared as fast as you could. You broke Jenny's heart, Charlie.'

He shook his head. 'You'd seen me at Bertrams arm in arm with my...' He paused. 'Donors. I wasn't ready to explain that to her. She's not you. She wouldn't have understood.'

'Is this what this is all about? Driving me home so you can worm your way back into her affections?'

The interior of the car was dark, yet still she saw her outburst had unnerved him. In fact, he looked as though she'd physically hit him.

'I felt bad afterwards. Believe me I did.'

'That's rubbish and you know it. Now drop me off here at the corner. I can walk the rest of the way.'

He said nothing more but pulled into the kerb.

She pushed open the door and made a point of slamming it shut behind her.

The turning into Coronation Close wasn't too far. She headed for it with a determination in her step. Tonight she had demolished two men with the sharp edge of her tongue. It felt good. Very good.

20

Doreen Hubert was not amused.

'You want me to stay yur and look after all this rubbish?'

Fists on hips and fast losing his famous patience, Robin scraped the bottom of the barrel for what little he had left. 'I need to deliver that bedroom suite I sold yesterday. The woman's paid me. She needs it today, especially the bed or she'll be sleeping on the floor.'

'I was going shopping. I need some things in town.'

'Can't you get what you need in Melvin Square or Filwood Broadway?'

Doreen sneered. 'They ain't got nothing much to shout about around yur.'

'It's dearer in town.'

'I like a bit of quality. Some of us don't know silk from a sow's ear, but I do!'

Robin rubbed at his aching head, hand across the brow, then at the nape of his neck. The ache had begun when he'd got up this morning anticipating this scene and his wife's reluctance to look after the shop. He'd broached the subject last night, but Doreen had told him she didn't have time to discuss it.

'I need to make a telephone call.' So off she'd gone to the telephone box that stood red and sturdy on the corner next door to the hardware shop.

First thing this morning, he had broached the subject again. The response was much as he'd expected. But it couldn't be helped.

How to appeal to Doreen? There was only one way he could think of to make her see sense.

'Look, Doreen. I need you to do this. We'll be losing good money if you don't.'

At mention of money, her head swivelled round as though it was made of rubber. 'How much?'

He took a deep breath and lied. 'Five pounds.'

'Blimey. Was it gold plated?'

He didn't rise to the bait. 'It was a very nice set and there's a chance they'll come back for a few other items. She had her eye on that chest of drawers, the small set that would suit a nipper.'

Doreen studied her reflection in the mirror of a late Victorian hallstand that hadn't yet been sold. One finger flicked at each corner of her mouth where the lipstick had smeared. 'I'll need two pounds to go shopping.'

'I've given you the housekeeping.' He didn't even try to keep the frustration out of his voice.

'It's not for housekeeping. It's for me. Didn't you pay that woman to look after the shop when you weren't around – and when you were!'

The insinuation was clear. She was accusing him of having Jenny Crawford working in the shop for his own needs. He could have retaliated that she was a bright one to talk, but this was not the time to dwell on it. He needed her to be here so had no option but to agree to give her two pounds. 'All right,' he said nodding. 'I'll give you two pounds as soon as I get back. The pawn shop key is on the hook. And don't upset anyone whilst I'm gone.'

'Perish the thought,' she said carelessly as she filed at one of her fingernails. 'Go on then. Clear off.'

Feeling a deep sense of relief, Robin left Filwood Broadway and headed for Coronation Close. That was the other reason he'd agreed to handing over two pounds and getting away quickly. The buyer of the bedroom suite was a Mr and Mrs Routledge and they'd just moved into number five.

The day had started well. He had a few pounds in his pocket. *Let's hope*, he thought, *that it gets even better and Jenny is at home.*

* * *

Back at the shop, Doreen was being a bit offhand with a regular customer who had brought in a four-foot-high aspidistra in a green glazed pot.

The customer was giving the same spiel that she did every time she brought it in. 'It ain't the biggest aspidistra in the world like that Gracie Fields sings about, but it's a nice one and the pot it's in is an antique. Me mother said so.'

Doreen wrinkled her nose. 'It looks a bit dusty. Are you sure it's still alive?'

'Course 'tis! I water it regularly.'

Doreen shook her head and said resolutely, 'We don't take plants. It's the watering. Somebody's got to be yur to do it.'

The woman was resolute but also shocked. On entering the shop, she'd worn a congenial look because she was looking forward to getting some money. Now, the possibility slowly fading, she looked at Doreen in dismay. 'Robin's accepted it before! Half a crown each time I pledge it.'

'Well, I'm in charge today and I'm saying we ain't taking it. There is a limit. We can't hand over good money for any old rubbish. We got standards, you know.'

The woman, a Mrs Clarke from Newquay Road, looked her up and down. 'Standards? You? I've seen better than you up at the dog track – the ones being let out of the trap!'

Doreen was in no doubt of what she was insinuating. Sniffily, she pulled herself up straight and pointed, 'There's the door. Now, you get out of it and take yur bleedin' plant with you.'

Perhaps the woman might have stayed and argued the toss, but just then the bell above the door jangled and a man entered.

'Ladies,' he said, touching the brim of his hat. 'I 'ope I ain't interrupting anything?'

'No,' snapped Mrs Clarke as she and the potted aspidistra pushed past him. 'I wouldn't pledge anything with that cheap tart if I was down to me last kipper.'

Once she'd gone, the new arrival closed the door, reached up and silenced the bell which had continued to jangle.

He was a bit on the thin side but good-looking and relatively smart. This, Doreen decided, was a customer worthy of her service. She adopted her most endearing smile and trusted that her lipstick had not stained her teeth.

'Good morning, sir. What can I do for you?'

His eyes raked her body as his smile matched her own. 'Good day, sweetheart.' He touched the brim of his hat. 'I've come to collect a little item I pledged. It should be there in the back of the shop.' He jerked his chin in the direction of the wire enclosure where the most valuable items were stored. 'Here's my ticket.'

Doreen allowed their fingers to touch and linger as she accepted the ticket and read the number and the customer's name. 'Thirty-four.' She fluttered her thickly mascaraed eyelashes as she smiled up at him. 'Mr Tucker.' Her voice was like treacle.

'That's me.' He smiled back.

'If you would like to come this way.'

With key in hand and wiggling her hips like she'd seen the film stars do, Doreen led him towards the rear of the shop. Ticket in hand, she went along the shelves. Thirty-two, thirty-three and thirty-five were there but no thirty-four.

Doreen tutted. 'I'm sorry about this. The silly woman we used to employ to organise this has got things out of order.'

Stuart was instantly panicked. 'But you still have it? You haven't sold it without telling me?'

'No. It has to be here somewhere.' Doreen began rummaging amongst the tickets hanging by string from each item.

'I want my property back. I've got the money to redeem it here.' He patted his breast pocket.

The last thing she wanted was to appear less efficient than that mouse Jenny Crawford. Anyone who didn't wear a decent amount of make-up and rarely had their hair permed was a mouse as far as she was concerned. The fact that Jenny's complexion was flawless and her hair naturally wavy and she had no need of those things was irrelevant.

'Look,' Doreen said, smiling up at him. 'How about we wait until the shop owner gets back. He'll probably have some idea of where she put it. Unless she fancied your pledge and ran off with it,' she said laughingly. The comment was a suggestion rather than a known truth. Still it seemed like the perfect way of killing two birds with one stone. Sorting out this man's problem and fouling Jenny Crawford's reputation appealed to her very much. 'Either way, we'll get it sorted. Fancy a cup of tea or would you prefer something stronger?'

The man she knew as Donald Tucker grinned. 'If you're offering.'

She closed in on him until there were only inches between her breast and his broad chest. 'I'm sure we can sort this out and whilst we wait you can tell me all about yourself.'

Whilst I plan to pin the misplaced piece of silver on Jenny Crawford.

The thought was warming, more so even than the few glasses of gin she was about to share with a total stranger.

* * *

Robin vowed he would never sell anything to Mr and Mrs Routledge ever again.

'At first, he was going to leave me to take the furniture up to the bedroom by myself. I told 'im straight that I needed a hand. It takes two to handle heavy furniture, especially upstairs.'

'But he caved in?' asked Jenny as she poured them both a well-deserved cuppa.

'Had to. I told 'im it was a case of that or me taking it all back to the shop. Not that I wanted to. That would 'ave been an even bigger nightmare.'

Jenny pushed a plate of ginger biscuits across the table. Robin ate one whole, then took another. Sweat had seeped into his shirt, leaving stains under his armpits. Jenny handed him a flannel and he wiped his face.

'Thanks, Jenny.' He looked up at her appreciatively. 'You're a good woman. Roy's a lucky man.'

Jenny sat down at the table opposite him, her hands cupping her face. So far, she hadn't touched her drink. Her eyes were downcast.

Robin noticed. 'Sorry if I was being too forward. I should learn to mind me tongue.'

Jenny shook her head. 'No. It's not you.' Her eyelashes, dark and entirely natural, flickered. 'I've told you that Roy's on his way home. I didn't think I would ever see him again.' She stopped and reconsidered the rest of what she wanted to say. It came out anyway. 'Quite frankly I never wanted to.'

Their eyes met in mutual understanding. There was no doubt in either of their minds that if things were different, they would be together. But things weren't different. The vows of holy matrimony to the wrong spouses were holding them tight.

'When do you expect Roy to come walking in through the door?'

She shook her head sadly. 'He might not be walking. I had a letter from the army saying that first he'll be in the fever hospital at Ham Green. Once they judge him fit, they'll bring him here.' The sadness in her eyes intensified. 'I tried to get more information. All they say is that they'll bring him home when the time is ripe. A man from some kind of medical unit came round here to tell me that he will need a great deal of rest. When I pressured him to tell me what to expect, he looked awkward.'

Robin wanted to say that no news was good news, but he was of a sensitive enough nature to understand what Jenny had determined. Roy was seriously ill.

'I haven't told the girls yet. Call me a coward, but it isn't easy.'

In a strange way, the silence that fell between them was almost deafening, not with lack of sound but with the realisation that their hidden feelings were evenly matched. They needed expressing, but how to do that in the circumstances they found themselves in.

With an air of reluctance Robin got up. 'I'd better be going.'

'I'll show you to the door.'

He'd hardly taken a step when a loud banging came from the front door.

'You expecting someone?'

She shook her head and with Robin behind her went out into the hallway.

'Good day, Mrs Crawford.' Constable Gilbert Gates was known to her and she was known to him. Everyone in the area knew him. He glanced at Robin, then looked away, almost as though he preferred not to see him there.

'Constable Gates. Can I help you?'

He took his notebook out of his jacket pocket and peered at it with short-sighted inclination. He cleared his throat before saying, 'I've a report from Mrs Hubert...' He cleared his throat again and looked pointedly at Robin. Of course he knew that Doreen was Robin's wife. 'It concerns an item of silver left there by a Mr Donald Tucker that appears to have gone missing. Mrs Crawford was apparently the last person to see this silver...'

Robin pushed past Jenny and joined the policeman. 'Gilbert, that piece of missing silver, as you put it, is with your colleagues at Broad Walk Police Station. I went along to the station to see what they might know about it. This Donald Tucker, he gave a false address. What's more, your plain-clothes officers were suspicious that it wasn't his real name... And we now know that it wasn't. His real name is Stuart Brodie. I think you'll find that his name is engraved on the side of the cup. He used to be a jockey.'

'He's been hanging around trying to contact his daughter. I think he wanted the money from pledging the cup so he could impress her,' Jenny added.

'Oh.' Gilbert Gates shut his notebook with an air of finality. 'That puts a different slant on things.' Gilbert made a big show of clearing his throat again, looked at Robin, then at Jenny, and said, 'The gentleman concerned appears to be getting drunk with... Mrs Hubert.'

It happened in a flash. Robin rushed past him and jumped into his van. The tyres screeched as he tore off around the horseshoe shape of Coronation Close and out onto the main road.

As the van skidded in a circle, Jenny caught a glimpse of the set of his chin and his fists gripping the steering wheel.

'My, my,' said Constable Gates. 'Mr Hubert don't look a happy man. Somebody's going to be in for it.'

Yes, thought Jenny. Doreen Hubert might at last have stepped over the mark.

* * *

The shop door crashed open and Robin was the proverbial bull in the china shop.

The man and woman sitting far too close for comfort with a bottle between them sprang apart.

Robin picked up the bottle and threw it against the wall.

'You,' he said, stabbing his finger at the man, 'have got some explaining to do. As for you!' This time his finger was pointing accusingly at his wife. 'I don't need you to explain anything. All I want you to do is to pack your case and get out!'

Doreen's jaw dropped before she regained her assumption that she was, and would always be, the one with the ace cards up her sleeve.

'If I go, the kids go with me!'

'Doreen, I ain't got much money, but at this moment in time I'm willing to spend every bloody penny I got to divorce you. There's plenty who would swear on a stack of Bibles about you and yur carrying on with anything in trousers. You're a rotten wife and a lousy mother! And I'll be well rid of you!'

She looked stunned. He knew it wouldn't last, but for a moment it warmed him – until she pulled what she thought was another ace out of her hand.

'Well, don't think that you'll be bringing that mousy little Jenny Crawford into your bed. She'll be in prison, she will. Stole this bloke's bit of silver and likely 'as been pinching other stuff when she was yur!'

'Ah yes.' Robin's eyes were smouldering fit to catch fire. 'Your piece of silver, Donald Tucker – or should I call you Stuart Brodie. You'll be glad to know that it's in safe hands.'

'I want it back. I need that money. I have expenses.'

'Well, if you want it back, you'll find it at the police station in Broad Walk.'

The look of surprise on Stuart Brodie's face was followed by a dash for the shop door.

Robin stood rooted to the spot. The main problem in his life was the woman he'd married, the mother of his children. He glared at her. 'Ain't you gone yet?'

His jaw was set firm. Doreen had held power over him for far too long. He wasn't sure he could afford a divorce and get custody of his children, but even that didn't seem to matter. If he was absolutely honest and despite his paternal feelings, they were more her children than his. They had the same nasty streak, the same selfishness as their mother, even showing him the same contempt that she did. In time, they might grow out of it, but time was precious. Living in the moment was all that mattered.

The cruel smile he'd been expecting was there on lips that had been red but were now smeared with the effect of the alcohol – or something else. 'Oh don't worry. I'm going. To be honest, I've been making plans for a while now. I've got a friend with a nice 'ouse.' She swung away from him. Her manner was that of a woman who would always better him, always have her own way. She half turned on her way to the stairs. 'Once it's sorted, I'll be back for the kids.'

* * *

Stuart Brodie was coughing badly by the time he got to Broad Walk Police Station. He wanted that cup back and although he'd been ill, he'd earned enough money on the illicit gambling scene to pay for a flight back to Ireland. It was there that he intended to die. He was leaving soon. Very soon.

The police sergeant behind the desk was so disturbed by his coughing that he got him a chair. 'Sit down here, sir, and tell me what it's all about.'

It took a little time and a glass of water before Stuart found his voice and explained about the silver cup and the misunderstanding with the pawn shop. 'They're not to blame. It's my own fault. I was trying to keep my return a secret. I wanted to surprise my daughter – and my wife. I was abroad and taken ill. I wasn't expected to survive.'

It was all a lie. The police officer showed sympathy. The lie had worked. All would be well. The cup was his again.

Grasping his chest with one hand, Stuart rasped his way to the bus stop. Luckily, it wasn't too far. The bus would take him to Temple Meads Railway Station. From there, he would have to walk the towpath alongside the Feeder Canal to his digs. Past the bitumen and chemical tanks, their chimneys spilling a yellowish smoke into the air above the cramped streets of terraced houses of Barton Hill where he was lodging.

He knew where the bus stop was but hadn't known it was so close to the playing fields used by local schools. The moment he saw Mary spilling out of the fields along with other girls from her school, she ran across the road and stood breathless and awestruck in front of him.

'Mary.'

He wanted to give her the silver cup of which he was so proud there and then, but he held back. If he did that, she would want to know the reason why. No matter his predicament, he didn't want her to share it. Sickness and death was too disturbing. They were for the old not the young.

'Where are you going?'

Her face was bright and full of hope. No. He did not want to destroy that hope, that verve for life.

'I'm off back to Ireland. I've a race to ride in.' Voice and expression matched in cheerfulness. It wasn't true exactly but he could see from her expression that she was impressed.

Mary sucked in her breath. 'A race?'

'That is so. There's planes flying over to Dublin from Bristol on Sunday. I'm that excited.'

Judging by Mary's expression, she too was delighted. 'Take me with you.'

'Take you?' He shook his head and was discomfited because he knew it wasn't possible. There was no future for him and wouldn't be for her either. 'Well I don't know about that.'

'I want to.'

Her open face, her exuberance, touched his heart. 'Well...'

'Please.'

He wanted to laugh, but if he did that he'd start hacking again.

A compromise was in order. 'How about you come and see me off, then when I get back, we can talk again about you coming with me.'

Mary's face was like a sunburst coming out from behind a cloud. 'When are you going?'

'Not until Sunday evening.' There was a flight before Sunday but no seats were available. He was sure someone would drop out and he would get away before Sunday, before having to lie to her even more than he had. By Sunday he should be gone.

'I'll be there. I promise I'll be there.' Her face glowed with hope and he couldn't possibly disappoint her.

He was relieved when the bus arrived. It wasn't easy to lie to her. Surely Thelma would keep an eye on her and she wouldn't turn up at the airport. He hoped that would be the case. He had to go. He had to leave.

'I'll see you in the field next to the airport,' she shouted out. 'We can have a picnic.'

'Of course we can,' he shouted back, though he had no intention of doing so. The plane was leaving that evening.

The cup lay in the brown paper carrier bag Robin Hubert had used when he took it to the police station. His fingers followed the hard lines of its sublime shape. The cup would be Mary's after he'd gone. And he was going to somewhere Mary could not possibly follow. In the meantime, he needed to leave it with someone who would make sure she would get it. Thelma was the obvious candidate, but he couldn't face her. The cup pressed hard against his side. He slid his fingers into his coat pocket and fondled the crisp brown paper. The only place he could think of taking it was the pawn shop in Filwood Broadway. He'd found out that Jenny was Thelma's friend. She'd been working there when he'd first pledged it.

That, he decided, was the place he would leave it, along with a note – his will in fact – detailing what should happen to it after his death.

Yes. That seemed as good a place as any.

21

It was a sunny Sunday morning and Thelma had brought out a couple of dining chairs into the front garden, setting them on the path beneath the living-room window.

Eyes closed and the sun warming her face, she lay her head back and waited for Jenny to come across. Her stomach was doing somersaults. There'd been no sign of Stuart these past few days. No news should have been good news, but in a funny kind of way, she wanted to know what he was up to. Just because he hadn't come knocking at her door didn't mean he'd given up on his plan to claim Mary.

She frowned into the sunshine. Why now? That was the question that still bugged her.

'You're going to get a red nose, Thelma Dawson.'

Thelma laughed as Jenny sat down beside her. 'I've been reading *Picturegoer*. A lot of film stars sunbathe, though mostly in the South of France. I quite fancy going to the South of France.'

'You might do one day. Who knows?'

Jenny's response was bright enough but she couldn't help the feeling that the opportunity of going to France might happen sooner than they expected – at least for those men old enough to join the army.

'Any news on Roy?'

Jenny took a deep breath. 'Next week.'

'How did the girls take it?'

'Gloria was over the moon. Tilly was her usual thoughtful self. She wasn't so fond of her father. Gloria was the one he doted on. And your little angels? What's going on there?'

'I read the riot act to Mary.'

'And her father?'

'Not a sign of him. He told her that his name was Donald Tucker. Did I tell you that before?'

Jenny sat up straight. 'I feel I should have known straightaway when he brought it in for a twenty-pound pledge and put two and two together.'

Thelma too sat up straight and shook her head solemnly. 'Stuart did like to play games. Liked gambling. Liked drinking too. And women of course.'

'Doreen took full advantage of that. She likes men too much that one. There they were drinking together and her suggesting to Stuart that I'd stolen it.'

'Nice woman!'

Thelma's expression was a picture in itself. Her tightly clasped hands gave the impression that she'd truly like to wring his neck.

Jenny eyed the late spring blossom now swiftly taking on its more robust summer sumptuousness.

'Nothing is ever straightforward, is it.'

Thelma gave her a nudge. 'Good job we've got good friends to see us through.'

'That's true.'

The two good friends sat back in their chairs enjoying the sunshine. The sight of the trees on the green, the roses, the kids playing all contributed to a feeling of contentment. There were problems, but somehow they would overcome them all.

After a moment of individual thoughts, Jenny said, 'I've asked the girls to share the big bedroom so their father can have a room to himself. Only until he gets better. They understood.'

'Hmmm.' Thelma's wordless comment was slowly delivered. She wondered just how long sleeping apart might continue and eventually couldn't help asking.

Jenny shook her head. 'Let's see what happens once he's better.'

Looking into the future was difficult at the best of times. All they could do was face whatever came and adjust if necessary.

'Fancy a walk?'

Jenny got to her feet. 'Yes. Why not.'

* * *

Mary watched them go. It was the moment she'd been waiting for. Her father was flying to Dublin to take part in a horse race. It was quite a thing at his age.

A thrill shot through her as she contemplated this picnic before he left. All she had to do was walk to the end of Inns Court Road and across to Whitchurch where planes regularly flew in and out.

A few more weeks and she would be fourteen and leaving school. There were a few jobs she could have for the taking, but she didn't want those jobs. She wanted to work with horses. Her mother told her it was a pipe dream – whatever that was. Her father wouldn't treat her like a baby and he'd worked with horses. He understood. Her mother did not understand and never would.

All night Friday and all day Saturday, she'd planned what she would take. Her clothes of course. And her copy of Anna Sewell's *Black Beauty* – her favourite book. Plus a few things for the picnic. Not much though. She didn't want anything noticed as missing.

In her heart of hearts, she couldn't believe that her father would really leave her behind. She chose to believe that at the last minute he would relent and take her with him.

Although she'd found it hard to sleep all weekend, on Sunday morning she awoke with a feeling of urgent excitement. She couldn't wait to leave home and go off on an adventure, for that's what she was sure it would be. Boring old Coronation Close would be left behind.

But what about her mother? What about Alice?

Tears stung her eyes, but resolutely Mary blinked them away. She was a big girl now. No! Not a girl. She was a young woman and could make up her own mind about what she wanted to do with her life.

She avoided contact with any of the friends she had in the street. When Alice asked her if she wanted to see if there were any tadpoles in the brook, she most certainly declined.

'You go off with your little friends,' she'd said in a lofty manner. After she'd seen the hurt look on her sister's face, she'd regretted saying it. But she couldn't take it back. She had to be grown-up about it.

The Sunday roast had always been enjoyable and consumed by all. Sometimes George and his wife joined them but not today. Perhaps if he had, his presence and wisdom might have made her change her mind.

Her mother had asked her why she hadn't eaten all her dinner. 'Roast beef is your favourite. And I've given you an extra Yorkshire pudding.'

She'd made the excuse of not feeling well and gone up to bed.

Once alone in her room, the door bolted in case her sister Alice dared to intrude, she'd dragged the suitcase out from beneath the bed. Once again, as she had three or four times over the weekend, she checked the contents. Everything she needed was there. She'd thought of everything – even her sanitary towels. She had enough to last for the next visitation of the monthly curse. How would her father react, she thought, when she asked him for money to buy the next lot? The very thought of it made her blush.

As the afternoon wore on, she'd buried her face into her pillow. From out in the street came the Sunday sounds of children playing, women chatting and a couple of men singing after a lunchtime session at the local pub.

Mary had forced herself not to fall asleep. The worst thing that had happened was her mother taking two chairs out front. She'd hoped she wouldn't sit there but venture over the road to chinwag with Mrs Crawford or further up the cul-de-sac with Cath Lockhart. The latter didn't happen so much of late. Cath was wrapped up in her brother and his family who had moved into number five. Not that he seemed that warm-hearted a brother, to her mind. She'd heard someone once say that you could choose your friends but not your relatives. She supposed that had something to do with it.

Oh how she wished her mother would leave the front garden!

Squeezing her eyes shut, she'd prayed for it to happen. 'Please God. Get her out of the way so I can go with my dad.'

Having a dad seemed such a special thing – probably because she never knew she had one. On the rare occasions she'd asked her mother about him, she'd been told he was dead, though she thought that on one occasion she'd said he'd gone away to sea. Whichever way, she had one now and didn't want to lose him again.

The sound of chair legs heralded the fact that her mother was making a move. Both her voice and that of Mrs Crawford carried up from around the side of the house. Then she had heard the garden gate which had a strong spring and always clanged shut.

Seeing as it was Sunday, she thanked God for his intervention and crept across the landing to her mother's bedroom at the front of the house. Carefully, desperate they wouldn't notice, she lifted a sliver of pink brocade curtain and looked out. Her mother and Jenny disappeared by the sign at the end of Coronation Close, the name having been altered back in 1936.

Relief washed over her. Now all she had to do was grab the little brown case and head for the designated meeting place.

All she hoped was that nobody in Coronation Close would notice her case. If they did, she intended telling them that it held carrots for the horses up in the Novers.

At one point, before she'd got too far, she thought she heard Alice shouting after her.

Mary broke into a run and didn't stop until she was sure that her sister and Coronation Close was far behind her.

* * *

Her father had told her to meet him at the far end of Inns Court Road where the fields stretched away on the other side towards Whitchurch and Bristol Airport. That was where they would have a picnic.

The grass was long and feathery all the way to the wire fence enclosing the airport runway and its buildings.

At one time, before the recently erected fence had been installed, it had been possible to get closer to where planes landed and took off. Perhaps at some time in the future her father had plans to take her up in a plane and fly much further than Ireland. Perhaps to Africa. She would quite like to go there and see zebras, lions and elephants. There were some at Bristol Zoo, but they were caged, not wandering the plains or jungles.

The sound of aircraft overhead attracted her attention. Three of them were flying in formation. One of the boys at school had proclaimed that they were training pilots at the airport in case there was a war. He'd also declared that's what he wanted to do once he left school. Comments had been made that only posh kids would get to fly, not the sons of working-class parents from a council estate.

Her added comment that she too would like to learn to fly was received with laughter and remarks that girls didn't get to be pilots. She wondered how it would be up there flying through white fluffy clouds. Today she would find out if her father would take her with him.

The sunny afternoon was fading into evening and still he hadn't arrived. With anxious eyes, Mary scanned the road she had crossed to get here and wondered whether she'd got the time wrong but decided she had not. Something must have happened to hold him up. That had to be it.

She sat there hidden by the long grass. Perhaps it was hiding her too well. Laying her little case to one side, she bobbed up above the grass and looked around. There were cows on the other side of the fence in the next field. One or two looked in her direction, chewing lazily on mouthfuls of grass.

A whistle sounded. A signal? Was he coming at last?

Mary looked around again. There was no one on her side of the fence but on the other side the cows began to move.

'C'mon, c'mon, c'mon.'

A man's voice. Then another, repeating the same sounds but in a different voice. A boy's voice.

Through gaps between the tangled thorn hedge, she saw men with sticks driving the cattle before them. The sight and sounds passed. No sound remained except for the crying of seagulls sweeping low, then soaring in the sky towards the airport.

Time was moving on. Mary was beginning to get hungry and the bottle of Tizer she'd brought with her was nearly all gone.

What now? she thought, panic tickling around the edges of what had been excitement.

Evening was turning into night. She found herself thinking of beef dripping on a thick slice of bread and sprinkled with salt. That would have been her supper. And she would have had a bath of course. She and her sister always had a bath and changed their underwear on Sunday night prior to Monday at school. The rest of the week they only had a wash and underwear was expected to last for the week.

Hungry now and thirsty, she was unsure what to do. Surely her father hadn't let her down. She'd put such faith in him. She couldn't bring herself to believe he wasn't the perfect person she'd thought him to be. There had to be a reason for him not turning up.

The warm day had gone. Night was drawing in with a star-spangled sky. There were few lights around except for those twinkling through the trees from the airport. There was also a brighter light higher above the rest.

Having had little sleep on Friday and Saturday night, her eyes began to feel heavy. Hungry, thirsty and tired, the thought of a cup of cocoa before bed plagued her mind. Her mother would bring her one, smile and pat her head – just as she always had when she was small. Oh to be there now.

But she couldn't go back. What if he came and found she wasn't here.

Darkness descended and the night sounds came with it. A sharp cry of a night creature, a fox perhaps or a rabbit trapped in its jaws. An owl swooped over the tops of trees that looked like black cutouts against a glowing shade of indigo.

From a distance, the bell in a church clock chimed the hour. Mary was too tired to count how many times it struck.

A jumper pulled from the suitcase gave her extra warmth and when her father finally came, she would feel warmer because he would be there.

22

Jenny looked in on her daughters. Their dark hair spilled over the whiteness of their pillows. Each looked deeply asleep and, dare she believe it, as content with their world as she was. Seeing them sleeping so peacefully made her regret having asked them to share a bed when Roy came home.

Thoughts about him coming home followed her into the front bedroom. This was where she slept with him when they'd first moved in, though it seemed a lifetime ago since she'd shared a bed with her husband. Theirs had been an awkward, jaded relationship, worse when they'd lived in the slums of Blue Bowl Alley. Always angry. Too free with his fists. Full of jealous indignation. Back then, she'd been almost a prisoner in her own home. Things had improved on moving to Coronation Close. She'd been happy and Oswald Mosley's Blackshirts had filled Roy's life in a way it had never been filled before – enough to keep him away nights.

The bedroom curtains were still open. A streetlight not far from her window threw shadowy patterns onto the bedroom walls. Looking out at the trees on the green and the few lights still on in windows of the other houses, her contentment intensified. Coronation Close and the people in it had become her world, whereas...

She looked at the double bed where she had lain with Roy. A double bed, yet it might have been larger for the distance that had come between them. There always seemed to be a gap between them. Gradually, the gap had widened to almost the width of a pillow. Neither had broached that gap and eventually it felt boundless.

The bedclothes, the sheets fresh on today, were turned back and then smoothed into place. She thought over her conversation with Thelma earlier, which had been quite an eye-opener. Thelma had told her about meeting up with Mary's father at a pub called The Rhubarb Tavern.

Thelma had been scathing about the meeting. 'I gave him a piece of my mind, I can tell you!'

Neither of them could quite understand his purpose in coming back now after leaving her high and dry.

'With a bun in the oven! He left me with a bun in the oven!'

It wasn't often that Thelma used a common phrase. It was noticeable to all that knew her that she was careful how she spoke since landing the job at Bertrams Modes. She'd been there a while now and her care with words had become an ingrained habit. Except when she was angry. Mary's father had made her very angry!

Jenny began undressing. Before she had chance to take off the last of her things and pull a nightdress over her head, she heard the clang of a garden gate.

From across the road, she saw a figure hurrying around the kerbstones edging the green and heading her way.

The streetlight blinked out as it usually did at this time of night. Around eleven o'clock, she reckoned. Even so, she didn't doubt that it was Thelma, the heels of her fancy slippers clattering over pavement and road alike.

Jenny struggled into her dressing gown, thrust her feet into her slippers and made her way downstairs.

The light from the hallway picked out Thelma's distraught expression.

'Our Mary hasn't come home.'

'You'd better come in.' On seeing her friend's worried expression Jenny opened the door wider. 'Is Alice all right by herself?'

'She's sound asleep, though I'm going to have to wake her and ask if she knows where Mary's gone. She said she saw her earlier and that Mary ran away when she shouted after her.'

'Did she have any idea where she might have gone?'

Thelma's expression was darkly foreboding. 'He's got something to do with it. I'll kill 'im if he's got her.'

Again Jenny noticed that slip of speech. Thelma wasn't just angry; she was distraught.

'Come on in. I'll get dressed and we'll go out and look for her. I'll just have to tell Tilly I'm going out and not to answer the door.'

Thelma paced up and down the living room as she waited.

Jenny came down dressed in the clothes she'd only just taken off. She grabbed a door key from the hook and suggested that Thelma should get dressed too.

It seemed to come as something of a surprise that she was still wearing a dressing gown and slippers. 'Oh, just look at me! What am I thinking of?'

'More important things than what you're wearing.'

Jenny waited at the garden gate until Thelma reappeared fully dressed and wearing a formidable expression.

'Where do we begin?'

Thelma counted off the possibilities on her fingers. 'The Novers. She was carrying a bag. It could have held carrots.'

'In a shopping bag?'

Thelma frowned as a truly worrying thought hit her. 'A brown one. Only I don't have a brown one.' The realisation seemed to knock her sideways. 'But I do have a small brown suitcase.'

'Oh Thelma!' Jenny's thoughts returned to Mary saying that she would leave home. The reasons were not that important. Once a child had reached the age of thirteen, they truly believed that they were adults. She knew of some kids who had left school early and started work at ten years old, their families insisting they needed the money. Thinking themselves adults because they worked, they also took on the habits of grown-ups – smoking and drinking. Growing up too quickly.

'Where does Stuart live?'

'I'm not sure. It might be Barton Hill. That's where I met him in that pub. He didn't let on the exact address of his lodgings.'

The two of them stood helplessly at the garden gate, unsure of which direction to go in.

Thelma shook her head. 'I don't know what to do?'

In the past, it was usually Thelma who took charge of a situation. Now it fell to Jenny, though she couldn't see that she could do much except offer support. Like Thelma, she didn't know where to begin.

'I think we should go to the police.'

'Have you got your watch on?' she asked Thelma.

'Yes.'

'Can you see the time?'

Thelma squinted at the face. 'Just about. Half past eleven.' She slapped her hand against her face. 'What am I going to do, Jenny?'

'Robin. Let's go and see Robin. He spoke to the police. Then we take it from there.'

Thelma took a deep breath. 'That's a good plan, but first things first.' She spun away and dashed up the garden path of number eleven. 'I'll knock up everyone on this side, you start at Mr and Mrs Arkle's. Ask if they've seen her.'

Not holding out much hope for this strategy, Jenny carried it out for Thelma's sake.

Mrs Arkle appeared out of her bedroom window before they began their rounds, demanding to know what all the noise was about. Unlike more modern women who wanted their hair permed and crimped, she was not wearing curlers. Long strands hung like fronds of black seaweed on either side of her face.

'A child's gone missing.' Thelma realised immediately that Mary wouldn't thank her for calling her a child but the police were likely to assume her meaning a small child of perhaps six or seven – until she explained that is. *But Mary isn't here*, she reminded herself. 'We haven't seen her since about four o'clock this afternoon. You haven't happened to have seen her, have you? Or any of your family? Might they have seen her?'

Mrs Arkle shook her head. Somebody in the room behind her – Mr Arkle obviously – asked what was going on. With heavily accented words, she turned and explained. By the time Jenny was knocking on the door of number three, Mr Arkle was outside his front door fully dressed and offering his services.

'We need to arrange a search party. I'll round up a few of our neighbours.'

Although short in stature, his legs appearing to be not much longer than his arms, Fred Arkle was off knocking on doors, sparing no amount of noise, including challenges to those who answered sleepily or made excuses that they had work to do in the morning.

Only one person suggested that the girl was probably out with a boy and would return when she came to her senses. That person was Percy Routledge.

A crowd of men gathered beneath the street sign.

Thelma couldn't stop from trembling. Cath came down and promised to keep an eye on Alice and on Jenny's two girls. Thelma nodded mutely. She couldn't bring herself to say that the only man who'd refused to join the search party was Police Constable Percy Routledge, Cath's brother. Even Bill, Cath's husband, threw a glower at the house where his brother-in-law lived.

Amazingly, it was Fred Arkle who divided the volunteers up into groups with great efficiency.

Jenny mentioned it to Mrs Arkle, who stood at her front gate in her nightclothes looking on with genuine sympathy and what seemed to be pride.

Little serious conversation had ever passed between them. What could she say to a woman who pretended not to speak English, had picked all the flowers and vegetables from the garden and sent her children out to sell them.

'Your husband's doing an excellent job. Very professional.'

It was difficult to read the look on Mrs Arkle's face. A half-smile lifting one corner of her mouth, a raising of her chin that hinted at pride. 'He did this in the war. Looking for those who had fled into the mountains.'

Jenny frowned. 'Where was that?'

She expected the reply to be France. The trenches. The terrible names like Ypres and Passchendaele. 'Back in Spain. Our children born there. Parents died there.' She shook her head sadly. 'Very bad things 'appened. Very bad. My 'usband English but helped. Led people up into mountains so they be safe and 'e searched for the lost. They ran into mountains but didn't know mountains. Frightened. Ran from guns and wicked men. Ran.'

Jenny stood speechless. Never would she have guessed at Mr Arkle's past. Suddenly, she saw all of them in a different light. She could forgive the Arkle family for picking all the flowers and selling the vegetables. What did it matter? All that mattered to Mr Arkle was helping people who were in trouble. Just as he was now.

'Right! Follow me!' Mr Arkle beckoned the group of men he'd organised.

'Jenny.'

Jenny discerned a new strength in Thelma's tone. 'What do you want to do?'

Thelma heaved a deep sigh of resolve. 'Can we pay Robin a visit?'

Wrapping cardigans around themselves to cope with the ongoing chill, they headed out of the Close.

The last bus had gone back to the bus station. The streets were empty. The few streetlights still lit threw pools of light over the pavements. Silence reigned.

Filwood Broadway was as dark as everywhere else. By day, the area would be bustling, mostly with women doing their shopping. By night, there was nothing.

Jenny headed for Robin's shop.

'I take it Doreen won't be there,' Thelma enquired.

'I don't know.' She shrugged.

She had no idea what had transpired when Robin had dashed off on the day she'd had to explain herself to the local bobby.

She rapped hard on the door. The glass shook in its frame. A light burned at the very back of the shop.

'Is he still up?'

Jenny nodded. 'He's doing his accounts. He hates doing accounts,' she added. She rapped again and dared to shout out, 'Robin. It's me. Jenny.'

Another light went on in the front shop, where furniture was piled around the walls and the more attractive items displayed in the window.

He swiftly undid the top bolt, the bottom bolt and then the

catch. Before he had chance to ask what they were doing banging on his door at nearly midnight, Thelma took the initiative.

'Mary's gone missing. We thought you might be able to help. Do you mind if we come in?'

Looking puzzled, Robin reached up to quieten the overhead bell and bid them enter. He looked from one to the other. 'She's not yur if that's what you were thinking.'

'How about Doreen?' asked Jenny.

His look soured at the thought of all that had happened.

'I told 'er to pack 'er bags and she did.' A flicker of disappointment flashed in his eyes before he added, 'She took the kids with 'er.'

'I'm sorry,' said Jenny though felt intense relief. No slanging match tonight. They were here on serious business and could well do without that.

Thelma gripped her cardigan more tightly around her upper body and pleaded, 'Robin. We... or rather Jenny thinks you might be able to help. She said that Stuart pledged a silver goblet or something and you reported it to the police. Did they come back to you about it?'

He nodded. 'Yes. It belonged to him. They said he came in and collected it.'

Thelma latched onto those words as a drowning man might grab a lifebelt. 'Mary might be with him. Did they give you an address?'

Disappointment sent the corners of her mouth downwards when he told her they did not.

Jenny got the strange impression that there was more to what Robin had told them. But for now the priority was finding Mary. Whatever secret he was hiding could wait.

Thelma shook her head slowly from side to side. Finally, she slumped onto a wooden chair.

Jenny rested her hand on Thelma's shoulder. 'Mr Arkle has done a marvellous job sorting out the search party. And he has experience. She'll turn up. I'm sure she will.'

23

Mary didn't know what time it was. All she did know was that she was cold, hungry and wanted to go to the toilet. The latter was easily achieved. There was nobody around and the grass was long.

She shivered. The warmth of the day had gone. A few droplets of rain bounced off her head and ran down her face. She hadn't brought something waterproof with her, not even an umbrella.

Tears of disappointment mingled with the rain trickling down her face. She now accepted that her father was not going to turn up. He'd lied to her.

Her shivering intensified and the darkness was becoming intimidating. She badly wanted her bed. She badly wanted to be indoors, not out here on a rainy night in a damp field. This was all a terrible mistake.

Picking up her case, she tiptoed through the grass, presuming it was the way she had come. She could see lights. It had to be those back on the main road, but she wasn't sure.

The darkness of the hedgerow was all around her. The lights beckoned. No matter what they were, she focused on them, seeing them wax and wane through the hedges. Sometimes they merely flickered. At other times, they were big and bold.

Taking her courage in both hands, she headed for what looked like a gap in the hedge. The track beneath her feet was muddy, but there'd been little rain so it wasn't slippery.

On the other side was more tall grass levelling out to a well-lit building. A long track of short grass stretched out in front of her. The grass to either side was longer making it look like a road. Ahead of her and to one side standing in a line outside the building were a series of aeroplanes. The truth was startling but also exciting. She'd wandered into the airport. Aeroplanes took off from along that track of short cut grass. If she was lucky she might see one. She'd only ever been here once to watch a display of aeroplanes doing tricks in the sky. They'd seemed so small, like birds or butterflies. Far away. High in the sky. This was the closest she'd ever got to one.

Suitcase bumping against her legs, she staggered on towards the airport building. The aeroplanes fascinated. Three smaller ones of the same colour were lined up on either side. Ahead of her, immediately outside the building, was a larger plane. It looked very different than the smaller ones, had solid wings and big propellers and writing along the side. As she got closer, she could see it said, 'Irish Sea Airways.' That must mean it flew to Ireland.

As she got closer, several people came out of the airport building and lined up at a set of steps leading directly up onto the aircraft.

Gripping her suitcase tightly, she frantically studied the features of those queued up, anxiously looking for the one face she desperately needed to see.

And there he was. He looked shocked when he turned and saw her.

Her eyes bristled with tears. 'You were going without me,' she wailed.

He showed no sign of embarrassment as those in the queue looked at him, looked at her, wondered what was going on.

'Mary, you can't come with me. Go home to your mother,' he said as he strode towards her.

'I don't want to. I want to be with you.'

Her voice carried to those standing waiting to board the plane to Ireland. They watched, fascinated by the scene and no doubt wondering what lay behind it. Who was the man? Who was the child? What were their links to each other?

One passenger was suspicious enough to call out. 'Are you abducting that child?'

'I'm her father,' Stuart snarled back.

'You're leaving me behind. You told me to meet you.'

He shook his head. 'Your place is with your mother, not with me. I had no right coming back into your life.'

'But you promised!'

Mary couldn't hold back the flood of tears. All her hopes and dreams that he stood for – working with horses, not in a factory where she would most likely end up – fell to the floor and broke into pieces. He'd lied to her. He'd let her down. All that excited anticipation she'd harboured ever since he'd arrived in her life turned to disappointment – perhaps even to hatred.

'Now come on, darlin'. You must understand. It was a mistake to think I could be a proper father to you. I've been a bachelor too long. It wouldn't work. I was daft to think that it would.' His voice was conciliatory.

With an air of straight-backed resignation, he began to walk back in the direction he'd come. The aeroplane was waiting. Those who had been queuing had disappeared inside the body of the aircraft.

'No!' Mary screamed, but he didn't look back. He kept walking.

The lights from the airport building seemed brighter now. There were also lights in the sky. They were coming lower and lower as though falling to earth.

Uncaring of anything else, Mary began to run towards what she thought were falling stars.

She heard somebody shouting her name and figures running from the field where she'd been sleeping.

Blinded by tears, she kept on going.

About to step on the first of four steps onto the flight to Dublin, Stuart froze when he saw what was happening – or rather the likely consequences of what was happening.

'Mary!'

Throwing his suitcase aside, he ran full pelt across the runway. This was where flights took off and landed and, at present, before his flight across the Irish Sea, another craft was coming into land. Mary was running towards it and most definitely in its path.

Mr Arkle shouted. Bill Lockhart shouted. Both saw the danger she was in and began running.

Mary paid them no heed. Her legs kicked out in desperation towards this new set of lights, not realising what they were or that they were getting closer and closer. There had been no wind, only rain at the end of this evening. But there was wind now blowing right at her.

Suddenly aware of her plight, she stopped dead, filled with horror at what was about to happen to her. And then suddenly a body barrelled into her. A pair of strong arms whipped her off her feet and pushed her to safety. She fell headlong, the wind knocked out of her as she landed flat among the longer grass. Behind her, the aeroplane landed in a whirl of sound.

Her eyes closed. Her head ached. She heard someone calling

her name repeatedly. A rough palm brushed her hair back from her forehead and she heard somebody say that she was all right.

Another voice, softly, more fearful. 'What about 'im?'

There was no answer. She fancied rather than knew that someone had shaken their head. Then she blacked out.

* * *

A doctor on the panel Thelma paid into on a weekly basis looked Mary over and advised two or three days of rest.

Bertrams Modes were kind enough to give Thelma three days unpaid holiday until Mary had recovered.

Mr Bertram apologised for not being able to pay her to stay home longer. 'It's all this talk of war. There's been increased demand for fabrics and clothes in general. People have been stocking up on luxury goods and in response our suppliers have put their prices up. I'm sorry.'

'I'll manage,' she'd said. 'I've got a bit put by.'

She did have a little nest egg she'd earned by making and selling things from old clothes she'd bought at jumble sales and down the Sally Army auction hall. Her intention was to hold onto that. There was no knowing when a rainy day might arrive and she didn't want to get caught in the downpour. She too was preparing in advance of a war that might or might not happen.

Bert said he could cover any shortfall if she found it a struggle.

'You're a good man, Bert Throgmorton,' she expressed between a bout of sobbing as she cried on his shoulder.

He smiled wanly. 'I try to be.'

She sensed he had more to say.

'What will you tell her?'

Thelma brushed the wetness from her eyes and blew her nose

into a clean handkerchief. 'I've told her he's gone to Ireland to work with racehorses.'

Bert nodded safely. 'Will you ever tell her that he's dead?'

'No.' She shook her head vehemently. 'She's upset enough as it is.'

Bert collected the teacups and took them out into the kitchen. 'You stay there,' he said when she attempted to get up from her chair. 'I'm a capable man. I do know how to do washing up.' He laughed.

Thelma sat back. Bert's laughter made her smile.

He came back in from the kitchen rolling his shirtsleeves back down and doing up his cufflinks. 'I was going to ask you something.'

He looked a bit sheepish. *My word*, she thought, *is this the moment when he finally sets a date?*

'Ask away.'

'Your Mary should be OK by Saturday afternoon. I've got a little something on and thought you might like to come with me.'

'A little what?' she said, smiling and frowning at one and the same time.

'An art exhibition. The Bristol and District Painting Society are holding an exhibition of their work at St Dunstan's Hall. It's a sale of work. Proceeds go to the St Dunstan's Society – you know, them that were blinded in the war.'

'I know what it is,' returned Thelma. The smile had dropped from her face. Many in the trenches had been blinded, some by mustard gas and some had lost their sight through their wounds. 'Are you taking some of the paintings you did of me?'

The sheepish smile came back. 'Only with your permission. I reckon I can get a decent price for the one of you in the red dress.'

Thelma felt herself blushing. 'Oh, Bert! It's a bit revealing.'

'It's breathtaking.'

Thelma covered her pink cheeks with her hands. 'You look at me through rose-coloured glasses.'

He shrugged. 'I'll pick you up at ten on Saturday morning. Will that be all right?'

She nodded.

'I suppose I'd better go. Will you be all right?'

Thelma raised her eyes to the ceiling. 'All seems quiet on the Mary Dawson front.'

'Has she said anything?'

'Nothing much. Just lays there looking sorry for herself and angry at her dad for leaving her behind.'

Their eyes met in mutual understanding. Stuart had been hit by the tip of the aeroplane's wing. It had been travelling fast enough to inflict fatal injury. The opinion of the man in the control tower, a former flier from the Great War, was that it had been over in seconds.

'The airplane company is dealing with the funeral. Paying for everything. I told them not to inform me of when it was. I would prefer Mary not to know.' She shrugged. 'It was a difficult decision, but I did what I thought was for the best. She'll get over it.'

Mary getting over it was what she was banking on, the solution like a single lifebelt floating on the sea before her eyes. Everything else was too confusing. She was too confused. Too frightened by what might have happened.

'And how's your George?' Bert asked.

'He's fine. I got word to him and he called in to see how things were. It's likely he and Maria will call in on Sunday.' A little smile lifted the concern on her face. 'She's due to have the baby. That should brighten all of us up.'

* * *

Mary lay in bed looking up at the ceiling. There were no shadows chasing sunshine, just a dull ceiling on a dull day. Outside, a light rain tinkled like fairy bells against the window.

Last night she'd blamed her father for letting her down, for not turning up, for lying to her. Now she was taking a different view. Her mother had sent people to look for her, determined not to let her go. The reason, as far as Mary was concerned, was that she'd been jealous that she'd wanted to be with her father. And now he'd flown off to Ireland without her.

Having the mismatched logic of a fourteen-year-old, she'd totally discounted the fact that he hadn't turned up. There'd been a mistake. Her mother had found out and warned him off. Alice had told her! That was her conclusion, though she had no evidence of that. Except Alice had seen her trooping off carrying her suitcase. That had to be it!

She turned over onto her side and sucked on her thumb, just as she had when she'd been a baby. Tears still stung her eyes and she was still weary from lying in a grassy field in the middle of the night with a damp drizzle falling on her.

She remembered that bit but only vaguely recalled what had transpired on the other side of the hedge. A series of bright lights from a central building had lit her way along a track. A grass track. She remembered the aeroplanes lined up. The queue waiting to board one plane that was bigger than the others – and then nothing! Just waking up in her own bed feeling tired and sore.

Her fatigue took over. In her dream, she was with her father in Ireland with horses – lots of horses. Shreds of reality broke the dream into fragments. Her mother would not let her go. Her mother was to blame for her dream being shattered. And she would never forgive her.

24

It was Saturday afternoon when Roy Crawford was to be reunited with his family. Jenny stood at the garden gate, their daughters standing either side of her. Her heart felt as though it was trying to burrow through her ribcage as she remembered how it had been between them.

Gloria, who was like a cat on a hot tin roof, unable to keep still and sizzling with excitement, asked, 'Do I look pretty, Ma?'

Jenny gently smoothed her hair back from her forehead. 'You look very pretty.'

Tilly was more apprehensive than excited. For some reason, she and her father had never got on so well. Her younger sister had always taken centre stage.

Jenny's thoughts turned to the sleeping arrangements about which she'd had second thoughts. Originally she'd asked if they minded sharing one room so that she could sleep in the other and leave Roy alone in the marital bed. On changing her mind she'd allowed the girls to keep their rooms, which meant she would be sharing with Roy. The prospect made her feel sick. It had been such a long time since they'd slept together.

A cab from the Blue Taxicab Company that waited for passengers outside Temple Meads Station appeared, a stately vehicle, its drivers clad in the old-fashioned way – gaiters, jodhpurs, a cap and a jacket shining with brass buttons.

Jenny sucked in her breath as the cab pulled in at the kerb.

Gloria could no longer control her excitement. 'Daddy!' She ran to the rear door.

The driver gently pushed her to one side. 'Let me open that door for your daddy,' he offered.

Jenny plastered a smile on her face. Inside it seemed that a whole squadron of moths were fluttering around a flame.

The driver helped Roy out.

Was this really Roy? Jenny tried to control her expression, to pretend that he hadn't changed at all. But the fact was that his eyes were sunken and his whole body seemed to have shrunk. His face was sallow and haggard – a yellowish colour. His clothes hung on him and fists that had been strong gripped a pair of crutches.

Gloria wore a look of total surprise, her eyes round, her mouth hanging open. This was not the father she remembered.

It was difficult to gauge what Tilly was thinking. She looked surprised but also, to Jenny's mind, oddly relieved.

She didn't discourage the driver from offering to bring in her husband's kitbag. It looked bulky.

Everything in the living room breathed home. A bowl of flowers sat in the middle of the table. There were also sandwiches and a Victoria sponge oozing homemade jam.

Jenny watched as Roy loped into the room on his crutches.

The cab driver left the kitbag and refused to take the tip her husband had given him. 'I don't take tips from His Majesty's soldiers. I was one meself once. Just the fare will do.'

After he'd gone, they all stood there, even Gloria – unsure of what to do next.

Roy balanced between his crutches. He too had not moved. Neither had he spoken.

Jenny finally found her voice. 'Is there anything I can do to help?'

He shook his head.

Gloria asked if he would like a piece of Victoria sponge.

'No.' His voice carried less power than Jenny remembered. It was no more than a croak. A frog in the throat. As though his larynx was sore.

'Bed,' he said without looking at any of them. 'I want to go to bed.'

'Yes. Of course.' Jenny guided him towards the door leading into the hallway.

Once at the bottom of the stairs, he transferred his weight from the crutches to the banisters that ran up each side. She followed on behind him, ready to catch him if he stumbled. He didn't. But his legs seemed unbending and weak. The stairs were going to be a problem.

The bedroom landing was small and bounded by three doors. He used the walls to make his way to the door of the front bedroom. Their bedroom.

There being no more walls, it was left to her to take over. Using both her arms to support him, she got him to the bed. In the past, she would never have had the strength, but beneath that uniform, he felt like a bag of bones. She knew he was suffering from more than one tropical disease but hadn't expected him to be this shadow of the man he'd once been.

'Draw the curtains. Please.'

There was no demand in his voice and rarely had she heard him say please. There had been incidents in the past when he'd forced himself on her and she'd feared it might happen again. After feeling the lack of body mass beneath that uniform he'd so wanted to wear, she knew nothing like that would be happening for a very long time. Or perhaps not at all.

Drawing the curtain blotted out the daylight. The room was cool, an island of calm whilst life went on outside.

He sat silently on the edge of the bed, staring down at his feet.

'I'll get your things.'

'My boots.' He sat there staring at them. He wanted her to take off his boots. Was he really that weak?

Meekly, she got down on her knees and undid his laces. One by one, she eased each boot from his foot. Like the rest of him, his feet were thin and bony.

After placing his boots under the bed, she stated her intention to get his kitbag. 'You'll need your shaving kit. And other things.'

He said nothing but sat there plucking lethargically at the buttons of his uniform, his eyes downcast.

Downstairs, the girls looked as perplexed as she felt.

'Help yourself to the spread,' said Jenny as she heaved the kitbag out into the hallway.

So far, neither girl had asked if they could go upstairs to see their father.

Having removed his jacket, Roy was lying on the bed with his eyes closed when she went back up.

'Is there anything in here you want?'

He turned his head and looked at the kitbag with what she could only describe as deep distrust – even hatred. 'There's a letter. Read it.'

With trembling fingers, she fumbled with the rope holding the canvas kitbag closed, then dipped inside.

The letter was in an official-looking envelope and was addressed to her – in a hand she recognised as being that of her husband.

As she read, a deep sickness took hold of her stomach.

The letter itself was typed and headed with the name of a military hospital in Singapore.

To whom it may concern.

Mr Royston William Crawford.

This man has succumbed to malaria, dengue fever and dysentery. On further examination it was discovered that he also has a severe lung infection. This infection has spread outside the lungs and into other organs of his body.

The only treatment we can advise is rest. Please advise a doctor to attend on a regular basis.

Jenny's mouth had gone dry. 'They're recommending I get a doctor. I'll get that done as soon as I can.'

'No.'

She stared at him, a small furrow between her eyebrows.

A chuckle escaped from low in his throat. 'I've had it. I'm at the end of the road. There's nothing anyone can do.' It seemed to take a lot of effort opening his eyes. 'I'd like to see the girls.'

She nodded numbly. 'Of course. I'll send them up with some cake and sandwiches.'

'No. I'm not hungry. Just the girls. You've read the letter. You know why.'

Yes. She knew. And he knew. They shared the knowledge that he was dying, yet neither of them could put it into words.

As for the girls, well, they were the most important thing he wanted to address in the brief time he had left. And it would be brief. The letter had not been specific, but it didn't need to be.

'I'll get them.'

When she went back downstairs, Gloria and Tilly were nibbling at sandwiches whilst eyeing the Victoria sponge. Bless them they were eating in proper order.

'Your father wants to see you.'

She was finding it hard to take on board that the man upstairs was the father of her children, the man who had fitted into the fascist attitude of Mosley's Blackshirts, even to enacting violence to their old neighbour Isaac.

The two young faces looked pensive.

Gloria swallowed what was in her mouth, brushed the crumbs from her lips and went willingly.

Tilly showed more reluctance. 'Do I have to?'

Her eyes were big and round, her voice pleading.

Gloria shouted, 'I'm coming to see you, Daddy,' her feet pounding up the stairs with obvious enthusiasm. Her father was home and she'd always been the apple of his eye.

A pang of fear shot through Jenny, a suspicion as to why Tilly had this attitude to her father. Everyone had heard of fathers who couldn't keep their hands off their daughters. But surely she would have known?

Gently taking hold of her daughter's arms, she sat Tilly down before asking her the dreaded question. 'Tilly. Has your father...' Her mouth was too dry to continue. She licked her lips and tried again. 'You don't want to see your father. Why is that? What's he done?'

Tilly's eyes were luminous with sadness, liquid with unshed tears. 'Because... because...' A single tear trickled from the corner of one eye and down her cheek.

'Slowly,' said Jenny, fearing the worst and wondering how she would live with it, live with him if the very worst was true.

'Because he's not my daddy. He told me he wasn't.'

Jenny shook her head in consternation. There was relief, but, also, if Tilly was telling the truth – and she didn't doubt it –

disowning a child was a cruel thing to do. 'That was very wrong of him. He is your father. There's no doubt about that and I don't know why he said that to you.' It was, she realised, a symptom of a jealousy he'd harboured over the years.

Jenny handed her a handkerchief and told her to wipe her face and blow her nose.

'Will you come up with me?' Tilly looked nervous and her voice was hesitant.

Jenny said that she would.

Gloria was lying beside her father on the bed. He had one arm around her.

Tilly stood beside the bed, looking unsure.

Jenny's eyes met those of her husband.

'Tilly wasn't sure you wanted to see her,' Jenny said it in a challenging manner. 'And don't be short with them. Treat them kindly.'

There were tears in his yellow-rimmed eyes as though it pained him to raise his arm, to invite his eldest daughter to join him, to show affection for what could be one of the last times ever. 'My girls,' he whispered as they snuggled in beside him on top the pale green coverlet. He kissed each of them on the forehead. Gloria snuggled up willingly, Tilly more awkwardly before she finally relaxed.

Feelings were like lumps of stone in Jenny's throat as she retreated to the bedroom door and out onto the landing. She swiped at her nose, sniffed back her tears. Roy was dying and there were things she could forgive him for and others she could not.

Robin Hubert had been her childhood sweetheart, but it seemed that in Roy's mind his significance had taken on greater meaning. It helped explain the reason he'd kept her a virtual prisoner in the grim rooms they'd lived in back at Blue Bowl Alley. He'd feared her having contact with him and the jealousy had festered in

Roy's mind. She might have been able to forgive him for that, but not for taking it out on Tilly.

Prior to him coming home, she'd felt as though she might be worn down by his presence, might even slip back into the former mouse she used to be. This new knowledge strengthened her. He was her husband and she'd vowed to look after him in sickness and in health. She would do that but no more than her duty. Whatever love she'd had for him was long dead.

When she next stepped across the landing to look back in, his eyes were closed. Gloria too looked to be asleep, her cheeks round and rosy. It proved otherwise when she opened her eyes and said, 'Can I have a piece of cake now?'

Back downstairs, Jenny left the girls cutting a slice of cake whilst she made her way to the red phone box out on the main road. The pennies dropped into the box with a heavy metallic thud – like a funeral bell.

The doctor would come within the hour, once it was established that her family was on his panel. Several people in Coronation Close contributed to a panel fund so that there'd be enough in there should they ever need emergency care.

On her return to the house, her daughters sat cuddled up together on the settee.

The table had been cleared, except for a plate of sandwiches and a slice of cake.

'Is that plate for me?'

'Yes.' Tilly got up and threw her arms around her mother.

Gloria's upturned face was still pink and her eyes were sparkling. 'Can I go out to play now?'

Jenny smiled down at her. 'Of course you can.'

Tilly looked concerned. 'Will you be all right by yourself if I go?'

'Yes. You go out and enjoy yourself. I'll be fine.'

It touched her heart to think they'd waited for her to get back and she was most definitely looking forward to a cup of tea. The cake and sandwiches would also go down well, but first things first. She needed to sort out a chamber pot for Roy, possibly also a hot-water bottle. A cup of tea first perhaps?

With tea in hand, she mounted the stairs and softly entered the front bedroom. For some reason, she half expected him to be sitting on the edge of the bed fully recovered. Daft, seeing as he was emaciated. But still, the old image was strong and slow to fade.

He was lying flat. Arms by his side. Eyes wide in their sunken sockets, mouth open, skin barely clinging to his cheekbones and so pale, so very pale.

With trembling hands, she placed the cup and saucer on the tallboy and looked down at him. She knew there were things she should do, close his eyes, make him decent, but she couldn't bear to touch him.

Roy Crawford, her husband and father of her children, was gone.

25

A month went by following Roy Crawford's funeral and the tragedy at the airport. The sadness was there, but the residents of Coronation Close were of a generation who accepted that life was not always fair but there to be lived.

Life went on as normal. The milkman still delivered from his horse-drawn cart, those that had jobs went to work and those that gossiped still gathered in groups at the garden gate or in the queue at the Cooperative Store.

Thelma Dawson did her best to jolly Mary along, though the shadow of her father's death lingered.

The bus was crowded and being August, the day was warm so she was glad to alight and walk the wide pavement to Bertrams Modes.

As was her habit, her walk slowed so she could admire the window displays. Bertrams was famous for its innovative displays, not just mannequins in the latest season's fashions, but some kind of theme, a background to enhance the elegant clothes on display.

Face bright with anticipation, her eyes swept over the very latest display, one only put into place the night before and unseen by anyone – including her.

At the sight of it, she stopped in her tracks and her jaw dropped. Pictures, paintings in elegant frames were hung along the back wall behind the mannequins. 'The Gallery' was painted above the pictures in gold letters. Thelma's cheeks burned and a gasp of surprise escaped her red-painted lips. There, at the very centre of the line of paintings, was one of a dark-haired woman in a red dress, her shoulders bare and a provocative smile on her lips.

'Oh my word. Bert Throgmorton, what have you done?'

Other people were regarding the display, for the most part voicing their admiration.

'I like the one in the red dress the best.'

'I like the squirrel.'

In winter, Thelma would have pulled the collar of her winter coat up to hide her face. At this time of year, all she had to hide her blushes was a headscarf. Not that – yet at least – anyone had linked the woman wearing the smart black dress with Peter Pan collar and cuffs with the woman wearing the red dress in the painting.

Her face burning, Thelma made a dash for the lane at the side of the building and into the entrance used by employees.

Mrs Apsley saw her come rushing in.

'Good morning, Mrs Dawson. I see our latest window display has attracted a larger audience than usual.'

'Yes. Good morning.'

She rushed on past without giving Mrs Apsley time to say anything more. Had she noticed it was her in the painting?

Oh why had she allowed Bert to paint her at all? Sculpting in clay had been his passion. Then he'd changed to painting and she was always his model. At first, she'd been flattered so long as nobody got to see the end products. She told Bert that she looked a bit provocative in some of them. The one in the red dress most certainly fell into that category.

'Thelma, I bring out the real you, a desirable woman.'

She'd quite liked his description, which had helped her decide to let him continue.

All day, she waited for someone to make the connection between the courteous saleswoman and the undeniably sexy-looking woman in the portrait.

Finally, a customer did notice and made comment.

'Excuse me, but I was admiring the window display and I must say you bear a striking resemblance to the woman in the portrait, the one in the red dress.'

The blush had hardly left Thelma's face that morning. Now it came back with a vengeance.

'Really, madam? I can't say that I've noticed. Now, what can I show you, madam?'

The woman addressed her companion. 'Of course it couldn't possibly be her. She's just a shop assistant. Artists don't use lowly shop assistants as models.'

They both laughed in the smug, satisfied manner of women who have never had to work long hours for their living or known poverty that forces a woman to do whatever she can to survive.

Mrs Apsley, Thelma's senior at Bertrams, moved as though she were gliding a few inches off the floor. Not a sound did she make as she walked her domain, checking that everything was top notch in the hallowed world of Bertrams Modes. She appeared like a wraith from the mist, but there was no doubt that she had overheard their rather rude comments.

'Excuse me, ladies. I believe you are mistaken.'

Her speech was as crisp as theirs, her demeanour that of a woman who knows she's more capable than most.

As Thelma blushed in the background, the two women

regarded Mrs Apsley with arched eyebrows unsure as to what she referred.

Mrs Apsley, a most cultured woman, informed them in no uncertain terms, 'It is a well-known fact in the art world that models were very often of the lower classes. Take Manet's barmaids. He did two. One at the Folies Bergère. Then, of course, there's Rossetti. His favourite model used to work in a milliner's.'

The lips of both women collapsed into pinched moues. Pink spots gilded already rouged cheeks.

It wasn't until lunchtime that Thelma got the chance to thank her superior for her intervention.

'Stop looking so mortified, Mrs Dawson. It's a beautiful painting and whoever executed that picture captured you very well indeed. Mr Bertram was quite drawn to it. In fact, he bought quite a few that morning at St Dunstan's. The idea of the gallery in the shop window was his. I think basically he wanted to show off his purchases without having members of the public trooping through his house,' she added with a light laugh. 'Mr Bertram is thinking of having an open evening to show off our latest modes and his pictures. He likes to think of himself as a man of taste. Would you be able to spare an hour in the evening to serve drinks and converse with our customers? You won't need to wear your uniform. Do you happen to have something that would pass as a cocktail dress?'

Thelma gave her answer immediately. Yes, she would like to attend, and yes, she did have something suitable that would pass as a cocktail dress.

One question was uppermost in her mind. Would the painting of her in the red dress be noticeable.

Mrs Apsley's eyes twinkled. 'My dear, I think it deserves pride of place.'

Thelma's jaw dropped, but she pulled it swiftly back from where it had fallen.

'Mr Bertram intends having our window dresser set out the mannequins in the main part of the shop, interspersed with his collection of paintings displayed on easels. He's also bringing in two or three models to float around dressed in our most expensive dresses and outfits. It should be quite an affair.' She smiled in that secretive way of hers. 'Our wealthiest customers are sure to attend – including those two from this morning. Mrs Digby-Platt and The Honourable Christal Wallaby.'

Thelma smiled down into her tea. 'Yes. I think I will very much enjoy that.'

Bert was over the moon that evening when she told him about the cocktail party. She waited until they had a drink each before giving him the details.

'My word,' he said, a slight blush coming to his face. 'That's a turn-up for the books.'

'Beats collecting the rent money.'

They clicked glasses.

'Here's to you, Bert.'

'Here's to us.'

Bert drove her home from the Red Lion on the Wells Road. It was barely ten o'clock, but the enthusiasm of a would-be painter was glowing in Bert's eyes. She knew he'd head for his studio before making his way home. He couldn't help himself.

After a goodnight kiss, Bert took his leave. 'I'll see you later in the week.'

Not the following night or the one after that even. Later in the week meant the weekend and they'd probably go to the pictures.

The house was silent when she got home, which came as something of a surprise. She'd expected to find Mary still up. It was usual for her to go to bed after Alice but not tonight it seemed.

Thelma made herself a hot drink. After switching off the main light and turning on the standard lamp, she sat in its light sipping at her tea.

The forthcoming cocktail party had come as quite a surprise and she was very much looking forward to it. Smiling to herself, she thought about which dress to wear. She'd chosen some truly old dresses to cut down and make more modern. A particularly lovely mauve dress was the first to come to mind. Beautiful fabric, though a bit clingy. Her mind skirted over a few more before she settled on the one that nagged her. The one she'd worn in that painting. The red dress. Just as the painting showed, it was the perfect combination, what with her dark hair, red lipstick and creamy shoulders.

The oil painting with all its allure would be sitting in its gold frame on an easel. Mannequins would be strategically placed. Professional models would glide amongst the guests, the mannequins and the paintings. And where would she be? Serving drinks. A mere saleswoman – unnoticeable. Except...

The red dress. Having her serving drinks and dressed as she was in the painting would make her stand out. Nothing could match her and the painting. The likes of those who had passed comment were sure to notice.

Whilst these thoughts had blazed a trail through her head, her gaze had been fixed on the dresser, where mugs and cups hung from hooks and plates and saucers stood upright behind them.

Every hook had been filled. Every space taken up with a plate or a saucer, each one commemorating a royal coronation, a royal marriage or birth. Kings and queens in regal poses were emblazoned on each one. The royal family were her passion. If a search for the most loyal royalist in the kingdom was ever held, Thelma was bound to be the outright winner.

On seeing an empty hook, her brow puckered.

When she got closer, she found what had been a mug celebrating the coronation of King Edward the Seventh lying in pieces at her feet. If it had landed on the rug, it might have survived. Unfortunately, it had landed on the area of dark-stained floorboards where the rug did not reach.

She sank to her knees.

'Oh no.' Her exclamation was a strangled wail. Her grief caught in her throat. Everything about it was in pieces and it wasn't just a case of the handle having snapped off after being dropped. Bending down to examine it, she picked up one tiny piece after another. Some of the pieces were ground almost to powder. As though someone had stamped on it.

She shook her head in disbelief. How could this have happened? Perhaps a cat had got in?

She checked the downstairs windows. They were all tightly shut. Only the ones upstairs would have been left open.

A mouse? Would a mouse be big enough to knock the mug off its hook?

She couldn't believe that it could. A rat might have more of a chance but...

She decided that no creature could easily prise a mug or cup from a hook. They were firmly fixed and the handle had to be *lifted* off. It was almost impossible to knock it off.

With a heavy heart, she brushed what had been one of her most treasured possessions into the dustpan. The only possibility was that one of the girls had done it. Just an accident. Only, deep in her heart of hearts, she knew that it looked trampled on. *Deliberately* trampled on.

Never mind, she told herself. It was only a mug. Just a mug. However, she couldn't escape the fact that one of her girls might have done this. Neither of them were around to admit to anything. That seemed odd. They would have stayed up to tell her what had happened, whether it had been an accident or not.

No, she couldn't believe it. Before taking the fragments out to the bin, she moved a delicate little mug depicting Queen Alexandra, the Danish wife of King Edward the Seventh, onto the lately vacated hook. The mug was her favourite of all her collection. King Edward was gone and his wife had filled the gap. It seemed very apt somehow but still it upset her.

* * *

The next morning, she studied the faces of her daughters for any sign of a guilty conscience. She saw nothing. Alice was frying two pieces of bread and two eggs, one for her and one for her mother. Looking very thoughtful, Mary was spreading dripping and salt on a piece of toast. Today, along with many other school-leavers, she was starting work at the tobacco factory.

Thelma sipped at her cup of tea. 'Right, Mary. Let me look at you. Come on. Look up so I can see if you look the part.'

'The part of what?'

Mary's tone was glumly couldn't care less.

'A girl off to work. There's lots of girls would like to be in your place.'

Mary shrugged disconsolately. 'I can't see why.'

Thelma drew in her chin. 'Because, young lady, they're a very good employer. You'll probably end up earning more than me – even at your age.'

Mary got to her feet. She was wearing a polka dot dress with a white collar and cuffs.

Thelma looked her up and down. 'You'll do very well.' She kissed her daughter on the cheek and gently caressed her chin. 'I'm sure they'll take you on. You'll get a good wage and their facilities are second to none.'

Mentioning wages once again resulted in a noticeable change in her daughter's attitude, just a flicker, then it was gone.

'I need the bathroom.'

Thelma looked at the clock again. 'I have to go. Let me know how you get on,' she shouted after her.

Still in two minds to mention the broken mug, she picked up her handbag tied a green and blue scarf around her neck and prepared to leave.

It's only a mug, she told herself. *It's not that important.*

Alice asked a question that took her mind off the smaller things.

'Are we going to the pictures on Saturday night?' she asked.

'We could do. I'll check and see what certificate it is. We can all go.'

Mary had come back from the bathroom. Thelma eyed her speculatively. She'd been very quiet of late ever since being told that Stuart had flown to Ireland. He hadn't, of course, but Thelma still maintained it was best that way. Telling her the truth, that he'd been mangled by a propeller from a plane coming into land, would have preyed on her mind. She couldn't do that. She'd sent the word round that she didn't want her daughter to know. It was too dreadful. She only hoped that nobody would break silence and tell her.

She glanced at the clock. 'Time I was off.' She kissed Mary's cheek. 'Best of luck on your first day. And don't be cheeky to anyone.'

26

On the same day that Thelma had wished Mary good luck with the interview for her new job, Jenny planned to go shopping at Filwood Broadway. Of late she'd made a point of shopping in East Street, Bedminster or only going as far as Melvin Square.

She kept her knitting in a tapestry bag with wooden handles. The bag held plenty of knitting needles, but she was getting low on wool. The girls would need new cardigans for the winter.

What remained of a green ball of wool sat in her lap next to a navy-blue ball and an off-white skein that she couldn't recall ever seeing before. Apart from those, she found lengths that were only good enough for sewing completed garments together – so long as they were the right colour, of course.

She pursed her lips. She needed to go to Rigby's to replenish her stock.

Would Robin be in his shop? Not necessarily so. He sometimes had to deliver or pick up furniture. She pushed him out of her mind, but it wasn't easy.

Roy had been gone for a while and she'd half expected Robin to call and ask how she was. He'd come to the funeral but had not made his presence that obvious to most. But she'd known he was there. She'd felt his presence in the church from where he stood at the rear close to the exit. Neither did he mix nor come for refreshments afterwards. She'd appreciated his thoughtfulness. Tongues would have wagged. Husband hardly cold in his grave and there's the fancy man, hanging around ready to pounce.

Only Robin couldn't, and wouldn't, pounce. She was now a widow, but Robin was still married, though separated from Doreen, a tartar of a wife who had made him very unhappy.

Walking to Filwood Broadway was fine. Arriving there made her feel nervous. She forced herself not to look over at his shop on the opposite side of the green to the wool shop.

Head down she pushed open the door. The shop bell jingled merrily. As usual, the stools ranged along the counter were occupied by several women. Mrs Rigby didn't insist on customers buying wool on every occasion. A number came in content to sit and chat with other women from the estate. Some knitted as they chatted. Others simply drank one of the innumerable cups of tea Mrs Rigby brewed in the back room.

The owner spotted Jenny and recognised her immediately.

'Hello, Mrs Crawford. Sorry to 'ear about your husband passing. My sincere condolences.'

Jenny thanked her. 'It's nice to see you all again.'

'And you, darling,' said one of the older women before taking a slurp of the milky tea she'd poured into a saucer.

'There's barely a ball of wool left in my knitting bag, only bits and pieces.'

Mrs Rigby waved a big brown teapot at her. 'I'm doing tea duty this morning, but my cousin Beryl can help you. Beryl's come to live with me. Couldn't leave her by herself, not now she's a widow. Didn't deserve that.'

Jenny looked round to see to whom she was referring until her gaze fell on the top of a head.

'Get on that orange box, Beryl, so you can serve this lady. And go careful. Mind you don't fall.'

A smiley face appeared, which appeared to be attached to a deformed body. The woman's back was bent and she leaned on a tall stick with her right arm. 'How can I 'elp you? Mrs Crawford, you say?' Her smile was broad. Her eyes twinkled.

'That's right.'

His wife. You ought to see the poor thing. She's crippled and sometimes he locks her in the bedroom.

The words sprang into her mind from nowhere. She knew immediately that this was Sam Hudson's wife.

At her request, the skeins of wool she required were stored on a shelf marked *Reserved*. Four of them, all double knit, she paid for and placed in her shopping bag. She'd pay for the rest one by one when she needed them.

'Can you confirm your address for the rest, Mrs Crawford, so I can put it in the ledger?' Beryl asked.

Jenny gave her the address. 'Number two Coronation Close.'

At mention of Coronation Close, the woman she was sure was Beryl Hudson beamed even more broadly at her. 'I've got a good friend lives there. Mrs Dawson. Do you know her?'

Jenny nodded enthusiastically. 'Yes. She's my friend. A great friend in fact.'

'I'd like to think she's my friend too,' said Beryl. 'Used to bring me wool when my swine of a husband was alive. He's gone now. Fell down the stairs and broke his neck.' She winked. 'They said it was an accident. You could say he met a bad end. But it weren't bad for me.' She winked again, which made Jenny think of a mischievous pixie, one whose cleverness should never be taken for granted.

The gossips in the shop tittered as they knitted and caught onto the subject.

'When we was first married, I chucked a clock at my old man,' said one of the women, her grey hair bundled like wire wool beneath a battered hat. 'Told 'im, don't you ever dare lay a finger on me again.'

'Did 'e?'

'What do you think?'

Cackles of laughter rattled around the small shop from wide open mouths, some of which were devoid of teeth.

'I threatened to put rat poison in my old man's dinner if 'e dared raise 'is fist to me again. I said to 'im, the way you wolfs food down when you gets 'ome from work you wouldn't know. Said I'd put it in 'is chitling. Wouldn't notice it what with the amount of vinegar and pepper 'e plastered it with. Was a bit careful from then on. Treated me a bit better. Never could be sure, could 'e?'

The cackling rattled around the shop. Jenny left with a smile on her face thinking that how, despite the harshness of their lives, there was a lot of love in those women – and a whole lot of resilience.

Thelma would be glad to know that Beryl Hudson was all right. She'd felt for her, had seen what she'd had to put up with.

'Give Thelma my regards,' called Beryl as Jenny left the chattering women and the jangling bell behind her.

Out on the pavement outside the shop, a man calling out 'any old iron', came level with her, blocking Jenny's view of Robin's shop. Once he'd gone past, she couldn't resist looking over.

Robin was leaning against the doorway, just as she'd seen him do many times before. A habitual stance, surveying what was going on in the world – principally in Filwood Broadway.

She stopped and held his gaze. Her ears thundered with the rush of blood. Would he make his way over? No. She was the widow, the one no longer tied in holy matrimony – or, in her case, downright unholy at times. His too, come to think of it.

Taking her courage in both hands, she crossed the road. Even at the halfway stage she could his beaming expression.

'Jenny. I've been waiting for you.'

'I thought you might have called in.'

He shook his head. 'I didn't think it would be right. You know 'ow people gossip.'

She smiled. 'That was very considerate of you. And how about Doreen? Is she gone for good?'

He chortled in a regretful way that said it all really. 'Would I be so lucky! She'll be round some time or other when she's short of money. Doreen has got the taste of a toff and the purse of a pauper!'

Jenny smiled a little sadly. Robin deserved better. She wanted to ask whether it was true that Doreen was in the family way. The hesitation in her voice and curious expression was noted.

'I 'eard the rumour too.' Happiness shone in Robin's eyes and sunny expression. He jerked his chin in the direction of the wool shop. 'There's more rumours in that shop over there than there is wool. If Doreen is up the spout it's nothing to do with me. And she's been seen with another bloke, one with a flash car and a gold tooth.' His face was wreathed in smiles. 'Ask them in the wool shop about that.'

Thinking about it she'd known from the first that it was nothing to do with Robin.

'So how are you?' he asked.

'Fine. I get a widow's pension and one from the army, though it's not much.'

Robin nodded in understanding before looking past Jenny to the green and the shops opposite. 'I was about to put the kettle on. Dare you chance coming in? There's something I want to talk to you about.'

Jenny glanced over her shoulder. Two women had come out of the wool shop and were now outside the butchers. They looked over before putting their heads together as though sharing some little snippet of gossip – most definitely about her.

She told herself she was a widow and would chance it. Let them say what they wanted.

The back room boasted only a small window. Robin filled the kettle and lit the gas.

'I've been wondering how you were,' he said to her as she pulled out a chair.

'I was wondering how you were too,' she responded. 'That day when the policeman came knocking… it was quite a shock.'

'That's what I wanted to talk to you about. Just a minute.'

He headed for the pawn shop side of the business, where the wire cage protected the pledges made – not that many of them were worth that much. This was Knowle West, not Clifton or Redland.

'I wanted to see you about this,' he said.

Jenny recognised the item of silver Stuart Brodie had brought in.

'It is quite valuable, though we're not talking thousands. No more than a hundred.'

Jenny gasped. 'That's a lot of money.'

The kettle whistled loudly and hot water was poured into a dull brown teapot.

Even though the kitchen window was small, the silver looked as though it had never lacked for care. It still shone as though it was new.

'Did the police give it to you? You didn't say.'

She had been taken totally by surprise. Seeing as Stuart Brodie had met his death, what was it doing here?

Robin began to explain. 'He had only months to live. He didn't want anyone to know. Especially Mary. And Thelma would have nothing to do with him. He pledged it in the first place so he could pay for some medical expenses until he could earn a bit and retrieve it.'

'But why do you have it now?'

Robin fiddled with the object. 'Stuart wanted Mary to have it but didn't want her or anyone else to know he was ill.'

'So he pledged it again?'

'Not exactly. He brought it in and asked me – or you, if you could oblige, and hand it to Mary. Not right away, but once she'd been told he was dead and got over it. By way of a will, he left a note. Here you are.'

Jenny read the note quickly.

To whom it may concern. I don't have long, but when I'm gone, I want my daughter Mary to have the silver trophy I won at Ballymena. All I have in the world is the trophy and a daughter. I know it won't make up for me being absent all these years, but it's the only valuable item I own. After waiting a respectable time, give this to her. I saw Coronation Close and know what a close-knit community it is. I know my last wishes will be honoured.

Signed by me, this...

His signature, scrawled in a weakening hand, followed the date.

'It's rather beautiful,' Jenny said softly.

Robin sighed.

Her gaze was attracted to the sight of his strong arms crossed over his chest. Because of his work, his muscles were well defined.

Before her face became hot with embarrassment, she shook the visions away.

'What I thought I would do is to sell it on to an antique dealer, then I can get my money back and the balance I can pass to his daughter – if Thelma would allow that. Do you think she would agree to that?'

Jenny returned her empty cup to its saucer. 'Mary might prefer a memento of her father – even though she didn't know him for very long or very well.'

Robin had to agree with her. 'You're right. Let her decide. That would be best.'

He ran a calloused hand through his hair as he thought it through. She so sorely wanted to reach out and do the same, or touch the hand that was doing it, clasp his fingers tightly, bring them to her lips and kiss each one.

She turned away so he wouldn't see the consternation on her face.

'Would you like your old job back?'

Her head jerked up.

He went on, 'Now that Doreen is gone, I could do with some help. Not that she ever helped.'

'Just like before?'

'I hope for more but realise I 'ave to give you time. But let's start there, shall we?'

There was pleading in his voice and in his eyes. She knew what he was saying and was fully aware of where it might lead. She missed her job. She missed him. But dare she risk the gossip merchants, some of whom had vile tongues.

Her thoughts turned to Thelma, who shone as a lighthouse to so many people. She'd lived her life to suit herself regardless of gossip. Three children from three different men, only one of whom had been her husband. If Thelma could be brave and win through, then so could she.

'Yes,' she said softly, her eyes fixed on him and smiling at him in a way she never had before. 'Yes. I'll come back to work for you.'

27

Something crunched under Thelma's foot. Even before she looked down and saw the crunched-up pieces of porcelain. A cold feeling enveloped her. She didn't need to see her reflection in the mirror to realise that this was a purposely vindictive act.

Out in the kitchen, Alice was preparing boiling eggs and making toast.

Thelma popped her head around the door. 'You all right there?'

Alice smiled. 'Won't be long. Three-minute eggs coming up.'

Mary was the culprit. Angry and flushed faced, she raced to the hallway and pounded up the stairs.

Mary was standing in front of the dressing-table mirror buttoning up her green overall. She didn't acknowledge her mother. It hurt. It angered.

Thelma stood with her arms crossed, barely able to control herself. 'The other day I found one of my collectibles smashed. Now today I found another. Is there anything you want to say?'

There was not a shred of reaction in Mary's face. She merely shrugged her shoulders. 'It must have fell off.'

'What both of them?'

Thelma stood behind her daughter. Both eyed their reflections. Their faces were mirror images of each other in colouring and features. Only their expressions differed.

'They didn't just fall off. They didn't just smash. They were ground into the floor. Now! What do you have to say for yourself?'

There was a cold look in Mary's eyes reflected at Thelma from the mirror. 'I have to go to work now.'

'What about breakfast?'

'I don't want any. All I want is to make some money. That's the only reason I'm taking this job. I want to get away from here! From you!' Mary grabbed all she needed for the day and pounded down the stairs.

Thelma just stood there. Tears stung her eyes and the anger she felt boiled inside her. What could she do to mend this terrible situation?

Not wishing to upset Alice, she polished off the boiled egg and toast, only leaving a sliver of crust behind.

Just as an afterthought as she grabbed her handbag, she asked her youngest daughter if she knew anything about the smashed china.

Suddenly Alice dropped the frying pan and burst into tears. 'I didn't mean to do it. I got angry. Mary's got a daddy. I haven't.'

Thelma felt as though she'd been slapped in the face.

'Oh Alice. You silly goose. Come here.'

It didn't matter that she'd be late for work. What did matter was that she'd been so sure that Mary was the culprit. How difficult it could be to truly see the emotions at play deep inside.

'Tell you what,' she said, cupping her daughter's tearful face with both hands. 'How about we clear it up together and then plan what picture we're going to see on Saturday night. How would that be?'

Alice nodded.

'And leave those dishes. We can do them together tonight. They won't hurt for now.'

Alice's face brightened.

Thelma wiped away the tears at the corners of her daughter's eyes and smiled down into her face. 'I'm sorry I didn't see how upset you were.'

It had been a very sad time of late. Her daughters had been more affected than she'd expected.

Alice took on an inquisitive look. 'Do you miss my daddy?'

Thelma nodded. 'Of course I do.' Thelma tried not to think of what might have been. What was gone was past, as far as she was concerned.

* * *

One of Mary's new friends at the factory asked her if she was coming along to the bus stop. She replied that she was not.

'I'm going to visit my brother and his wife. She's having a baby. They live in Montpelier.'

'See you tomorrow then.'

They waved each other goodbye. Mary headed for the bus that would take her to the grim rooms George and Maria lived in.

The house was one of a terrace that in previous times might have been home to just one family. There were four rooms on each floor. Like everyone else in the building, George and Maria rented two rooms.

The hallway was an unappealing shade of olive green. The stairs and banister leading upwards were dark with varnish that had been very popular in Victorian times. It hadn't been redecorated since.

Before placing her foot on the first tread, she stopped and called up the stairs, 'George?'

There was no response.

The threadbare carpet moved beneath her foot as she proceeded to the next stair and called out Maria's name.

She thought she heard a reply but couldn't be sure. But at least it seemed as though somebody was in.

Mary pounded up the rest of the stairs and pushed open the door to her brother's apartment to find Maria lying half in and out of the armchair in a room that doubled as kitchen and living room.

'Mary!' She reached out a slim trembling hand. 'Please. Help me to the bed.'

All thought of self and her endeavour to seek sympathy from her brother and his wife fled like early morning mist.

Using all her strength, she proceeded to help Maria into the adjoining room and onto the bed.

Maria asked her to open the window.

With grating reluctance, she pushed open the lower half of the sash window. Flakes of paint showered off as she did so.

Mary went back to the bed. 'Shall I get the doctor?'

Maria shook her head. 'Mrs Allen from downstairs is gone for the woman.'

'The woman?'

'Lying-in woman. Midwife you say here.'

Mary eyed Maria's stomach with increasing alarm. She'd never seen a stomach do that before, pulsate and change shape as it progressed from her midriff down to her loins.

'The baby is coming. I cannot hold on!'

Maria's cry of anguish burst into her thoughts. Seeking sight of the midwife, Mary looked out of the window, which was barely two feet from the side of the bed. There was no sign of anyone who resembled a midwife.

Maria touched her hand lightly, then grasped it as another spasm gripped her stomach. 'You have to help me, Mary.'

Mary gaped at her. 'Help? Me?' The idea scared her to death. 'What about our George?'

'At work,' said Maria amid rapid breathing. 'You must help me bring the baby. I will tell you what to do. I helped my mother bring my brothers and sisters.'

Mary nodded mutely and cleared her mind. Concentrate. She must concentrate. This was no time for dwelling on why her father had left her behind. Not now. She was faced with something she'd never done before, but for Maria's sake, for her brother's sake and everyone else – including her mother – she had to deal with this.

As per Maria's instructions, she boiled water, fetched towels and helped her out of her underclothes. She spread layers of newspaper beneath her naked thighs and although her sister-in-law was lying there half naked – a factor that would have once embarrassed her – Mary forced herself to concentrate on what was happening. Helping this baby be born was all that mattered.

Maria howled as a huge contraction heaved her belly from side to side and downwards at the same time. 'It... comes!'

Mary stared as the crown of the baby's head appeared and, finally, with a slither its whole body.

Without being ordered, she wrapped the baby in one of the towels she'd gathered.

The look on Maria's face was not so much one of relief for nearing the end of her ordeal, it was because she could look at her baby's sweet face.

'I will name her Francesca.'

Mary leaned forward to scrutinise the baby more closely. She hadn't thought to check whether it was a boy or a girl. Now she knew.

The thud of footsteps coming up the stairs preceded the arrival of George and the midwife.

'Out,' said the formidable-looking woman when George looked as though he might stay. 'The delivery room is no place for men!'

Although she herself hadn't been singled out, Mary chose not to stay but joined her brother in the other room.

'It's a girl,' she exclaimed.

George slung off his coat and threw it onto a chair. His pink face and breathing made it seem as though he was the one who had given birth. 'Well, our Mary. Are you going to wet the baby's head with me?'

She looked at him askance. 'What does that mean?'

'Celebrate! Celebrate my daughter's arrival.'

'Francesca. Maria has named her Francesca.'

'Then here's to Francesca.' He drew the cork from a bottle of port and tipped an inch into two glasses, then added a bit more to the one nearest to him.

'To my daughter,' he said with obvious pride.

He slugged some back.

Mary did the same – too quickly for someone unused to alcohol. A fit of coughing ensued.

George patted her on the back. 'Sorry, Mary. I shouldn't have encouraged you. But after all you've done...' He shook his head in disbelief. 'I don't know what would 'ave happened if you hadn't been yur. I'm grateful that you were. I wouldn't have wanted my Maria having the baby all by herself. So you're number one for godmother – if you don't mind that is.'

Mary gawped at him. All thoughts of moaning to him about her absent father and her mother's perceived part in the event left her head. Surprised and delighted, she clinked glasses with him this time, even though his was empty. Her face was a picture of delight.

'Unless you're going anywhere that is,' said George a little more seriously. 'You ain't gettin' married or anything are you?'

'No,' she replied resolutely. 'I'm not going anywhere. Except home. I am going home.'

* * *

She'd expected a telling-off when she got home. She knew she was late.

Alice passed her by the garden gate. 'I'm going to Hamblins' for some fish and chips. Do you want some?'

'Yes. I would.'

Alice gave her a questioning look. 'You look like the cat that got the cream.'

'Don't be daft. You don't even know what it means.'

'Yes I do. You look as though somebody's given you a five-pound note.'

Mary knew that Alice had gathered all these sayings second-hand. As her mother had pointed out, Alice had big ears. She'd thought it literal when she was younger and had made a point of studying her sister's ears to see just how big they were. At one point, she'd even called her Big Ears, like the Enid Blyton character. She now knew that her mother had meant that Alice listened to everything adults said.

Mary's lips curled in a smug smile. 'I've done better than that. I was there when our George's baby was born. Her name's Francesca.'

Alice's eyes opened wide. 'So that's where you were. Ma did wonder.'

'So why are you going to the chip shop. Is nothing cooked?'

She smiled smugly. 'Because there's a visitor.'

Refusing to say who it was and enjoying the look of consternation on her sister's face, Alice skipped off.

Feeling curious, Mary went round the side path and into the back door. She found her mother in the living room sitting at the dining table. A man she recognised as Mr Hubert who ran the furniture shop in Filwood Broadway was also sitting at the table.

They both looked at her intently as she entered the living room. Her gaze clipped from one to the other.

Back at George's place when the baby was born, she'd felt quite grown up. Now, beneath her mother's rather surprised-looking gaze, she began to feel like a child again.

'Before you tell me off for being late, I've got something to tell you. Our George has got a little girl. They're naming her Francesca.'

Her mother's eyebrows shot up. Following that both hands went up to her face. 'A girl? How do you know?'

This was Mary's ace card. She almost smirked when she said, 'I was there. The midwife hadn't come so I helped Maria give birth.'

Her mother's face was a picture. If she'd been going to tell her off for being late, Mary was sure it wouldn't happen now. Her mother was now a grandmother and looked as pleased as punch about it.

Mr Hubert looked at her mother and asked if she wanted to carry on or would she prefer he left.

'Stay.' She held out her hand as though she might pat him. Her eyes were focused on her daughter. 'Sit down, Mary. Mr Hubert has something for you.'

At a nod from Thelma, Robin Hubert passed a brown paper carrier bag across the table.

Puzzled, Mary looked down at it. 'What is it?'

'It's yours. To do with as you please.'

Mary frowned. Gingerly, half expecting it to be a kitten or a puppy, though it was too still and solid for that, she held the two edges of the bag apart. Once she'd discerned what it was, she drew it out.

She looked at her mother for explanation.

'Look at the engraving.'

Mary traced the engraving with her finger as she read it.

The Marlborough Stakes, Donegal Racecourse.
Winner, Moonfleet. Jockey Stuart Brodie.

Her hand went to her mouth and covered a strained squeak.

'Your father pawned it with Mr Hubert because he had no money and it was the most valuable thing he owned. He gave instructions for it to be given to you when he was no longer around.'

Mary shook her head. 'But surely he'd want it himself. He's gone back to Ireland.'

Thelma shook her head. Robin looked solemn. He clasped his hands together.

'Your father was ill. He knew he didn't have long but wanted to leave you something to remember him by. He left me instructions to wait before passing it on.'

Seeing her daughter's confusion, Thelma went round to her side of the table and put a loving arm around her shoulders.

'Mary. Please forgive me. I lied to you about him going back to Ireland. He was very ill and wanted to see you before he died and leave you something to remember him by.'

Confused, Mary looked up into her mother's face. 'He died?'

Thelma nodded. 'He died saving your life. You were running along the runway and an aeroplane was coming in. He saved you, but he couldn't save himself. He got hit by a propeller.'

Mary stared at the silver goblet. 'He didn't leave me.' It was a statement rather than a question and just saying it lit up her face.

Thelma, her eyes misted with tears, answered, 'He didn't leave you. Not purposely.'

Mary hugged the goblet to her. 'He didn't leave me.'

'No.'

Her mother exchanged looks with Robin. 'I'm very grateful to you.'

Robin got up. 'Happy I could help. And Mary...'

She looked up at him.

'If you want to change if for cash, I can sell it for you.'

She shook her head vehemently. 'No.'

The sound of Alice returning was accompanied by the strong smell of fish and chips.

Robin headed for the door. 'Time I was going. But I think we're on for the pictures on Saturday night?'

Feeling a lot lighter than she had for a while, Thelma nodded and smiled. 'I'm up for that. Let me see you to the door.'

A sense of calm descended on number twelve Coronation Close that night.

Bert was a bit late arriving. They agreed on not going out but just sitting, reading the newspaper, listening to the wireless and, in Thelma's case, doing a bit of mending. She didn't get to tell him what had happened until the girls had gone to bed.

After he had all the details, he patted her shoulder and kissed her cheek.

'You're a game woman, Thelma Dawson.'

She looked at him perturbed. 'And what's that supposed to mean?'

'No matter what's thrown, you catch it and either throw it back or keep it as a memento of your life on this earth. My mother thinks the same too.'

Thelma chuckled at the thought of his mother saying that about her.

'Has she seen that painting you did of me in the red dress?'

'No, but she's going to. She's had an invitation from Gilbert Bertram to this cocktail party. She's known him for years.'

'Oh my word!'

He rubbed her shoulder affectionately. 'Don't worry. I'm sure she'll love it.'

'But it's a bit...'

With a sly grin, he pointed out the obvious. 'Her son – yours truly, my dear – is the artist responsible for painting it. He can do no wrong.'

28

'Len Hutton scores 364 runs against the Australians...'

A great roar of approval went up from the audience at the Broadway Picture House.

'That man will go down in history,' stated Bert with great gusto.

Robin agreed with him, before turning to face Jenny and squeezing her hand. Even in the reduced lighting of the front stalls she could see his faint smile and even the light of adoration in his eyes.

'Everything's going to be all right,' he whispered.

She met his look with a smile and a slight nod towards her daughters.

He acknowledged her wishes to be discreet whilst in their presence, but she knew he wanted things to go further. Robin was hog-tied to Doreen and so long as he paid her maintenance, she'd be in no hurry to give him a divorce.

Thelma's daughter, Alice, was also with them, but Mary, now she was a working girl, had gone out with her new friends from the factory.

'We're going to do a bit of window shopping in Castle Street. Then a coffee in Carwardines.'

Thelma's first impulse had been to say there was no way that she was going by herself into the middle of Bristol on a Saturday night. Before it could be said, she'd reminded herself that Mary was no longer a schoolgirl and bit her lip.

'Enjoy yourself and don't be late home.'

She'd assured her mother that she wouldn't be late and she had every intention of enjoying herself.

A bag of toffees was passed around.

'Toffees. My favourite,' stated Thelma. 'It was a toss-up between toffees and sherbet lemons. I like them both. I think we all do.'

Jenny didn't voice that toffees stuck in her teeth and lemon set them on edge. Thelma had bounced back from her problems like a newly blown-up beach ball. Mary had taken the death of her natural father very well, to the extent that she expressed pride that he'd saved her life whilst giving his own.

The brightest star to have entered Thelma's life was her newly born granddaughter Francesca. If you could believe what Thelma said, she was the sweetest, cleverest baby ever to be born. Jenny had listened to every word and not once reminded her that the sweet little mite had only just been born. Whether she'd be beautiful, clever or walking by the time she was six months old could not yet be known.

'Give her chance to grow up, will you.' She'd said it laughingly of course.

Thelma had sighed and expressed her desire that she remain a baby forever. 'Wish mine had.'

Thelma was also all agog about the forthcoming cocktail party at Bertrams. Mr Gilbert had overruled Mrs Apsley about Thelma serving the drinks.

'She's very popular with our customers. Yes, she can offer a few drinks, especially to those customers with whom she is on friendly terms. But primarily I would prefer her to... to...' He'd looked up at the central glass orb hanging from the ceiling as he searched for the right word.

'Butter them up,' Mrs Apsley had offered.

'Do you know anyone who might be willing to circulate with a tray of drinks? I am willing to pay them the going rate of course.'

Thelma had immediately thought of Jenny. 'I believe I do. She's well-spoken and presentable.'

Jenny had jumped at the chance. Her income had reduced since Roy's death so she intended grabbing every opportunity to earn extra. The small wage she would earn at Robin's shop was useful but a little more would be welcome.

Coverage of the cricket and Len Hutton's winning score was replaced by dull men with serious expressions pointing at a large map spread out over a desk. The commentator informed them that Germany was making demands about a place called the Sudetenland in a country called Czechoslovakia.

'Never mind the news, get on with the film,' grumbled Thelma.

The Lady Vanishes. Directed by Alfred Hitchcock.

The characters were travelling through a fictional country, where it seemed downright dangerous to voice anything that might upset the uniformed elite. There were spies and secret messages, women dressed as nuns who were no such thing. A man on holiday with his mistress. Two cricket fanatics desperate not to miss the test match at the Oval. A young couple who everyone knew would end up together by the end of the film after sorting out the plot and making it a happy ever after.

* * *

'That was good,' said Thelma as the National Anthem finished and everyone moved as one to the exit. 'Goodies and nasties.'

'Or goodies and Nazis,' said Robin.

No doubt he hadn't meant to lower their spirits, but he'd touched on something very current about the film. From what they were led to believe, the fictional country it portrayed could just as easily have been Germany, the uniformed men marching about as if they would stomp everyone underfoot, others who would betray their fellow man just to show they were loyal.

'It's a clear night,' Bert said suddenly. 'Just look at all those stars.'

Faces turned upwards. Awestruck, they took in the spangled aspects of those stars set like diamond studs in the sky – though not all.

'Those stars are dancing,' Alice said suddenly and with childish glee, she pointed to the south towards the very end of Inns Court and the sky above the fields and the airport.

'That's not stars,' said Bert. 'That's aeroplanes coming into land. Quite a few aeroplanes.'

Robin watched their steady movements. There were indeed quite a few.

'It's been like that for a few days. I hear they're setting up a training corps. Just in case.'

Nobody asked him what he meant. Because they knew. There might not have been any explosions showing on the screen this evening, but that didn't mean they weren't living in dangerous times. The news, the aeroplanes, the queue for enlistment, the distribution of gas masks were an escalation of preparations for war; a taste of things to come.

29

The main thing Jenny noticed on entering the area at Bertrams where the cocktail party was to be held was the smell. Perfume and face powder contributed to the overall impression of wealth. Women in silk dresses and white summer gloves floated like water lilies over what was by day the sales floor.

As per Thelma's instructions, she was dressed in a plain black dress. Bertrams Modes had provided a crisp white apron and starched cap.

'You look a picture,' Thelma whispered to her.

'I'm a bit nervous. All these posh people...'

'Didn't you work at the Hatchet once?'

Jenny pulled a woeful look. 'The Hatchet's a pub and I never even pulled a pint, let alone waitressed. I did some cleaning for them. Roy would have had a fit if I'd dared go behind the bar.'

'Right,' said Thelma, her eyes shining brightly as she surveyed the clientele. 'Let's go and see how much commission I can earn.'

Whilst Thelma went off to circulate, a fussy little man in a penguin suit furnished Jenny with a silver tray and several champagne glasses. Each was half filled with champagne.

'Only half measures?' she said jokingly.

His look was dismissive. 'There are two reasons for this. One, we are serving ladies. They only sip at champagne. Two. You won't spill any.'

She opened her mouth to say that she had a steady hand, but he was already instructing another waitress brought in for the occasion.

Jenny began circulating amongst women who spent as much on a dress as some families she knew spent on their monthly groceries. The voices she heard in passing were full of rounded vowels and fully expressed consonants. Not for them even a hint of accent. Theirs were the voices of the well-educated and well-heeled. Only a few thanked her for their champagne. The rest only saw the tray and not the person holding it.

Thelma nodded and exchanged comments with customers she knew, asking them if there was anything she could help them with.

'We have silk scarves in from Italy. Don't you think them beautiful? And each one is individually painted. They're quite expensive, of course, and very individual. If you should decide to buy one, it will be unique. Yours and yours alone.'

One of the things Thelma had learned about wealthy women was that they coveted that which no one else had. To be unique was a flamboyant show of wealth, signifying their cleverness and their ability to pay for something others could only dream of.

A silk scarf was chosen, interspersed with tissue paper and placed in one of the smart black carrier bags with Bertrams Modes emblazoned on the side in gold lettering.

Full-length cheval mirrors had been placed at intermittent intervals.

Thelma smiled at a model who had twirled her way between a mirror and the customer. The latter was fondling the material and asking Mrs Apsley if she thought the colour – a shade of aquamarine – would suit her. Mrs Apsley assured her that it would.

'I fully accept that I would need it in a slightly bigger style.'

Thelma coughed to cloak the laugh that threatened. The model was slender and young. The customer was in her fifties and the dress would need to be a lot larger to fit her. At least three times larger, in fact.

But Mrs Apsley would assure her that they could get it in a larger size. Like Thelma, she knew which side her bread was buttered and had learned over the years how to make a woman feel she was a princess – not a pumpkin!

Not only were the wealthy elite enjoying viewing the mannequins with their steadfast smiles and elegant poses, and comments about Mr Gilbert's collection of paintings. Not all of them were complimentary.

'I've gone beyond pictorial paintings. I have a liking for abstract works by the likes of Pablo Picasso.'

'Hunting scenes, that's the stuff!' The speaker was a woman of broad proportions wearing a tweed suit. Both her persona and her outfit seemed out of place amongst the other more elegant ladies.

'Mother, I don't know why I brought you here.'

'Because I complained that I didn't see enough of you and that you mixed with the wrong people.'

Thelma froze. She didn't know the woman, but she certainly knew the identity of the man.

'I rather like the lady in red.' He waved his empty glass towards Thelma's portrait. 'I think I know her.' He looked directly at her and winked.

Thelma felt as though her face was on fire.

Without formally acknowledging her, Charlie Talbot called for more champagne.

To Thelma's horror, Jenny began to head his way but froze when she saw him. Her pink lips parted with surprise. The last thing she'd expected was for Charlie Talbot to be swanning around the sales floor of Bertrams Modes.

Thelma had not told Jenny of his new venture as a car dealer, nor that she'd seen him. The past was best left behind, though sometimes, as in the case of Stuart Brodie, pigeons did come home to roost.

So far, Charlie hadn't seen Jenny, so absorbed was he in placating his mother. But Jenny had seen him.

Thelma rushed to stand between her and him whilst she apologised. 'I didn't know he was coming,' she said as softly as she could.

Jenny had a full tray of drinks. She barely considered what she going to do next. Her chin was uplifted in that defiant way she had when determined to see something through. She took a deep breath and declared, 'I'm being paid to do this. I'll be fine.'

Head held high, Jenny wove her way past Thelma until she was standing there, silently offering the tray of drinks.

For one terrifying moment, Thelma thought she might throw the whole tray over him. She wouldn't blame her if she did. On the other hand, she'd assured Mrs Apsley that Jenny was very presentable and could mix with the best.

Heart in her mouth, she was barely aware of the models pivoting around her, carefully manicured hands resting on hips or raised to rest behind their head.

Jenny held the tray in front of her as if she really were invisible, but Charlie Talbot was the one person in the whole room who couldn't stop staring at her.

He took two glasses. 'Here you are, Mother. One for you. Why don't you take it over there and have a closer look at that painting? It's very good.'

She didn't look too enthused. Her face brightened when she spotted an old friend. 'Lucinda! Fancy meeting you here.'

Charlie looked relieved.

Jenny began to head away with her tray of champagne. She should have known better. He followed her.

'Jenny. I've been wondering how you were.'

She nodded mutely and kept her eyes downcast. At one time long past, she'd thought herself in love with Charlie Talbot.

'Nice to see you. Excuse me, I must circulate and serve...'

He stepped in front of her, a brick wall who seemed to have no intention of letting her pass. 'How are things with you?'

She could have admitted that she was a widow. If she'd still been in love with him, perhaps she might have. 'I'm fine.'

She failed to ask him how he was. It just didn't matter. And that was when she knew for sure where her heart was. Her heart was at home in number two Coronation Close. That was where she belonged, with her family and friends. It mattered that war clouds were gathering on the horizon, but she knew that surrounded by those she loved and those who loved her, she would get through it.

'Excuse me. I have a living to earn.'

He looked surprised when she pushed past him, which made Thelma smile. Jenny had been a bit cowed when she'd first moved into Coronation Close, but she wasn't now.

Fresh air wafted through the shop door, fluttering the gossamers and silks of some of the dresses. The man who entered took off his hat and waved at her.

'Mr Cuthbert Throgmorton,' he announced himself to the young lad dressed in bellboy outfit as he handed him his hat and coat, then made a beeline for Thelma. 'My mother was coming, but she's enrolled in the local amateur dramatic society and there's a rehearsal tonight. She just couldn't let them down.'

Jenny came over with champagne and exclaimed, 'Your painting of *The Woman in the Red Dress* is wonderful.'

Although she wasn't supposed to, she handed Thelma a glass of champagne, taking the last glass herself.

'A lovely evening,' she said as they clinked glasses in a toast. 'Oh, and by the way, Thelma. Beryl Hudson has moved into the wool shop. Apparently, Mrs Rigby is her cousin. She sends her regards. Sorry I forgot to tell you before.'

'That calls for another toast,' said Thelma. They clinked glasses again.

More fresh air wafted from the open doorway. Charlie Talbot was leaving with his mother, who might have been just a wee bit drunk.

It was a pleasure to see the positive glow on Jenny's face. There was something so vital about it, so full of hope.

'I'm staying behind to help with the washing up,' she told Thelma when Bert offered to give her a lift home. 'I'll make my own way. Besides, I think you two might want some private time together after such a successful night – for both of you.'

Thelma and Bert acted on her suggestion. Arm in arm, they left Bertrams Modes behind. The pinkness of her cheeks was now only due to the night air. She'd walked on air tonight and nothing that could happen or be said would dampen her lust for life.

She sighed. 'This was a perfect evening, Bert.'

'I thought so too. Shall we pop into a pub on the way home and celebrate?'

She hugged his arm close. 'I'm in the right company, so why not?'

AUTHOR'S NOTE

I was born and grew up at 116, Glyn Vale, Bedminster, Bristol 3. No postcodes then, just a single number.

Most places in this book really existed – with the possible exception of Coronation Close. The only one I know is in Warmley, which is East Bristol.

The characters are all fictitious but are representative of the women – and men – I once knew.

It's around one hundred years since the first council house was built in Bristol. Two million have been sold under the right to buy. A lot have been bought by private landlords – such was their regard for the quality of build.

Bye, bye, council houses. You fulfilled a great need and deserved better. We could do with them now.

A few notes of historical fact.

The third news of the day, that is the last news broadcast on BBC Radio, was exactly as it was announced and listed – 9 p.m. Basically the last news of the day.

Gas masks were distributed in 1938 and men were invited to enlist as the prospect of war became ever more possible.

Pre-war Bristol Airport was at Whitchurch, not Lulsgate Bottom where it is now. Back then the runway really was just short grass until more and more training flights began in earnest once it seemed war was inevitable.

Incidentally, this airport was the only one in England to remain a civil airport once war began. It was from here that flights journeyed to neutral Lisbon and back again – just as they did from Casablanca to Lisbon.

ACKNOWLEDGEMENTS

Many thanks to everyone involved in polishing this book to the best it can be. Editors, cover designer, marketing and publicity people. You're all great.

Thanks also to my partner Chris who takes over the cooking when I'm engrossed in writing my books. Also for mixing cocktails, which he is ace at doing.

ABOUT THE AUTHOR

Lizzie Lane is the author of over 50 books, a number of which have been bestsellers. She was born and bred in Bristol where many of her family worked in the cigarette and cigar factories. This has inspired her new saga series for Boldwood *The Tobacco Girls*.

Sign up to Lizzie Lane's mailing list here for news, competitions and updates on future books.

Follow Lizzie on social media:

facebook.com/jean.goodhind
x.com/baywriterallatı
instagram.com/baywriterallatsea
bookbub.com/authors/lizzie-lane

ALSO BY LIZZIE LANE

The Tobacco Girls

The Tobacco Girls

Dark Days for the Tobacco Girls

Fire and Fury for the Tobacco Girls

Heaven and Hell for the Tobacco Girls

Marriage and Mayhem for the Tobacco Girls

A Fond Farewell for the Tobacco Girls

Coronation Close

New Neighbours for Coronation Close

Shameful Secrets on Coronation Close

Dark Shadows Over Coronation Close

The Strong Trilogy

The Sugar Merchant's Wife

Secrets of the Past

Daughter of Destiny

The Sweet Sisters Trilogy

Wartime Sweethearts

War Baby

Home Sweet Home

Wives and Lovers

Wartime Brides

Coronation Wives

Mary Anne Randall

A Wartime Wife

A Wartime Family

Standalones

War Orphans

A Wartime Friend

Secrets and Sins

A Christmas Wish

Women in War

Her Father's Daughter

Trouble for the Boat Girl

Sixpence Stories

Introducing Sixpence Stories!

Discover page-turning historical novels from your favourite authors, meet new friends and be transported back in time.

Join our book club Facebook group

https://bit.ly/SixpenceGroup

Sign up to our newsletter

https://bit.ly/SixpenceNews

Printed in Great Britain
by Amazon